MAKE ME YOURS

Chad slowly reached out and brushed his hand gently over the mass of curly hair, then down her cheek. She looked back into his eyes as he tilted her chin upward. They both leaned closer in that moment as their lips hovered inches apart. Then Chad lowered his mouth onto hers.

It was just a small touch at first, a simple brush of their skin. Then it was deeper, swiping, delving, savoring. She tasted hot and sweet. Like ripe black cherries drizzled with melted brown sugar. It was way better than he had imagined, and very hard to stop. Chad forced himself to pull back, fully aware that they were in a very public hallway, and any one of his coworkers could easily walk by.

"Are you sure you want to go to the beach?" Chad asked softly. "Because I can think of a more satisfying way to spend the afternoon."

Rebecca didn't respond right away, nor did she pull away in outrage or insult. But he could sense her hesitation. He pulled back to look at her face.

"I leave tomorrow," she stated simply.

"I know." Chad brushed a finger over her soft lips. "I do too. So this seems like the best opportunity to explore whatever *this* is."

Also by Sophia Shaw

Published by Dafina Books

Make Me Yours

SOPHIA SHAW

Dafina BOOKS

Kensington Publishing Corp.

http://www.kensingtonbooks.com

DAFINA BOOKS are published by

Kensington Publishing Corp.
119 West 40th Street
New York, NY 10018

All Kensington Titles, Imprints, and Distributed Lines are available at special quantity discounts for bulk purchases for sales promotions, premiums, fund-raising, and educational or institutional use. Special book excerpts or customized printings can also be created to fit specific needs. For details, write or phone the office of the Kensington special sales manager: Kensington Publishing Corp., 119 West 40th Street, New York, NY 10018, attn: Special Sales Department, Phone: 1-800-221-2647.

Dafina and the Dafina logo Reg. U.S. Pat. & TM Off.

ISBN-13: 978-0-7582-6528-9
ISBN-10: 0-7582-6528-X

First Kensington mass market printing: January 2013

10 9 8 7 6 5 4 3 2 1

Printed in the United States of America

For Naima Rebecca:
Your spirit and determination inspire me.

ACKNOWLEDGMENTS

In MAKE ME YOURS, I was excited to return to Chicago, one of my favorite places! It is a city filled with diversity, culture and natural beauty. The perfect backdrop for this story.

To the *real* Chad Irvine—thank you for letting me use your name, and your height. All other similarities are purely coincidental ☺.

To Scott—thank you for putting up with my crazy schedule and making me laugh whenever I need it the most. Most of all, thank you for being the man I've always dreamed of, but never thought I would be lucky enough to find.

Love always,
Sophia

Chapter 1

"This place is pretty nice," William Holmes stated to his friend and coworker, Chad Irvine, as they drove down the fairway of an eighteen-hole golf course. "I was a little disappointed when they said we were going to Myrtle Beach this year, but this is not bad at all. It's not the Bahamas like last year, but it will do."

As he drove the golf cart, Chad nodded while looking around the perfectly manicured landscaping: He took a small bridge over a pond, then stopped near the putting green of the fifth hole. Both men hopped out and grabbed their putters from the bag of rented clubs strapped to the back of the buggy.

"I still can't believe I let you talk me into teeing off at seven-thirty in the morning," William continued as he prepared his stance for a long putt.

Chad chuckled. William had been complaining about it since Chad had booked the round of golf about a month ago.

"Come on, you must admit it feels good," he

urged William. "It's a beautiful day on a spectacular course. And there's no one out here but us. What could be better than that?"

William completed a measured stroke before he replied, putting his ball within a few inches of the hole. "No one's out here because they're all sleeping in, Chad. That's what people do on these trips. Then they have a massage, eat a big lunch, and maybe do one of the afternoon activities. Didn't you read the itinerary?"

Chad executed his putt with a perfect stroke, which sank his ball to complete a birdie. He smiled with satisfaction.

"Well, we'll finish eighteen holes before lunch so you can relax all afternoon if you want," he replied to William as he watched his friend sink his ball on the next try.

"That's right. I'm going to stretch out on the beach in my Speedo!"

Both men laughed, knowing he would do no such thing. Though it was mid-September and the weather was still in the eighties, William was not the type to lounge around half naked in skintight swim trunks. He was five feet, eight inches tall and rail thin, unlikely to wear anything less than the cargo shorts and short-sleeved golf shirt he had on now.

Chad, on the other hand, was the opposite of his friend in almost every way. He was six feet, three inches tall and around 230 pounds of thickly carved, solid muscle. His rich, warm, copper skin was also a stark contrast to William's very pale complexion, pink from sun exposure. The huge difference in their physical appearance was a constant source of teasing and jokes between them and their other friends and coworkers. But their friendship was based on the similarities in their personalities and work ethics. Despite having very different backgrounds, Chad and William were both smart, hardworking, high-performing professionals strongly focused on their careers.

They had both been hired by Sheppard Networks almost right out of university over ten years ago, and rose quickly and steadily to high-level positions. William was a senior technical architect responsible for designing the company's best-selling remote access solution for business customers, and Chad was the financial controller for the business products department. They had worked closely together on many large projects over the years and built a reputation as a successful team. This five-day all expenses paid vacation to Myrtle Beach was a Sheppard Networks Platinum Club reward for the company's top ten performers and their spouses. Chad and William had been on the list for three of the last five years.

The friends continued to tease and taunt each other as they played through another four holes. They stopped by the clubhouse for a few minutes to take a bathroom break and purchase two bottles of orange juice, then continued to the tenth hole. It was a short 110-yard par three, but with a ridge of trees along the back of the green and two large water hazards. Chad checked his watch while William adjusted his form to tee off. It was quarter to ten, so they were making good time.

"Nice shot!" Chad exclaimed as they watched

William's tiny white golf ball fly in a perfect arc down the middle of the fairway, over one of the ponds, and then roll to the edge of the green.

William grinned in obvious delight, then stepped back so Chad could take his turn. About a minute later, Chad pulled back to take a restrained swing with his seven iron. But something bright caught his eye off in the tree line just as he was following through to hit his ball, and he lost his focus. Chad knew right away that his aim was off and that he had used too much force. He watched with dismay as his ball flew over the green and disappeared into the foliage behind the hole.

"Well, at least it didn't end up in the water, right?" William stated with an amused look on his face.

Chad twisted his mouth with annoyance, but didn't bother to respond. As they walked to the cart, his eyes drifted to the trees again, directly in line with where his ball had landed, wondering what had distracted him to begin with. He drove them through the short fairway and parked on the path near the putting green, then headed off into the brush to try and find his ball.

The foliage turned out to be denser than he had anticipated, thick with bushes between a row of mature, majestic live oak trees. Chad's limit for looking for a lost ball was about five minutes, max. He bent low, hoping his ball would be visible from where he stood, saving him the effort of maneuvering his large body through a barrier of prickly branches. He slowly walked along the edge of the grass, using his club to push leaves and loose dirt around, but there was no sign of the small white sphere.

He let out a deep sigh, then looked behind him to the tee, trying to reassess the vector of his swing. The ball should have landed within the area he had estimated, so it must have dropped down deeper into the trees. William was still struggling with his putt, so Chad decided to have one more quick look around.

About thirty seconds later, he spotted the familiar white orb with the Sheppard Networks logo clearly visible. It was a few yards into the bushes, nestled against the wide trunk of a massive tree. Chad pushed his way through the shrubbery, then stopped as he heard rustling from above him. He looked up into the thick branches above, and a second later caught a glimpse of a round, tubular object catapulting down toward him. Instinctively, he leaned back with his hands lifted, but not fast enough. The heavy metal object clipped him at the side of his head before he managed to catch it with both hands.

"Rahtid!"

The loud expletive came from somewhere up in the shady green canopy, and the Jamaican slang caused Chad to raise his eyebrows in surprise. He looked down into his hands and quickly realized that he had caught some sort of camera lens, one that was probably quite expensive judging by the weight and size. He then touched the tender spot on his skull to check for blood. Though his finger came away clean, the area was a little tender. Chad looked up again, trying to locate the negligent owner. There was more rustling, then a flash of orange color and additional cursing.

Several seconds later, he was still looking up into the tree, waiting for the clumsy person to finally emerge.

"Oh, thank God!"

The exclamation came from behind him, so Chad quickly turned around with his eyes flashing to demonstrate his annoyance. The sharp retort he was ready to bark back died quickly on his lips as his gaze dropped to the tiny woman standing in front of him.

"Is it damaged?" she continued, her attention completely focused on the lens.

Chad let her snatch it out of his hands, then silently watched as she spent the next minute or so doing a thorough examination. He was immediately struck by her unconventional appearance and intense focus on her task. She was short and slender, wearing a loose orange hooded sweatshirt over gray leggings, and knee-high purple rain boots. Her hair was a thick mass of small corkscrew curls held back from her face by a white cotton scarf folded into a triangle and tied at the nape of her neck. A large, serious-looking camera hung from a strap around her neck. She looked like a kid.

"Sweet Jesus!" she finally declared with an accent that was clearly Caribbean, her eyes closed and head thrown back with obvious relief.

"You're welcome," Chad finally stated after a few seconds. His voice was deep and thick with sarcasm. It was irrational, but her obliviousness to his presence annoyed him.

She finally looked up at him with large round eyes. Their golden copper color was several shades lighter than her creamy chestnut skin tone. "Sorry," she stated, blinking a few times. "I was certain the lens would be completely smashed. It's the only wide-angle lens I brought with me. The whole morning would be wasted without it. I can't believe it fell from that height and is still okay."

"That's because it made a soft gentle landing on my head," Chad growled back.

Her mouth opened in surprise. "I'm sorry," she stammered, clearly unprepared for his sarcastic tone.

"I'm lucky you didn't crack my skull open with that thing. What are you doing climbing around in trees on a golf course anyway? Forget your lens, you could have broken your little neck! Never mind injuring unsuspecting golfers!"

Chad didn't raise his voice, but his annoyance was obvious. She took a couple of slow steps back as though moving away from a hungry bear.

"Okay, I'm really sorry," she replied again, both hands raised with her palms facing him. "I've been out here since before sunrise and lost track of time. But I certainly didn't mean to cause any trouble."

She looked around them with darting eyes, still backing up. Chad let out a deep sigh, feeling a new wave of irritation with her skittish behavior. He wasn't going to hurt her, for god sakes.

"Thank you again for saving my lens," she stated softly before turning and walking behind the trunk of the tree she had climbed out of.

"Wait," he called after her, surprised to see her take off so quickly.

Chad followed her path to call out to her again, but she was nowhere to be seen. He continued around the circumference of the trunk, looking for any sign of her until he was back where he started.

"Hey, what's going on?" William yelled from a few yards away. "Are you still trying to find your ball?"

Chad looked over at his friend, his brow still wrinkled with a frown. "No, I found it," he replied, pointing to his ball still resting against the tree.

"Are you going to play it? There are a couple of people getting ready to tee off behind us," William explained.

Chad looked around the area again, then touched the tender spot on his head to see if the recent encounter had really happened. There was definitely going to be a small bruise. "Nah, let's move on to the next hole," he finally stated as he scooped up the white orb and headed back to finish the tenth hole.

"Are you sure?" William asked, clearly puzzled, when Chad reached the edge of the green. "What should I put down? Five strokes?"

"Yeah, that's fine," Chad replied.

"What took you so long and who were you talking to?" William continued as they walked to the cart.

"Didn't you see that girl?"

"What girl?"

Chad looked over at him as they climbed into the vehicle. "The girl by the tree," he explained.

"I didn't see anyone. I only heard your voice. Why, what happened?"

"There was this girl in the tree taking pictures,

and she dropped a lens, that's all," Chad explained briefly, letting out a long sigh.

He felt William looking at him oddly, but didn't elaborate further. The tension was slowly seeping out of his body, leaving him puzzled by his reaction to the odd female with the melodic voice who had appeared out of nowhere and disappeared even more quickly. Now it was clear his annoyance was an overreaction to the situation, and his words to her were unfair. He remembered the alarm reflected in her bright copper eyes and felt like a big bully.

What the hell had gotten into him? While his head was still a little sore, the minor injury was barely worth noticing. Maybe it was just his surprise at her fragile size coming down from such a dangerous height that made his heart beat faster with concern.

"Okay, this one is a par five, four hundred and thirty-one yards," William stated as Chad stopped the cart next to the tee for the eleventh hole. "According to the map, it cuts to the left around the middle of the fairway, and has a couple of sand traps next to the green."

"Okay, then let's get to it!" Chad replied with exuberance in an effort to refocus his energy back to the game.

The two men hopped out of the cart and grabbed their drivers, ready to tee off with the greatest distance possible. They played the hole aggressively, landing in the rough through a couple of strokes; then they both finished the hole one over par. By then, the friends were back to ribbing each other and bouncing around ideas about how to spend the rest of the day. It was almost noon when they returned to the clubhouse, and they were back at the resort by twelve-thirty.

"Just in time for lunch," William stated as they walked through the hotel lobby.

"Sandra and her husband should have a table for us by now," Chad replied while he quickly looked through the messages on his phone. "Yup, they're at the poolside restaurant. I'll meet you guys there in a few minutes. I want to see if I've got a new room yet. I won't last another night on that double bed."

"No problem."

The friends separated as William continued toward the restaurant at the rear of the hotel overlooking the pools and ocean, and Chad turned down a hall on his right that led to the registration desk. There were several people being checked in, so he stood in line, browsing the other messages on his phone as he waited for his turn. Out of the corner of his eye, Chad got a glimpse of something orange and purple to his left. He looked up quickly, turned toward that direction, but the blur of color was gone.

"Can I help you, sir?"

Chad blinked a few times, wondering if the image was real or just his imagination.

"Sir?"

The voice calling out to him finally registered, and Chad faced the front desk again to find a young girl with a bright smile patiently looking at him.

"Yes . . . sorry," he said as he approached her. "I checked in last night, but my room wasn't available for some reason, so you gave me a temporary one. Can you see if there is a king bed available now?"

"Sure, sir. I apologize for any inconvenience. What is your current room number?" the girl asked.

Chad pulled the key pass out of his pocket and handed it to her.

"Okay, Mr. Irvine, it looks like we do have your room ready now. And you've been given an upgrade to one of our executive suites. I'm sure you could use the extra space," she added with a teasing smile.

"That's great, thanks," he replied politely, not missing her flirtatious reference to his imposing size.

"Here is your new key. Would you like me to get a bellhop to help you move?" she asked.

"No, that's okay. I'm meeting friends for lunch, and I'll move my things after, if that's all right."

"No problem, Mr. Irvine. My name is Amy. And please let me know if you need anything else during your stay." She flashed another bright, inviting smile.

"Thank you, Amy," he replied with a respectful nod.

Chad turned away from the desk. Before heading to the restaurant for lunch, he found himself unable to resist taking another look around the open lobby for the mysterious girl from the tree who had nearly knocked him out.

Chapter 2

Rebecca Isles didn't get back to her hotel room until almost one o'clock in the afternoon. After her awkward encounter with the big, angry giant, she grabbed her gear bag and ran off the golf course, not stopping until she reached her rented scooter parked in front of the clubhouse. There were very few people to be seen in the area, as one would expect on a Thursday morning, and a quick look around confirmed to Rebecca that no one was paying her any attention.

Once she carefully put her equipment into the large storage bag, Rebecca paused for a moment to catch her breath and calm herself, then went up the stairs and into the building.

"How did it go?" a heavyset man asked as he walked across the lobby toward her.

Rebecca let out a deep breath and smiled back at the general manager for the course, George Matthews.

"Hey, George, it was good. I got at least two

hundred shots, so definitely time well spent," she replied once he stopped beside her.

"Good stuff, good stuff," he replied.

"Thanks again, for letting me on the course so early."

"It was no problem at all, Rebecca."

"Well, hopefully you'll like what I've done and have all the pics you'll need for the new marketing ads," she added.

"I'm sure I will. How long will you be staying in Myrtle Beach?"

"I'm not sure. I don't have my next assignment confirmed yet, so I'm open right now," Rebecca explained. "At least over the weekend, I think. I have a couple of other sites I want to visit, like some of the local plantations. Maybe a couple of other golf courses."

"I can make a few calls to some of our resort partners, if you'd like," George offered.

"No, no, that's okay. That's not necessary. I just want to wander around a bit, see what catches my eye."

He nodded, smiling, and there was a glint of hope in his eyes. Rebecca instinctively knew what was coming next.

"I'm finished at three o'clock—" he started to say, but she cut him off before he could finish the offer.

"Thanks again, George," she told him sincerely. "I really appreciate your help today. And I'll make sure I send you some of the shots after I submit them to your marketing department."

"Oh, it was no problem, Rebecca. But I'll see you before you leave town, right?"

"Sure. I'll send you a note over the weekend."

He smiled wider, filled with hope, and Rebecca felt like crap.

She waved bye and made her way back to the scooter. The minute she buckled the helmet, her stomach started to rumble with hunger. The hot coffee from five o'clock in the morning was not going to sustain her until lunch. There was a granola bar in her purse, but Rebecca had a craving for something more substantial. Twenty minutes later, she was sitting in a pancake house on South Kings Highway.

While she waited for her eggs Florentine to be delivered, Rebecca took out her iPad in order to plan the next few days. She had arrived in Myrtle Beach on a Sunday afternoon, after more than two hours on a bus from Charleston. She had been there now for almost three weeks taking pictures for her client's three local properties, updating her Web site, and now waiting for the next assignment.

The gap between projects was one of the hardest parts of her career as a freelance travel photographer. Though the lag had never been more than two to three weeks over the last three years, Rebecca still felt anxious until she knew where she was going next and when she could expect to get paid. One of the first things she learned in her new career was to use every opportunity to increase her portfolio of marketable images.

Despite the challenges and uncertainty, Rebecca could hardly complain about her lifestyle. She was living her dream of traveling around the world taking photos of incredible people and places, and making a living off it, even if it was a very modest one. If she were still alive, her mother would be so proud of her. There were certain sacrifices, money being one of the biggest. Her net income was hardly something to brag about, just enough to buy equipment and pay for her food and expenses. Then there was her lack of a residence since leaving Jamaica on her first assignment. Living out of a suitcase was challenging, but manageable once she had developed a system and learned to make do with just the essentials. Now, Rebecca finally felt like she was living the adventure, taking one week at a time for as long as it lasted.

Surprisingly, the hardest thing to cope with was the loneliness. No matter how many people she met and new friends she made, Rebecca still woke up most mornings feeling completely alone in the world. It wasn't as acute or heart wrenching as those months after her mother's death; instead it was like the dull pain from an old injury. She was learning to live with it, and when it was particularly difficult, she would Skype her sister in California or a couple of her best friends back in Jamaica.

Her breakfast arrived pretty quickly, and Rebecca continued to research local sites while she ate. Myrtle Beach had tons of attractions, big and small, including dozens of golf courses. As she clicked through various Web sites, her thoughts went back to George.

Rebecca had met George very soon after she had arrived in Myrtle Beach and checked in to the beachfront resort that was to be her home base for the next three weeks. All her major assignments in the last three years had been in support of Royal Dunegan Luxury Hotels and Resorts as they updated their marketing pictures to reflect a new brand image and extensive renovations to most of their top locations around the world. Free accommodations in one of their hotels was included in her fee for each of the cities she worked in. Rebecca had been introduced to the resort manager, Stokely Adams, immediately after arrival, and he gave her a quick tour of the property. When they got to Stokely's office, George was waiting for him, and Rebecca was introduced. George was then very quick to offer her access to the golf course he managed whenever she needed it, and she graciously accepted. They ran into each other at the resort several times over the next couple of weeks and spent a little time together over meals or drinks. His interest in something more than casual friendship became very obvious, and Rebecca made an effort not to encourage his subtle advances. George was a nice, pleasant man, but not at all her type.

The situation was much like the encounters with countless men whom she had met from the Caribbean to Southeast Asia, and numerous countries between. While she was happy to make new acquaintances and had an interest in getting to know the local residents, she very rarely met anyone who sparked an interest for a more meaningful relationship. Making friends was always easy for her, even back in school, particularly with boys. Her older sister, Nadine, used to chastise her for being a tease, and letting all the boys think that they had a chance for something more with her. It was an accusation that Rebecca always hotly denied, insisting that it was just easier to make friends with males, but that they were only ever platonic. But now that she was older, Rebecca was mature enough to admit that wasn't exactly true.

Since leaving the small, safe hometown of Runaway Bay, Jamaica, and meeting people from many different cultures, Rebecca understood quickly what Nadine had been trying to tell her. It didn't matter that her intentions were pure and she never deliberately hurt anyone's feelings; pretending that she didn't know those feelings existed could be as bad as encouraging it. While accepting George's help could have gotten her access to additional Myrtle Beach attractions to photograph, Rebecca did not want to encourage his attentions any further.

It was almost noon when she left the restaurant and headed back to the hotel in the north end of the city. She made a brief stop at a drugstore on the way to pick up some toiletries, and pulled into the resort parking lot about thirty minutes later. She had just parked the scooter in the back of the resort when her cell phone rang.

"Hello?" she answered.

"Hey, Becca, how are you doing?" a deep male voice replied.

"Hi, Uncle Devon," she stated brightly. "I'm doing well. How are you?"

"I'm good, dear. How is the project going? Are you wrapping things up?"

Devon Thompson was a very close family friend whom Rebecca had known all her life. He was also a senior manager at Royal Dunegan, and had recommended her to their marketing department for her first photography assignment four years ago.

"It's going well. I sent in the final images a couple of days ago. I think they're happy with them," she explained with a shy giggle. "So I'm hoping they have something else for me soon."

"They are very happy, my dear. You're doing an excellent job. We've just started to use the pictures you took in Malaysia and Indonesia."

"Really? That's great. I can't wait to see which ones they used."

"I'll send you the proofs when they're finalized." He paused for a moment. "I spoke to your sister a few days ago. She says she hasn't heard from you for several weeks."

Rebecca looked down at the ground and nibbled on her lower lip, knowing there was a lecture coming.

"She just wants to know you're okay, Becca. You should call her more often," Uncle Devon continued.

"I know, I know. There's no excuse. I'll give her a call soon. I'm hoping that I can get some work in California while I'm here in the United States. Then I can visit her."

"Becca, you have time between jobs to go visit her if you want."

She opened her mouth to give an explanation, but nothing came out. He was right. She had the time and money to go to San Francisco if she really wanted to. But the relationship with Nadine was complicated, and Rebecca just wasn't ready to deal with it head on. But she could manage a phone call more often.

"You're right, Uncle Dev. I'll give her a call, I promise," she finally replied softly.

"Good. On another note, Richard said that they'll need you in Florida next, maybe for the whole fall season to shoot in Orlando, Saint Petersburg, and Daytona. So you could stay at my place in Winter Garden and negotiate a higher fee."

Richard Kent was the head of marketing with the hotel chain, and her prime contact for her assignments.

"Really? That would be great! Thank you so much."

"It's no problem at all. Let me know when you've confirmed things with Richard and I'll have the place ready for you."

Rebecca suddenly felt choked up, and swallowed hard to contain the tears that threatened to fill up her eyes. "Uncle Dev, I don't know how to thank you . . . for everything you've done." Her voice was thick and tight.

"Enough of that nonsense, Becca. Your mom was like a sister to me and I promised I would make sure you girls were okay after she was gone. So I don't want her spirit cursing me. You know what she was like when she was mad."

Rebecca burst out laughing, and wiped the moisture from her eyes. Devon laughed with her.

"So how are things in MoBay? How is Evelyn doing?" she then asked.

Though Royal Dunegan had its international main office in Chicago, Devon still lived in Jamaica with his wife, managing the Caribbean operations.

"You know how things are—they don't change much," he replied. "Evelyn is doing well in real estate. She sends her love."

"Well, I'm hoping to get back there soon," Rebecca told him. "I miss it more than I realized."

They talked for a few more minutes as he caught her up on some local gossip, before saying goodbye. Rebecca then slung her equipment bag across her shoulder and went into the hotel lobby. As she passed through the spacious area near the check-in counter, she smiled and waved at several of the hotel staff she had become acquainted with over the last couple of weeks. One young man in particular lit up when he saw her as she approached the elevators, and quickly ran over to where she was.

"Hey, Rebecca," he stated with a big smile. "How did it go today?"

"It went great, Juan. How's your day going?" she asked in return.

"It's all right. Did you hear about our open mic event later tonight?" he asked. Juan was part of the entertainment staff, and was a fun guy to hang out with.

"No, I didn't. When is it?"

"It starts at eight, and we're setting up the stage next to the outdoor restaurant. So I better see you there," he demanded with a teasing smile.

Rebecca laughed. "I'll be there," she promised

before waving good-bye and stepping into the elevator.

A few minutes later, she opened the door to her room, walked into the spacious suite, already visited by the maid. It looked exactly like the images found in glossy high-end travel magazines, complete with the perfect view of the Atlantic Ocean. She let out a deep breath and smiled as she dropped her bag on the plush sofa in the living area.

Rebecca felt like pinching herself sometimes. How on earth did an island girl, not quite twenty-six years old, find herself living in four- and five-star resorts week after week? She sighed again and went into the bedroom to change her clothes into something more suitable for the warm weather. Now wearing comfortable blue cotton shorts and a white tank top, she headed back down to the ground floor of the hotel with her iPad, the digital SD card from her camera, and an external card reader. There was a perfect shady spot on the property just back from the beach where she planned to lounge for the afternoon and get some work done.

Chapter 3

Over lunch, Chad, William, Sandra, and her husband decided to join an afternoon tour that included a visit to the historic Brookgreen Gardens, an area called Broadway at the Beach, and the new city boardwalk. The bus left the hotel at one-thirty, so Chad cut his lunch short in order to move his luggage to his new room before meeting the others in the lobby a few minutes before the departure time. They arrived back at the resort at six o'clock, in time to get ready for the company dinner with cocktails at six-thirty.

Chad was not a big drinker, so he opted to spend some extra time in the room, getting settled in and making a few phone calls. As promised, he was now in a large, executive suite with a full living area and a spacious private bedroom with a king-size bed. Chad took a few minutes to hang up the shirts and pants he had packed, leaving out one of each to wear that evening. He then grabbed his toiletry bag and took it into the adjacent bathroom where he laid out the various items for easy use.

Back in the bedroom, he undressed and neatly folded up his used clothes, then returned to the bathroom, naked, and stepped into the large glass-enclosed shower. As he lathered up his thick, muscled body, his mind wandered to some of the issues that would be waiting for him back home in Chicago, not the least of which was his attempt to buy a new home with the help of his mother.

Chad was the only child of Denise Crothers, formerly Denise Irvine, a prominent business owner with a small chain of beauty supply stores across the city. She had raised him as a single mother and they had a very close relationship. Even though Denise got married about ten years ago to Chad's stepdad, Samuel Crothers, who had two grown children of his own, she remained very involved in her son's life—maybe too involved, according to most of his ex-girlfriends. The thought made Chad smile because he knew that it was true, and honestly, he didn't mind since she was a smart woman with great instincts about people and business. But he also had complete faith that once he found the right woman to spend the rest of his life with, his mom would give her blessing and back off. Until then, he could count on her to run interference with anyone she found not good enough for her son.

Before he left Chicago yesterday afternoon for this trip, Chad had put in an offer on a duplex in the city. While out this afternoon, his real estate agent, Susan, had sent him a text message to say the sellers had sent back a counteroffer, higher than he was willing to pay. He had forwarded the note on to his mom, and the advice in her reply was to walk away.

Chad was torn. The property was in his ideal location in the Bucktown area, still downtown Chicago, but with a neighborhood feel. But it wasn't the single family home he'd originally had in mind, with a backyard and a garage. And his mom was pretty adamant that he should look in the suburbs and buy a home more suitable for raising a family. He also was hesitant to continue negotiations while out of town.

As he stood outside the shower and toweled off, Chad went through the short list of objectives he had written out when he first decided to sell his one-bedroom condo in Lakeshore East and buy something more established. He'd been seeing someone at the time, a girl named Angela Boone. They had only dated for about six months, but at one point, he had wondered if she was "the one," and what would happen if their relationship developed into something more serious, like living together or even getting married. Chad had been raised with a traditional view of a man's role in a relationship, meaning he should provide an appropriate home, and his condo wasn't going to cut it. Though things didn't work out with Angela, the idea of getting a bigger, family friendly house stuck in his mind. And once he had mentioned it to his mom, it took on a life of its own, and she had him signed up with a real estate agent in record time.

Chad quickly dressed in dark blue slacks and a striped blue and white shirt, finished with simple silver cuff links and polished brown shoes. He checked his watch and decided he had a few minutes to call his mom and still arrive at the restaurant just in time for dinner.

Denise Crothers answered after the first ring. "Hi, baby. How is your trip going?"

"Hi, Mom. It's going okay. There's a company event tonight, so I only have a few minutes," he explained right away so she wouldn't be offended when he got right to the point. "So, I saw your note about the duplex in Bucktown. You don't think it's worth what they're asking?"

"It's a beautiful property, move-in ready," Denise stated. "It's probably a fair price for someone who's looking for something in the city. But, sweetheart, it's not for you."

"I don't know, Mom. I really liked it. It's close to work and almost brand new."

"Yes, and with no green space or garage. You may as well stay in a condo."

Chad let out a deep breath. His mom was right; other than more square footage, the duplex wouldn't provide the change in lifestyle that he was looking for.

"Now, I did see a few really nice listings in Bolingbrook."

"I think that's too far, Mom. My commute would be close to an hour," he interjected.

"Or what about Oak Park? It's just outside the city limits."

"We'll see. I'll let my agent know I'm turning

down the duplex. Then we can look at a few more properties next weekend."

"Okay, dear."

"Thanks, Mom," he stated, checking his watch again.

"Oh, it's no bother, Chad. I'm actually enjoying myself."

They said good-bye a moment later. Chad grabbed his wallet and headed downstairs to the restaurant for dinner. When he arrived, the hotel staff directed him to tables set up outside where most of his small group of coworkers were just getting seated. He quickly found William, who had already secured a seat for him with several other people they often worked with, including Sandra. Within moments, the restaurant staff started to bring out a selection of appetizers.

It was a warm night with a light cool breeze and the poolside dining atmosphere had a tropical feel. While the guests ate their four-course meal, a band with a lead singer started playing classic sixties ballads. By the time dessert was served, the drinks were flowing and there was a distinct party atmosphere building. The music gradually became more upbeat, prompting a few people to hit the makeshift dance floor in front of the stage.

At about five minutes to eight o'clock, a handsome young Latino man borrowed the mic from the band to make an announcement.

"Hi, everyone. Welcome to the Royal Dunegan Myrtle Beach Resort and Spa. We hope you're enjoying your stay with us so far. My name is Juan, and

I'm your entertainment manager. We have quite a
night planned for you all. But first let's give a round
of applause to our resident band, Beach Bums!
They'll be playing for us all weekend."

The guests all clapped in response.

"Now, I hope you have some talented folks in the
audience," Juan continued dramatically. "Because
tonight is Open Mic Night! So, if you can sing,
dance, or tell a joke, this is your opportunity. The
top three performers will each win an amazing
prize, so don't be shy. I'll be at the bar to sign up
anyone who wants to participate. We'll get started
in about ten minutes."

Juan handed the microphone back to the
lead singer, and the band started up again with a
Motown hit.

"So, who's going to go up there?" Sandra asked
with a big smile.

Chad and William looked at each other, then
back at her before they all burst out laughing. They
had been together on enough President's Club
trips and corporate off-sites to know that they were
all equally conservative and way too low-key to per-
form in front of colleagues and other strangers.

"Come on, Chad! I'll bet you a hundred dollars
you can't get up there," Sandra's husband, Eddie,
teased.

"Wow, that's a pretty rich wager, Eddie," William
stated while they all laughed harder. "I'll do it for
fifty!"

"Billy boy, you would have to pay *us* fifty dollars

each before we'd let you sing," Chad stated in a dry tone.

While William looked insulted, the others at the table burst into loud hilarity. The teasing continued until the performances started. The first was a woman named Janet Humphries from the Sheppard Networks party, a top salesperson with a vibrant and outgoing personality. She chose to sing a big Lady Gaga hit song and did her best to put on a good show. Unfortunately, Janet's enthusiasm far outweighed her actual singing talent, and she was obviously too inebriated to care. But she definitely got the party started, and the crowd cheered wildly at her big finish.

The open mic performances continued for another hour showcasing a variety of talents, mostly singing, but also four comedians, two magic acts, and a really good highland dancer from Canada. Judging from the applause, the dancer was the top winner by far.

"Okay, everyone, we have some stiff competition tonight," Juan announced with a big grin from the stage, and the audience cheered, clapping loudly. "Our final performer is all the way from the Caribbean, so let's give it up to Rebecca!"

Though Chad and William were facing the outdoor stage, and their table provided a clear view of the competition, the two men had not been paying much attention after the first ten or fifteen minutes. They had been discussing the scheduled options for the next day while William moved quickly onto his second beer and Chad slowly sipped his first. Neither noticed the woman who walked onto the stage with a thick cloud of brown spiraling curls surrounding her face. She was wearing a sparkling silver tank top and the tiniest gray satin shorts with black platform wedges that made her lean legs appear a mile long. It was her voice that grabbed their attention.

The accompanying music started up with a strong drum beat and the steady strum of the electric guitar. It was the intro to a classic eighties song, and William paused midsentence to look up. Chad's gaze soon followed. For the opening bars, the girl on the stage was looking down at the ground, standing very still except for a slight bob of her head to the rhythm of the music. Then she started singing in a powerful, throaty voice with a strong blues tone, sounding very much like the vocalist Melissa Etheridge.

William and Chad looked at each other, then back at the stage. Everyone around them seemed to stop talking at the same time, captured by the unexpected performance. It was impossible to believe that the tiny black girl on the stage, with her chic, urban style, was belting out a powerful rock song about a wayward lover. While she started out fairly static, singing into the mounted microphone, by the first chorus she was moving to the rhythm, swaying with the words. The audience clapped wildly, and some of the older guests started singing along. She seemed inspired by the response, and sang the rest of the song like it was her own.

The applause at the end was thunderous, with

catcalls and enthusiastic shouts. The tiny girl smiled shyly before stepping down from the stage.

At first, Chad was too caught up in the entertainment to notice anything beyond the raise in his heart rate and the goose bumps on his skin. Unlike William, he wasn't a rock music fan. His style leaned more toward R & B, reggae, and soul, but he could still appreciate a good song, particularly one that was very recognizable. The singing wasn't perfect, but the performance was honest, emotional, and unexpected. That's what he was thinking as he watched the young woman walk toward the back of the restaurant, presumably to wait for the contest results.

"Wow, she was awesome, wasn't she?" Sandra asked once everyone was seated again. "That was my favorite song in junior high! Remember, Eddie?"

Her husband nodded while guzzling his beer.

"She was really good," William added. "And very hot!" He grinned brightly at Chad, raising his eyebrows up and down to emphasize his point.

Chad shrugged in response, indicating ambivalence. "She's cute, but not really my type," he replied, leaning close enough to William so only he could hear.

"That's right, you like them stacked," William stated, chuckling.

It was obvious that the alcohol had loosened his tongue and inhibitions. Chad shrugged since there was some truth to the statement. He had always been drawn to shapely women with soft curves. Not that he couldn't appreciate beautiful women of all shapes and sizes, but there was something about a pair of double Ds. . . .

His wayward thoughts were interrupted by Juan, who was back on the stage with the mic in his hand.

"Ladies and gentlemen, can we have all our talented performers back on stage?" he requested. "As I stated before, we have wonderful prizes for our top three performers, and you will choose our winners with your applause."

He looked over at the seven people now standing next to each other on his right, then proceeded to call out each of the names so that the audience could pick the favorites with the appropriate volume of cheers and claps. It was not surprising that the petite singer named Rebecca was the clear first-place winner by far. Four of the performers left the stage in good spirits, leaving the top three anticipating their prizes. Juan then announced that second and third place would get a complimentary spa visit and a bottle of rum in that respective order.

"And for our first-place prize winner, we have a safari jeep tour of the South Carolinian lowland. Congratulations, Rebecca," Juan added, handing her a gift certificate while everyone clapped.

Rebecca beamed brightly, clearly thrilled with the prize, before leaving the stage. She was still smiling as she walked through the tables, politely accepting congratulations from random guests as she passed them. . . . Until she got to where Chad sat with his coworkers. She froze for a few seconds as her light brown eyes locked with his, opening wide with surprise.

Chad immediately recognized his mysterious wood nymph. He blinked a few times and raised out of his chair, though he wasn't sure why. He only got halfway up before she was gone.

"What was that about?" William asked.

Chad shrugged and shook his head dismissively, but his heart was beating like a drum in his ears.

Chapter 4

Rebecca stood in the bathroom near the restaurant, looking down at her first-place award. The high of singing on stage and winning a contest was still buzzing in her veins, but it was the sight of that angry bear that occupied her mind.

She knew she had overreacted when she saw him. It wasn't his imposing frame and surly attitude, though that combination probably caused most women to scurry away in fear. Rebecca had dealt with men her whole life, and found that the biggest ones were usually the gentlest, like giant stuffed animals. So it wasn't his size that sucked the air out of her lungs. It was his eyes, deep, rich brown and burning with intensity as they locked with hers.

Rebecca let out a deep breath and shook her head before looking in the mirror at her oval face framed by an untamed cloud of curls. Her naturally pink lips were still moist and glistening with clear lip gloss, so Rebecca only smacked them together to freshen up the shine. The silvery silk top she wore hung off the shoulder with a cowl-neck that draped low in the front. It revealed her best attempt at a generous cleavage, aided by the superpowers of a strapless push-up bra. She was in the middle of adjusting her breasts so they were propped up into eye-catching mounds when another woman entered the bathroom.

"Congratulations," the middle-aged blonde said. She had a pretty, friendly face and smiled broadly at Rebecca in the vanity mirror.

Rebecca smiled back and replied, "Thanks."

"Do you sing professionally?"

Rebecca snorted and shook her head. "Not at all."

"Well, you should think about it. You were such a natural up there. And you chose to sing one of my favorite songs! I'm a huge Melissa Etheridge fan."

"So was my mom. She used to play that song all the time," Rebecca replied.

The tragic significance of the statement must have been visible in her large, round eyes. The woman smiled sadly and stepped closer to her. "Well, I'm sure your mom would have loved your version," she stated in a soft voice.

There was a short awkward pause.

"I'm Sandra, Sandra McLean."

"Rebecca Isles."

They smiled at each other again. Sandra then turned to the mirror in order to freshen her makeup.

"Are you here in Myrtle Beach on vacation or for work?" she asked the younger woman.

"A bit of both right now," Rebecca replied. "I came here to do a project, but it's finished and I have a few days before my next assignment. So I'm going to relax a little and visit some of the local sites."

"What sort of project?"

"I'm a photographer, and I have a contract with the Royal Dunegan chain of hotels and resorts."

Sandra paused while combing her hair, clearly intrigued by the information. "Really? So you just go around taking pictures for them?" she asked.

"Pretty much!" Rebecca replied with a light laugh. "There's a little more to it than that. I'm an independent consultant, so they still have to buy what I produce, and I work for other clients as a freelancer. But the bulk of it is for the hotels. They pretty much dictate where I will be week to week."

"Wow! How long have you been doing that?"

"Full time? About three years."

Their conversation was interrupted as several other women entered the bathroom. Sandra went back to her primping and Rebecca quickly washed her hands before turning to leave.

"It was nice meeting you, Sandra," she stated politely.

"You too."

Outside the bathroom, Rebecca checked her watch. It was a few minutes to ten o'clock. She wasn't quite ready to head up to her room, so she decided to go back outside and have a drink while listening to some music. The crowd had thinned out a bit, but there were still a decent number of guests enjoying the summer night air. Approaching the outdoor bar, Rebecca recognized a couple of the bartenders.

"Hi, Antonio. Can I have white wine, please?"

"Hey, Rebecca. You can have whatever you want after that performance!" he replied. "So how about I make you one of my special cocktails?"

He was flirting with her, and Rebecca knew it right away. Not the typical customer service flirting that bar or restaurant staff do to make guests feel good and tip well. It was clearly a "call me when I'm done with my shift" vibe. Antonio was a good-looking guy, tall and lean, a deep chocolate brown with neat shoulder-length dreadlocks, but Rebecca wasn't interested, not even a little bit. She had learned very early in her career traveling that there were always men looking to get together with a woman who would only be in town for a few weeks. That situation almost always ended with awkward emptiness or heartbreak. So Rebecca had made a pledge not to get involved until she was ready to have a steady address.

Antonio didn't spark enough interest to rethink that plan, but there was no need to be rude. "Sure, why not?" she replied, friendly but without encouragement.

"Great! One 'Tonio Tonic' coming up!"

She watched him pour a variety of liquids into a shaker with a few ice cubes, give it a vigorous shake, and pour it slowly into an oversized martini glass. The concoction came out a reddish gold color. He put it down carefully on a coaster in front of her.

Rebecca picked it up to sniff it. "Dark rum, mango, and pineapple juice?" she asked.

"Nice!" Antonio replied. "What else?"

She took a sip. "I'm not sure. Another liquor? Something sweet?"

"Yup. It's apricot brandy."

Rebecca sipped it again. It was strong, but really good. "I like it. Thanks, Antonio," she told him, raising the glass in a silent cheer.

"I aim to please, so let me know if there's anything else you need."

She nodded in agreement, then turned in her bar seat to watch what was happening in the outdoor room. The volume of the music had increased and people were now dancing to a popular radio hit.

"Can I have another beer, please?"

Rebecca looked over at the man who was now standing beside her. He caught her glance and smiled back, showing her his gorgeous blue eyes and brilliant white teeth.

"Hi, I'm Todd Bordeaux," he announced, facing her. "You're the girl from the contest, right?"

"That's right," she replied, a little reserved. As cute as he was, there was something about him that screamed "salesman," to Rebecca, even in his gray polo shirt and relaxed chinos.

"That was a great show," he told her, reaching for his fresh bottle of beer.

"Thank you." She was looking out at the dance floor, but could tell that he was watching her.

"What was your name again?" he finally asked.

"Rebecca."

"Well, Rebecca, would you like to dance?"

The DJ was playing a pretty good song, and

Rebecca was feeling the beat in her bones. What was the harm?

"Sure, why not," she told him.

They both put their drinks down and Todd escorted her to the dance floor. He turned out to have pretty good rhythm—nothing fancy, certainly nothing worthy of a *Soul Train* line, but nothing embarrassing either. After a couple of songs, Rebecca began to relax and lose herself in the music. Dancing was something that she loved, but rarely got the chance to do these days. It was the perfect night to let loose and work up a sweat under the stars.

They must have been out there for about forty-five minutes before the music changed to a romantic ballad. Rebecca indicated to Todd that she needed a drink, then headed back to the bar. The remnants of her cocktail were long gone, so she requested a bottle of water instead.

"Wow, Todd! I didn't know you could move like that."

Rebecca looked to her right and found that Todd had followed her off the dance floor and was now standing in front of a group of men. The comment was made by a slim, shorter guy with a pinkish skin tone.

Her dance partner just shrugged and laughed. "I have many talents, Billy Boy," he replied.

"Maybe, but you can't hold a light to your friend here. Are you going to introduce us?"

Rebecca suddenly found four pairs of eyes focused on her. She slowly lowered the bottle in her hand and turned to face the men. "Hi, I'm Rebecca Isles," she stated with an amused expression on her face.

"Nice to meet you, Rebecca," said the ringleader Todd had called Billy.

"Unfortunately, I work with these jackasses," Todd told her, like an apology. "This is William, Neil, Sean, and Chad."

Each guy nodded after his name, except for the last. He had been sitting during the conversation, hidden by the others. When he stood up, she noted as their eyes met that he was a good three to five inches taller than his peers.

Like the other two times Rebecca had found herself the focus of his intense gaze, she froze.

"So, what brings you to Myrtle Beach in the middle of September?" Neil asked, or maybe it was Sean. Rebecca wasn't sure.

"I'm here for work," she replied.

"On a conference? What company are you with?" the other one asked.

She shook her head. "I work on my own. I'm doing an assignment with the resort."

"An independent consultant?" one of them suggested.

"Something like that," Rebecca stated.

There was a short pause as the men looked at her speculatively. Except the tall one at the edge of the group. He looked out at the dance floor, stiff as a robot, as though she didn't exist. Something about the hard cut of his profile irked her.

"That's a pretty cool prize you won," the shorter guy, William, stated. "It's one of those jeep tours through a wildlife park, right? We're booked on a similar tour for tomorrow. When are you going?"

"I'm not sure," she replied, trying to be polite. "That's what it sounds like. I'll have to call them to see what's involved."

"Well, if it's the same excursion, then you can join our group. We leave at noon," he continued.

The other men around him were already nodding with encouragement, but Rebecca shook her head. "Sorry, I can't make it tomorrow. Saturday is the only day I have free at this point," she explained.

"That's too bad," Todd said. "Hopefully, you won't have to take the tour alone."

"I'm sure I'll find someone to take along," she stated with a nonchalant shrug and a flirtatious smile.

When the tall, broody one glanced over at her for a quick moment, Rebecca almost grinned at him, but checked herself. He was listening after all. She stood a little taller with her shoulders a tad wider.

"So, you guys all work together? Here for a company getaway?" she asked.

"Yup, we're with a systems firm, based in Chicago," Todd explained.

"And what do you guys all do? No, wait! Let me guess," Rebecca teased. "You are in sales?"

Todd raised his eyebrows with surprise while the rest of the crew laughed.

"How did you know?" one of the others asked.

Rebecca smiled broadly and took a drink of water. "I have a knack for reading people," she told him. "Okay, who's next? William, is it? I would say you're into something technical, maybe an engineer?"

William nodded, grinning.

"That's not so impressive. Look at his hair cut! It practically screams tech geek!"

"Hey! That's brilliant tech geek to you!" William shot back.

"Okay, okay," Rebecca replied, walking slowly toward the guy who had teased William. "Neil, right? I would say you are a . . . lawyer, maybe?"

There was another cheer.

"He's a contract negotiator," Todd confirmed. "Now do Sean."

She turned to the fourth friend, making a big show of looking him up and down. "Hmmm, I would say you're in sales also," she guessed.

They all groaned.

"No?" Rebecca queried, glancing between them.

"Nope. Marketing," Sean clarified, grinning broadly because he had stumped her.

"Rats! Well, three out of four isn't bad, right?"

She then slowly turned until she was looking at the fifth man in the group. He was facing the others now, but his face was still expressionless.

"You still have Chad," said William. "Guess what he does."

Rebecca lifted her chin to look the giant in the eyes, feeling relaxed and giggly from the rum and camaraderie. She raised an eyebrow in silent challenge.

"She won't get it," Chad finally stated with firm confidence. His voice was deep and smooth as silk.

"Oh, really?" she countered. "How much do you want to bet?"

He just stared back in silence, but the heat in his dark eyes intensified.

"You're not going on the safari tomorrow, Chad. Let's say that if she guesses right, you go with her on Saturday," William suggested.

The others chimed in with support.

"No, that's—" Rebecca started to say, but her voice was drowned out.

"Agreed," Chad stated.

The others laughed and cheered like it was a fraternity challenge.

Rebecca was suddenly questioning why she ever went down this path. As much as her competitive nature made her want to win, she wasn't sure the prize was worth it.

As though sensing her dilemma, Chad raised an eyebrow to mimic her earlier expression. His full lips curved into the semblance of a smile.

"It's a bet," she stated, unable to resist his goading.

Chad smiled broadly, showing strong, straight, beautiful teeth. "Well?"

Rebecca ignored him and instead decided to take her time, make him sweat. She took several slow steps until she was right in front of him. Her deliberate appraisal started around his shoulders, trailing over their broad sculptured strength, and lingered on the hard expanse of his chest. She took a sip of her drink. "Chad, right?" she quizzed softly.

"That's right. Chad Irvine," he replied as though unaffected by her examination.

"Chad," Rebecca repeated, stretching out the single syllable.

She then walked around him until she had a full view of his back. Though men like this weren't really her type, Rebecca had to admit he was an impressive specimen. He was built like a prize stallion, with firm, arched muscles clearly defined through his shirt, even in a relaxed position. It was a body carved in a gym with a strict diet and a precise regimen, not on the sports field having fun. Something told her that his life and his job were equally as rigid.

"Well, Chad Irvine. My guess is that you are an accountant."

His eyes widened with surprise, and Rebecca knew instantly that she was correct. The shouts and cheers from his friends confirmed her victory.

Chapter 5

Chad had to grudgingly admit he was pretty surprised. Sure she had been pretty accurate with his coworkers, but they were easy. Todd was the poster boy for your typical sales guy, and William could not look more like a techie with his ten dollar hair cut, pocketed white shirt and serviceable brown loafers. But people were usually surprised to find out he was an accountant. He immediately wanted to know how she had come to that conclusion, and intended to find out when the moment was right.

She looked up at him, obviously quite proud of herself, and he couldn't help but smile. "That's an impressive talent," he stated. "It looks like you have a date."

"Just so you know, Rebecca, we tried to talk Chad into coming with us on the tour. But he had no interest," William added with a chuckle. "What did you say, buddy? That the last thing you wanted to do was spend four hours crammed into a little jeep?"

"Something like that," Chad replied with a wry twist of his lips.

The other men laughed and teased Chad for a few minutes; then with the fun over, they moved to another spot at the bar to get more drinks.

Rebecca turned toward him once the others were out of earshot. "Listen, it was just harmless fun. So please don't feel as though you have to come along on the trip with me," she stated, obviously uncomfortable with the idea that Chad would not enjoy the excursion. "I can easily find someone who wants to go along. Or, I'm fine to go on my own."

Chad was already shaking his head. "Don't listen to Billy. He likes to exaggerate," he told her softly. "You won fair and square, and I always pay my debts. Plus, a jeep ride with a pretty woman is much more fun than with those clowns."

Her eyes widened in surprise at his compliment, but she smiled politely. "All right then," she finally stated.

There was an awkward pause as he watched her sip her drink.

"So, now that we've established what I do, why don't you tell me what kind of project requires you to climb up into trees in the middle of a golf course," he suggested.

She visibly froze for a few seconds, then let out a deep breath, and her reaction told him that she had been expecting the topic of their first encounter to come up eventually.

"I'm a travel photographer," she finally stated.

"Really?" Chad replied, unable to hide his surprise.

"Yup. I had the morning free, so I got out early

and used the time to add to my portfolio. I guess I lost track of time."

The final sentence sounded like an apology. It reminded Chad of how she had run off that morning, likely because of his boorish attitude. "That explains the camera lens that almost killed me," he added with a disarming smile, touching a spot on the top of his head. "I probably overreacted, though."

Rebecca let out a loud snort followed by a giggle. She looked up at him with twinkling eyes.

"Point taken," he stated, also chuckling.

"Are you okay? No permanent damage?" she asked, her eyes showing genuine concern.

"I'm told I'm hard headed, so I barely felt anything," Chad dismissed. "Is your work always so dangerous?"

She turned to fully face him, leaning one elbow on the bar. "That was nothing. Part of the adventure is investigating where to get the best shot. You can't always do that on the ground."

"Interesting. So, you're a professional photographer."

She nodded.

"And are you local?" he probed when she didn't freely add any more information. "I mean, I hear a Caribbean accent, but are you now living in South Carolina?"

"No, I only arrived a couple of weeks ago to do work with the hotel. I think Sunday will be my last day, then I'm off to Florida for a while."

"That's quite a travel schedule."

Rebecca shrugged. "It's part of the job description."

"And where do you call home?" Chad asked.

"Nowhere, really. I've been on the road for the last few years. But I guess it's still Jamaica."

"So, you've been traveling continuously? Alone? That must be hard."

"Not really. I think of it as an adventure. I get to see the world doing what I love. What could be better than that?" she asked him.

Chad didn't know what to say. He had never met a woman like her. While he wanted to ask her a ton of other questions, about her family, her solitary lifestyle, her ambition, he resisted, not wanting to pry.

"What about you? Are you also from Chicago, like Todd?" Rebecca asked to fill the silence.

"Yup. Born and raised. My mother is Jamaican also, but she came to the states when she was pretty young."

"Really, which part of the island?"

"I'm not sure, to be honest."

"Sorry to interrupt," William stated as he walked over and stood between them. "But some of us are heading over to a pool hall nearby to play a few games. You guys in?"

Chad looked at Rebecca with raised eyebrows, silently asking if she wanted to join them.

"Sorry, but I'm heading up for the night," she politely declined. "I have an early morning."

The added sentence was aimed at Chad with an impish smile. He grinned back, but was really disappointed that she couldn't hang around longer.

"Give me a minute, and I'll meet up with you guys," Chad told William.

"Cool. It was nice meeting you, Rebecca."

"You too," she replied.

Todd also came over to say good-bye. "Thanks for the dance," he told her, flashing his megawatt smile. "Happy to do it again tomorrow night if you need a partner."

She laughed at his offer and suggestive wink. "Thanks. I'll keep that in mind." She waved at all the men as they walked away

"So, why don't you give me a call tomorrow to confirm things for Saturday?" he stated.

"Okay. But, you really don't have to feel obligated to go. Honestly," Rebecca insisted.

"Not at all, I'm looking forward to it," Chad countered.

She looked skeptical, but pulled out her iPhone and turned it on. "Okay. What's your room number?"

He gave her the details, including his cell phone number. "If you don't get me in my room, just send me a text message."

"I will," she confirmed.

They looked at each other for a few seconds.

"All right, I'm off," she finally stated.

He smiled, strangely satisfied to see her awkwardness. "I can walk you up to your room, if you'd like," he offered, conscious of the fact that she was a woman alone at night.

"Thank you, but that's not necessary. I'll be fine, and your friends are waiting for you."

"Okay. Well, it was nice to meet you, Rebecca. Again."

"You too, Chad. Enjoy the rest of your night."

With that, she walked past him and off toward one of the hotel entrances. Chad stood there for about a minute until she disappeared into the building, then he smiled to himself. She really wasn't his usual type, without the curves and big city polish. But for some intangible reason, his interest was more piqued than he could remember in a long time. The rest of the weekend suddenly had unexpected potential.

"Ah, you made it," William said with a big smile once Chad joined the other men at the front entrance of the hotel.

"Yeah. I told you I'd be here in a few minutes," Chad replied.

His friend shrugged. "I just assumed that you had found other nighttime activities, that's all. That girl is hot and it was pretty hard to miss the sparks between you," William observed. "Just so you know, I think Todd is a little miffed that you cock-blocked him on this one."

The last sentence was made in a low whisper so the others wouldn't hear. The minivan taxi arrived at that point and the men all piled in. Chad entered last and caught a glimpse of Todd's face before sitting down. The other man didn't seem upset or even slightly bothered. He was laughing about something the rest of the group was talking about, his face a little flushed from the drinks throughout the evening. But Chad wasn't about to let something like this grow or fester. Todd was an essential part of his team at work, and while they weren't exactly best friends, they were friendly and worked well together.

He waited until they were dropped off at the pool hall a few miles away to address the situation.

"Listen, Todd," Chad said as he stopped his coworker with a light hand on his shoulder. "I'm cool to back off if you want."

Todd's face showed confusion at first, but the lights came on quickly. "You mean, the girl at the hotel? Rebecca? Don't worry about it, man. It's nothing."

"Yeah, well, I don't need to go on the trip with her if it's an issue for you," Chad added.

"Seriously, it's nothing. She was fun to hang out with for a minute, but there's nothing there. As long as she brings back some pics of you squished into a little jeep, I'm good," he replied, slapping Chad on the arm and chuckling at the idea.

Chad smiled briefly with a quick flash of his teeth, but his eyes were all business. "Yeah, that's not going to happen."

"We'll see," Todd shot back before sauntering over to the rest of their group as Neil and Sean started the first game. The boisterous and competitive playing went late into the night until the pool hall announced closing time.

On Friday, everyone from Sheppard Networks met for a breakfast meeting and a morning workshop. After lunch, they split up for preregistered activities. While the other guys went on the safari, Chad joined Sandra, Eddie, and several other members of their party on a casino cruise.

Chad wasn't really into gambling, but it was either

that or several hours at one of the amusement parks. His plan was to play with a couple of hundred dollars until it was gone, then hang out for the rest of the boat ride watching others waste their money. But the afternoon was much more fun and profitable than he had anticipated. He doubled his money at the blackjack table while having a pretty good time. Once he decided to stop pushing his luck, Chad cashed in his chips to spend the rest of the cruise enjoying the Southern Carolina coastline as the sun began to set.

The group arrived back at the hotel some time after seven that evening. Chad and Sandra agreed to meet William and a few other coworkers for dinner at seven-thirty, which gave them a few minutes to stop in their rooms. Chad used the time to change his shirt and reply to a few e-mails, including one from his real estate agent with a few listings to view. His mom was copied on the note, and the very next message was her offer to have a look at a couple of the homes for him over the weekend. Shaking his head with an amused smile on his lips, he replied to both women to say that he was fine.

He also checked for any phone messages to his room, or text messages on his phone from Rebecca to confirm their plans for the following morning, but there weren't any. Surprised but not concerned, Chad then grabbed his wallet and room pass and headed to dinner.

The resort was very busy as new guests arrived for the weekend, or to have dinner at the hotel restaurant. Once he stepped out of the elevator and walked through the expansive ground floor, Chad

found himself casually looking around to catch a
glimpse of Rebecca among the other guests. She
was nowhere to be seen.

The evening went by much like the last two, with
a delicious full dinner, drinks flowing too freely,
and a few hours of planned entertainment provided by the hotel staff near the outdoor bar. This
time, it was a comedy show with a series of local professional performers. The acts were funny, but
Chad remained distracted. He kept scanning the
room and repeatedly checking the message indicator on his phone.

It was minutes to ten o'clock when he finally
caught a glimpse of her near the bar. She was sitting
alone at a table for two, eating a dessert, something
chocolate and covered with whipped cream or ice
cream. Chad watched her, as covertly as possible, as
she savored each sweet spoonful while giggling at
the antics of the headliner. She seemed completely
comfortable and relaxed on her own in a room
filled with couples, families, and groups of friends.

The show ended moments later, and the guests
started to mingle while music played in the background. Chad declined a trip to the bar with
William and others, choosing to keep his current
view of Rebecca visible in his periphery. She finished her dessert, chatted with Juan and several
other staff members as they walked by, and danced
in her seat when there was a song that she liked.
She even politely accepted a drink from a guy at the
bar, but declined his invitation to dance. He felt a
little guilty about his surveillance, but not enough
to stop. Then he watched as she got up and walked

into the hotel, stopping to say hello to Sandra on the way. Not once did she look at her phone, or attempt to send him a message.

Chad was perplexed. It must have been visible on his usually stoic face.

"What's wrong?" Sandra asked as she rejoined the table, handing Eddie the beer she had purchased for him at the bar.

"What?" he asked, surprised at her question as it pulled him out of his thoughts.

"You look concerned about something. What's wrong?" she repeated.

"Oh. Nothing," he replied, sitting up in his chair and smiling back.

"So, what's the plan for the rest of the night?" she asked both men. "It's only ten-thirty and the night is young."

"Sorry, I think I'll pack it in a little early tonight," Chad told them. "Now you lovebirds can have some time to yourselves."

Eddie wiggled his brows suggestively and Sandra giggled. Chad couldn't help smiling at their teasing before walking over to the bar where the rest of their party were hanging out.

"Hey, Chad, what's up?" William asked with a toothy grin.

Neil and Sean also nodded to recognize his appearance.

"I'm heading up for the night," Chad told them.

"All right, old man," William stated, slapping him on the shoulder. "Are you still on for your date tomorrow morning?"

Chad was about to answer when he felt his phone vibrate.

"One sec," he told William as he pulled the BlackBerry out of his pocket and checked the new text message. He didn't recognize the phone number, but the message was simple:

Are we still on? The bus leaves at 9.

Chad smiled to himself as he quickly typed in a reply:

Meet you for breakfast at 8?

Then he waited for a few seconds for the response.

OK.

"What're you all giddy about?" William asked after a few moments.

"Nothing," Chad answered as he put his phone away.

"Ahhhh. I recognize that goofy grin. It's a girl, isn't it?" his friend teased, clearly on the tipsy side.

Chad just shook his head, refusing to participate in the juvenile banter. "Good night, boys," he said to the group. He tapped William on the cheek like a naughty child, then headed into the hotel and up to his room.

Chapter 6

Rebecca was filled with nervous energy. She was up before six o'clock on Saturday morning, dressed and ready for the day by seven. Unable to sit in her room and watch the clock tick by, she went for a walk along the beach to use up some time. Despite her best efforts, Rebecca was still over fifteen minutes early for breakfast. After requesting a table near the front entrance where Chad could easily see her when he arrived, she ordered a cup of coffee to drink while she waited.

Though she was fully engrossed in reviewing pictures on her iPhone, she knew the minute he stepped into the room. Something about Chad's confident posture drew all eyes to his impressive size as it filled the entranceway. Rebecca was about to raise a hand to grab his attention, but he found her first and headed over to the table in long, smooth strides. She rose out of her seat awkwardly as he approached and they hugged briefly.

"Have you been here long?" he asked, motioning to her nearly empty cup of coffee.

Rebecca laughed nervously. "I got here a little early," she confessed.

"Ahhh. You're a morning person."

It was a statement rather than a question, and it made Rebecca look at him quizzically. "I am," she confirmed. "How did you know?"

They were interrupted by their waiter, who took their orders and brought Chad a cup of coffee. She waited patiently as he added a generous amount of cream and sugar to his drink.

"Well, other than your fondness for early morning adventures, like climbing trees at the crack of dawn . . ."

"It wasn't the crack of dawn," she inserted defensively. "Okay, I did get to the course before sunrise, but the tree climbing came later. And I wasn't just gallivanting, okay? I was working."

He just smiled tolerantly, with one eyebrow raised. "Gallivanting?"

"You know what I mean," she shot back, her accent a little thicker than usual.

Chad sipped his coffee, obviously amused at how easy she was to tease. She took a deep, dramatic breath and flashed him a big fake smile. He laughed.

"Go on," Rebecca prompted.

"You look too energized for this early in the morning."

"Maybe it's the coffee," she suggested, taking a small sip from her cup.

"Nah, it's not artificial. I can see it in your eyes. You've already had a full morning while the rest of us are still half asleep," Chad said.

"Really? You get all that from my eyes?"

"It's a gift, " he stated simply with a shrug.

Rebecca burst out laughing at his dry humor. It was unexpected and very appealing. It also broke the ice for her.

"So, tell me about this adventure we're about to go on," he continued. "Do I need to increase my accident insurance before we leave?"

She giggled again. "No, I think we'll be okay."

Their breakfast arrived at that point. They spent the next twenty minutes eating and discussing their plans for the excursion. Rebecca outlined their schedule beginning with the bus that would pick them up at nine o'clock for the thirty-minute drive to the safari office. They would then have a museum tour and info session followed by the three-hour jeep ride through the South Carolina lowlands.

The morning went as planned, and the vibe between the two stayed relaxed and lighthearted. Once they reached the safari headquarters, they joined the rest of their tour group, around ten other people of various ages. The group completed the small tour of the historical museum, then headed out to a safari vehicle, an oversized utility jeep modified with enough benches to seat up to fourteen passengers. It was spacious and comfortable, with open sides and plenty of leg room. Chad and Rebecca had a row to themselves, and he fit into the space comfortably. With that concern out of the way, he seemed even more interested in the tour.

Three hours flew by as their guides stopped many times to point out culturally significant locations and interesting ecological sites. Rebecca used the opportunity to take several hundred photos of wildlife and untamed landscape. Chad seemed content to relax while taking in the sites, and occasionally pointed out things for her to shoot. He even helped her climb up a low wall in order to get a better view of an American alligator as it peeked its eyes out of the water. It was an awesome shot, and he seemed as thrilled as she was to see it captured.

At twelve-thirty, they were on their way back to the safari headquarters. Rebecca sat back in her seat and watched the scenery go by. In those moments of calm relaxation, she acknowledged that it had been a very nice morning. It wasn't just the excursion, it was also the company. She looked over at Chad as he sat beside her with his face turned away as he also looked out at the passing landscape. He was still as quiet and serious as he first appeared, but he was also funny, helpful, and easygoing. Rebecca found him to be a puzzle.

"Are you hungry?" he suddenly asked, turning to look down at her with those bright brown eyes.

Rebecca was caught off guard, immediately conscious of the fact that she had been staring at him for an uncomfortable amount of time. "I'm a little peckish," she replied.

"Peckish?" he quizzed, raising one of his brows.

She shook her head at his teasing. "Meaning a little hungry. I could do with a snack," she elaborated.

"Thanks for the definition. Let's stop for lunch on the way back to the hotel. There's a Brazilian steak house I was hoping to try."

Rebecca was surprised by the casual offer, but only nodded in agreement. The cold intense giant of a man that she had encountered in the forest was definitely not her type, but this version of Chad Irvine was growing on her. His light teasing and relaxed company was easy and uncomplicated. It was nice.

The restaurant Chad mentioned was on the way back to the resort, so they took a taxi for the fifteen-minute ride. He spent the drive talking about the last Brazilian restaurant he had been to in Chicago, going into great detail about the menu and the way the meat was grilled and served. His face displayed pure desire and his eyes flashed with the memory.

"Wow, you're really looking forward to this, aren't you?" she finally stated as they walked into the eatery.

Chad laughed. "What can I say? I'm passionate about good food, that's all. There's almost nothing as satisfying as perfectly grilled meat."

"Really? I can think of a few things. . . ."

Rebecca was about to add "and they have nothing to do with grilling!" but managed to cut the sentence short before her tongue ran on without thought. It was her natural, flirty nature bubbling to the surface, and the innuendo was obvious in her tone. But it was so out of place with their friendly and platonic interactions so far. She immediately felt Chad stiffen beside her, and could have kicked herself.

Thankfully, they were approached by a hostess and escorted to a table in the rear of the dining room that was quite busy with the lunchtime rush.

Once they were seated, Rebecca quickly glanced at Chad, hoping the moment had passed, but he was looking at her intently. Though his face was expressionless, the speculation in his eyes dashed her hopes.

"This place seems nice," she babbled, looking around.

"I said there was *almost* nothing as satisfying as a good steak," Chad continued as though she hadn't spoken.

She cleared her throat, trying to buy some time to decide what to do. There were a few sassy comments on the tip of her tongue that she was so tempted to fire back, but Rebecca tried hard not to. Something about his quiet focus said Chad was not the type of man who was easily toyed with or who participated in harmless flirting. But that possibility tempted her even more.

"So, what are these things you find more satisfying, Rebecca?"

It felt like the first time he used her name. It was soft and smooth, almost like a caress.

"Handmade Spanish chocolate hazelnut truffles," she finally stated. "And dulce de leche crème brûlée." Rebecca closed her eyes and licked her lips to simulate the sensations of eating a rich, sweet dessert.

"Really?" Chad replied, clearly skeptical. "So you're more passionate about what comes after the meal?"

She couldn't help but smile at his twist of her meaning.

Their waitress arrived at that moment to take their drink orders and explain the logistics of the meal. The large variety of grilled meat would be served to them fresh off skewers, while hot and cold side dishes and salads were laid out for customers to serve themselves. Chad and Rebecca followed the direction the waitress indicated and made a trip to the buffet table, and the meat started to arrive as soon as they were seated again. There was beef tenderloin, sirloin, prime rib, pork loin, ham, chicken breast, turkey breast, lamb . . . the list went on and on, and the skewers of tender, hot meat never seemed to end.

Rebecca had a healthy appetite, but could not get past the first three servings. Chad, on the other hand, had no trouble keeping up. She spent half the meal watching him savor the food while they chatted about his work and the President's Club trip. For a big guy, he was a very polished eater.

Finally, he set down his fork and let out a deep, satisfied sigh. Rebecca couldn't resist making a comment. "Was it good for you?"

Chad gave a big, slow smile that turned into a chuckle. It made him look younger, almost boyish. Rebecca smiled back.

"It was," he stated. "But I could still do with a little dessert."

She blinked a few times, trying to decipher if he really meant dessert, or if he was flirting about something less innocent. Another server arrived at that point carrying yet another offering.

"And here it is," Chad announced. "Grilled pineapple sprinkled with brown sugar and cinnamon. You have to try some; it's delicious."

Rebecca followed Chad's instructions and accepted a slice. It was warm, juicy, tangy, and sweet at the same time. She sighed with appreciation, letting out a soft moan. He watched as she ate another piece, his eyes locked with hers. He took a piece and they both savored the fruit without a word, but also fully aware of the change in the air between them. The moment seemed to stretch on forever.

"Good, isn't it?" he finally asked.

She was still fuzzy about whether to take his words literally, or respond to what his eyes were saying. She nodded as she swallowed her last piece while her pulse started to race.

"Do you want anything more?"

Rebecca didn't know how to respond. Her mind was suddenly mush and her usually clever tongue was tied. What was wrong with her? Why was she suddenly so awkward and flustered?

"They have other desserts on the menu, if you'd like something," Chad offered.

Then it hit her with complete clarity. He was seriously flirting. It was subtle and skillful, but it was clear. They could have something more if she wanted it. Rebecca smiled back with renewed confidence. The energy between them was almost palpable and her reaction to him was now undeniable. It wasn't something Rebecca had planned for or sought out, but it was a very exciting and attractive offer.

"No, thank you. I'm okay," she finally replied.

Chad nodded quickly. "Okay, I'll get the check."

He motioned to their waitress, and Rebecca pulled her wallet out of her bag.

"No need," he stated while pulling out his own money. "I'm taking care of it."

"Our bet didn't include you having to buy me lunch," Rebecca countered.

"My invite had nothing to do with our bet, Rebecca," he replied as he handed the folder of cash back to the waitress. "Plus, the safari was quite fun, so it was hardly a penalty."

"Ahhh, so lunch was offered out of guilt," she teased.

"Guilt had nothing to do with it." Though his expression was pleasant, his tone hinted at something more. But the moment passed as they made their way out of the restaurant and into an available cab called by the hostess.

"What are your plans for the rest of the afternoon?" Chad asked as they got closer to the hotel.

"Nothing really," Rebecca replied with a neutral tone.

"I was going to hang out at the beach, maybe rent a Jet Ski. Seems like something I should do at least once this weekend. Would you like to join me?"

"Yeah, sure. Sounds like fun."

Chapter 7

Chad was torn.

It was almost two forty-five, and he was about to head down to the lobby to meet Rebecca, then out to the beach as they had planned. But he had no interest in sunbathing, Jet Skiing, or any other related activities. The only thing he could think about was what Rebecca Isles would taste like. Would her skin feel as silky as it looked? The questions seemed stuck in his head since they met for breakfast, and he couldn't shake them. So the invite to lunch and to an afternoon of frolicking in the water were only meant to keep her close until he could figure out what the hell to do.

He knew what he wanted with Rebecca was pointless and impractical. They were both here in Myrtle Beach for one more day, then they'd go their separate ways. As much as she sparked something irrepressible in the pit of his stomach, it would only last for one night. And then what? Nothing else was possible. So why start it?

Chad had never been interested in one-night

stands, had never pursued one before. He had always entered into meaningful, committed relationships and was content to wait until he met a woman who was worth getting to know more deeply. Yet, right this minute, as he stood in front of the elevator pressing the button, none of those ideals mattered. His thoughts were screaming with desire for one woman, here and now. Her untamed spirit and unconventional life made her presence seem fleeting and unattainable. Like a moment he needed to capture now or he'd miss it forever. Tomorrow was too far away to care about.

For the length of the elevator ride, Chad wrestled back and forth between his baser instincts and his better judgment. He saw Rebecca as soon as the elevator doors opened, standing at the far end of the lobby at a secluded spot near the rear exit of the hotel. She looked refreshed in a pretty yellow sundress. The straps of a black bathing suit were tied around her neck.

"Hi," she stated with a friendly smile as he approached.

"Hi. You haven't been waiting long, have you?" he asked, stopping in front of her. She smelled like sweet, soft bath gel.

They were both in flip-flops, and Chad suddenly felt like a giant towering over her petite frame. His practical side reared its head again, insisting that she was too tiny and delicate for him. It reminded him that she wasn't like the women he typically pursued who had more height and a bit of size, and could handle him.

It was only a fleeting thought.

"No, only a few minutes," she replied easily.

"Good."

He remained still, making no move to head toward the beach, and after a few awkward moments, Rebecca looked up at him quizzically. His thoughts must have been clear in his eyes because she immediately stilled. A couple more seconds passed, then she let out a deep breath and her gaze slid to his lips. Chad slowly reached out and brushed his hand gently over the mass of curly hair, then down her cheek. She looked back into his eyes as he tilted her chin upward. They both leaned closer in that moment as their lips hovered inches apart. Then Chad lowered his mouth onto hers.

It was just a small touch at first, a simple brush of their skin. Then it was deeper, swiping, delving, savoring. She tasted hot and sweet. Like ripe black cherries drizzled with melted brown sugar. It was way better than he had imagined, and very hard to stop. Chad forced himself to pull back, fully aware that they were in a very public hallway, and any one of his coworkers could easily walk by.

"Are you sure you want to go to the beach?" Chad asked softly. "Because I can think of a more satisfying way to spend the afternoon."

Rebecca didn't respond right away, nor did she pull away in outrage or insult. But he could sense her hesitation. He pulled back to look at her face.

"I leave tomorrow," she stated simply.

"I know." Chad brushed a finger over her soft lips. "I do too. So this seems like the best opportunity to explore whatever *this* is."

He kissed her again, fearing it could be the last

time to experience it if she refused his suggestion. Again, it moved swiftly into something steamy and smoldering as he teased and stroked her lips. Then Rebecca opened her mouth to him and he almost groaned from the silky hot wetness of her tongue. So sweet . . .

There was no need for further discussion. He took her hand and they walked together back to the elevators. Neither said a word as they entered the lift with several other people and Chad pressed the button for his floor. He then led her to his door, and unlocked it as quickly as possible. Once inside, he carefully removed the bag she had over her shoulder and put it on the closest chair. They stood in front of each other, only a step apart, their breathing elevated with anticipation. Chad stayed still, fighting the urge to pull her close and devour every inch of her. He waited for her to make the first move, to set the pace that was comfortable for her. Then he would happily follow suit.

Finally, Rebecca reached out a hand and pressed it against the hard slab of his chest, covered by a light T-shirt. She then pressed against the muscle, testing the strength and firmness, adding her other hand to the investigation.

"You're very . . . big," she finally stated.

Chad couldn't tell if she was appreciative or put off. "Did you just notice?" he asked, running his hands up her arms.

"I noticed. It's just . . . now you seem taller, wider."

Her hand continued to explore his upper body, stroking up to his collarbone, brushing over the expanse of his shoulders, and back over his pecs. They hovered near his nipples.

"How tall are you?" Rebecca asked.

"Six three."

The palms of her hands scraped over his sensitive buds, sending a shiver up his spine. Then she was lightly gripping the edge of his shirt and raising it up. Chad didn't need instructions. He grabbed the fabric near the back of his neck and pulled it over his head with one quick motion, then tossed it aside.

"*Rahtid!*" she whispered as she took in his naked torso, padded with rippling muscles, but also practically covered with two tattoos. One was a large intricate fire-breathing dragon that started on the left side of his chest and wrapped over one shoulder with the tail ending on his back. The second was high on the right pec, and included two Chinese symbols done in calligraphy brush strokes.

Rebecca smiled up at him, clearly amused to discover what was hidden under his clothes.

"College days," he stated as an explanation.

"Right," was her sarcastic comeback.

Chad pulled her closer so their bodies were almost touching. She was still smiling.

"And this?" Rebecca asked, brushing a delicate finger over the Oriental words. "You're an assassin?"

He pulled back, surprised at her words.

"That's what it says, right? It's Mandarin for *assassin,* or *killer*?" she continued.

"Yeah! You read Mandarin?" he demanded, completely astonished.

Rebecca shrugged one shoulder, then leaned closer to him and pressed her lips along the groove between his pecs. He stopped breathing.

"Only enough to be dangerous," she whispered, kissing his skin and tickling it lightly with her tongue.

Chad leaned down and pulled her into a deep, thorough kiss. This time, she welcomed his tongue into her hot mouth, and teased him with the soft, delicate brush of her own. He pulled her so close, their bodies were completely meshed, and yet he ached to get closer. The steamy exchange went on and on until their breath came out in labored gasps. Chad's hands roamed all over her back, stroking down its slim length and cupping her round bottom in his hands. Then he needed more.

He took the edge of her dress and started to pull it up. Rebecca broke the kiss and stepped back from their embrace. She then slipped the straps of her dress off her shoulders and pulled it down into a puddle on the floor. Underneath was a black two-piece bathing suit with a bralike top that cupped her perky breasts, and very sexy boy shorts riding low on her hips. Her body was sleek and lean in the limbs and torso, but a nice handful in all the right places.

Chad quickly took the lead. He reached into the pocket of his swim shorts and took out his wallet, put it on the chair next to them, then shed the shorts. When he straightened up, he was completely naked for her scrutiny. His pulse raced as her eyes trailed down the ripples of his stomach, the defined contours below his belly button, and slowly dropped to his penis, now standing at full attention. The heat of her gaze was like a hot caress, and his erection pulsed harder.

They stood there for seconds, just looking at each other as the anticipation heightened and their bodies tightened. It was the most sensual thing Chad had experience in a long time. And they hadn't really done anything yet.

"Take off your bathing suit," he asked in a throaty voice. "I want to see all of you."

Rebecca followed his instruction, slowly undoing the top and dropping it on the floor. Her naked breasts were creamy chestnut perfection, firm and round with thick dark chocolate tips. Chad could not wait to lick them, feel the texture on his tongue. But he remained patient, watching as she rolled down the swim bottoms and kicked them aside. To his surprise, her pubic area was completely bare and smooth as silk with a full Brazilian wax.

She noted his focused stare and looked down at herself. "It's a habit I picked up in South America," she whispered. "Does it put you off?"

Chad could have told her how erotic he found it, and how completely intoxicated he was from the sight of her, but he didn't want to talk. He wanted to touch her, taste her, bury his throbbing cock deep into her.

He quickly grabbed his wallet, took out a condom, optimistically placed there earlier, and rolled it on.

"Come here," he requested instead, reaching out to take her hand.

Rebecca stepped forward and into his arms. The

smoldering spark between them ignited into a blue hot flame. He stroked his big hands all over her body while she pressed her lips against his chest. Chad cupped her bum, caressing her round curves, and pulling her tiny frame up higher until she stood on the tips of her toes. His rigid arousal rubbed against her torso with burning urgency.

Needing her even closer, he gripped the top of her thighs and lifted her up until her hips met his. Rebecca let out a gasp of surprise and instinctively wrapped her legs around his lean waist. Her weight was like nothing to him. He ran a hand up into her hair and pulled her head back gently so he could look into her face, only inches from his own. His other hand followed the valley between her butt cheeks until he reached the silky folds of her vulva. Her eyes widened as Chad moved two fingers further, reaching the delicate nub of her clit. He circled it with just the right amount of stimulating pressure.

"Oh God!" she moaned, biting her lower lip. Her eyes remained locked with his.

Chad continued the caress with steady patience, feeling her delicate flesh swell and dampen with excitement. His heart rate increased along with hers until it was beating like a drum. His loins began to ache with a need so intense it made his knees weak, but he didn't waver from his goal. Rebecca got wetter and her hips began to grind against his hand. He stroked her faster, feeding off her reaction, driving toward her undoing. She was so close, now groaning through clenched teeth. Chad paused for a moment to slide his thick middle finger into her hot, tight sheath. Her flesh pulsed against his digit.

"Oh, yes!" she almost screamed in a tight voice. "Yes!"

He stroked in deeper, their still eyes fixed with an invisible bond. She bucked her hips and began to quiver. The pleasure in her golden eyes made his heart pound faster. Chad went back to her clit, prepared to send her over the edge, unsure how much longer he could last in his current state of painful arousal. His penis was nestled against her bottom, sliding along the valley, throbbing with the need to feel her wetness.

"That's it," Rebecca whispered, suddenly completely still.

Seconds later, her eyes closed tight and she came with violent strength. She moaned uncontrollably while her body vibrated with powerful shudders. Chad was entranced, holding her body like delicate china as the shivers raced through her in never-ending waves. Feeling her intense climax in his arms was almost as satisfying as his own. Almost.

As Rebecca's body stilled, Chad wrapped his arms around her back to pull her close and keep her warm in the air-conditioning. He was so weak with need, his legs felt shaky. He carefully carried her the few steps across the width of the room until her back was against the wall. She leaned back slightly, her eyes drowsy in the aftermath. Chad lifted her body until the tip of his penis found the opening of her sweet cocoon. Rebecca clutched his shoulders as he slowly penetrated her depths.

Every fiber of his being wanted to slide in hard

and deep until she encased him to the hilt. But she was so tight, so tiny and delicate in his arms that Chad could only go in slow strokes while her body adjusted to his thickness. It was the sweetest torture, and he trembled from the effort of his restraint. It was too much.

"Jesus, Rebecca. I want you so bad," he groaned deeply.

"Then take me," she whispered, and flexed down with her hips, taking another inch of his thrust.

"Damn it, damn it," Chad muttered as his control unraveled.

He gripped her butt in one hand and slapped the other on the wall above her head for stability. He withdrew from her body, then buried himself as deep as possible in one swift penetration. It was incredible and it was his undoing.

Chad pressed his lips at the base of her neck before his body took over, taking her over and over again, groaning with every thrust, completely lost in the sex. She met his pace, gripping his shoulders and stroking his back. The explosion crashed down on him swiftly, sucking the breath from his body, and rocking him to his core.

"Jesus, Rebecca! Jesus!" he whispered.

They stayed in that embrace for long minutes until Chad returned to earth, naked in the front of his hotel room, standing pressed against the wall in the middle of the afternoon.

Chapter 8

That night, as the sun was setting, there was a party in full swing on the beach, hosted by the resort. There was music, food, and buskers performing a wide variety of acts. The area was packed with hotel guests and other customers. Rebecca watched the crowd from the balcony of her room on the seventh floor.

Chad was somewhere down there. She tried to make him out, searching for a bear of a man with eyes the color of dark chocolate. But she couldn't see him, and went back into her room after a few minutes to finish packing. Earlier in the evening, shortly after Chad had left to meet his coworkers for a company dinner, Rebecca received confirmation of her trip to Orlando, and planned on leaving tomorrow on a noon-hour flight.

Usually, she was excited to start a new project. It was the anticipation of her work, the chance to capture the experience of a new environment on film, but it was also the place itself. Every city she had been to over the last three years was unique in architecture, history, culture, food, sites, and people. Traveling alone, she had the freedom to do and try whatever she wanted, and often spent as much time exploring as she did working. Many of her favorite shoots in her portfolio came from wandering around foreign streets, snapping whatever interested her.

Yet this time, as she looked at her packed bags on top of the bed, she didn't feel excited. Instead, she felt sad, maybe even a little remorseful that it was so sudden and so soon. It was ridiculous, considering she had only met Chad Irvine two days ago. And they had only spent a few hours together. But those hours were undeniably incredible. Rebecca had spent the last couple of hours reliving some of the moments in her mind. The relaxed fun during the safari, the flirting through lunch, then the surprising proposition in the lobby. The mind-blowing intimacy was almost a blur. Details were overshadowed by the general taste and feel of him holding her up against the wall, then cuddling naked on the couch as they both recuperated.

It had all happened so fast, but it felt so natural in the moment. Even now, as she waited for his text message, Rebecca had no regrets other than how brief their encounter would be. Yes, she had a rule against starting relationships while traveling, but Chad was the perfect exception to the rule. There was clearly no hope for anything more long term—neither of them pretended differently—but the memories from this morning, afternoon, and night were going to last her for long enough to make it worthwhile.

Rebecca was pulled out of her thoughts by the vibrating of her iPhone, indicating a text message. It was a simple note from Chad:

Are you available at 9:30?

She let out a deep breath, not realizing that she had been holding it, and replied:

Yes. Where?

My room?

Okay.

It was almost eight-forty five, so she had enough time to freshen up and put a few essentials into her purse. Choosing what to wear took much longer than she planned. Rebecca finally settled on a light T-shirt dress in a sapphire blue. It looked casual and simple, and wouldn't be conspicuous if she was heading back to her room in the middle of the night or first thing in the morning. Rebecca slipped it on over a pretty copper brown bra and matching thong, and stashed an extra pair of underwear in her purse. She brushed on a little mascara and lip gloss, slipped on pretty silver platform flip-flops, then headed out the door.

When she arrived at Chad's room almost fifteen minutes late, she took a couple of deep, calming breaths before knocking. He opened the door within a few seconds.

"Hey," he said with a bright smile.

"Hi," Rebecca replied as she stepped inside. "Sorry I'm a little late."

"No worries. Though I did wonder if you had

changed your mind." His tone was flippant, but his eyes said it was true.

"No, not at all. I just lost track of time, that's all," she replied dismissively.

"I'm glad," Chad added as he walked toward the sitting area where the television was on. "Come in, have a seat."

"How was your dinner?" she asked once she was sitting down on the two-seater sofa. He sat beside her with his back to the arm so they faced each other.

"Boring," he told her with a chuckle. "But I was distracted, so I really shouldn't judge."

"Oh, you were distracted, were you? By what exactly?" The tease came out naturally.

Chad's eyes sparkled. "I couldn't stop thinking about you naked, so it was pretty hard to concentrate on corporate talk."

"I see," Rebecca added, feeling flushed by his words.

"Did you have dinner?"

"Yeah, I ordered a sandwich up to my room."

"Good, because I brought you something," he told her.

"Really? What?"

There was a plain white bag on the table that she hadn't taken note of. Chad picked it up, reached inside, and pulled out a black take-out container. He placed it in her lap.

"What is it?" she asked, puzzled.

"Open it."

Rebecca did as instructed, and found a huge slab of cake inside.

"Chocolate cheesecake drizzled with raspberry coulis," he told her as he produced a plastic fork. "I didn't want you to miss dessert."

She looked from the container up to his face and back down again. It was a very sweet gesture.

"Thank you, Chad. It looks delicious."

"Go ahead and have some," he told her, sticking the fork into the dense cake and scooping up a small chunk.

She allowed him to feed the forkful to her. It was incredibly smooth, sweet, and delicious. "Mmmm, that is so good!"

Chad fed her another scoop.

"You're going to have some too, aren't you?"

He ate the next scoop and closed his eyes while savoring it. "That is good," he replied, and Rebecca giggled at his expression.

They spent the next few minutes sharing the cake until Chad put the last piece into her mouth. He placed the empty box down on the coffee table.

"So, what did you do for the evening?" he asked.

She shrugged. "Just some packing, confirming my travel plans for tomorrow."

Chad nodded. He reached out to take hold of her wrist, urging her closer to him. Rebecca slid over until she was pressed against his side. He draped his arm across her shoulder.

"To Florida, right?"

"Yeah, Orlando to start."

He rubbed his hand up and down the bare skin of her arm. "What time is your flight?"

"I have to leave for the airport by ten-thirty in the

morning," she told him. "What time do you guys leave?"

"Not until later in the afternoon. The shuttle arrives at two o'clock."

They sat in silence for a few minutes while the news played in the background. Chad's hand moved into her hair where he played with the curls, massaging her scalp. He gently turned her head to face him and pulled her into a kiss. It was a soft and gentle caress with his lips. They spent a few minutes enjoying the simple touch, teasing each other with light pecks and tender brushes. Chad urged her even closer until she sat in his lap, her legs draped over his. The kiss deepened as he coaxed her lips open and stroked into her mouth with his tongue.

"I'm glad you came back," he whispered against her mouth.

"Me too," she stated.

He pressed sweet kisses against her temple while his hand swept up her body and cupped one of her breasts. Rebecca let out a satisfied sigh and her head fell back with anticipation. Chad moved his lips along her neck, teasing the tendon with his tongue. His fingers continued to tease her sensitive mounds until the nipples were taut and swollen.

"Stand up," he requested, then helped her to her feet.

Rebecca stepped in the space between his knees, and Chad moved to the edge of the couch to help her pull her dress up over her head. She tossed it away. He reached behind her to grip her bottom and pull her to him, pressing his lips against her stomach. She ran her fingers over his head, playing with the stubble of his hair. His hands went higher on her back to undo her bra. It too was thrown aside. He pulled her back into his lap, facing him with her knees straddling his hips. She gasped as he sucked one of her nipples into his mouth, scraping the tip with his hot tongue.

"I couldn't stop thinking about you all evening," Chad whispered against her skin.

He sucked harder on her puckered flesh, sending sharp, intense pleasure up and down her spine, then moved to the other breast.

"I was thinking that the next time, we would have all night. And we could take it slow," he continued between sucking, kissing, and licking her tight nub.

"Hmm-hmm," she murmured in agreement, finding it hard to focus on his words.

Rebecca pushed him back and began unbuttoning his shirt from the top down, hungry to see and touch his incredible body again. Chad let her take over, relaxing back so she had full access to his naked torso. She was like a kid in a candy store, licking and sucking on the hard, velvety planes of his body. It was exciting to have him pliant under her caresses, and to feel the strength of his arousal blossom against the apex of her thighs.

Her hands worked their way down his stomach until they reached the belt of his pants. Their eyes met as she slowly undid the buckle, popped the button, and undid the zipper. The thick length of his penis was outlined through his boxers. Chad clenched his teeth as she ran a flat palm from the base up, rubbing the sensitive tip before stroking down again. She repeated the motions a few more times, fascinated by the heavy thrust as it extended further against her hand.

Chad watched her with hooded eyes, jaw clenched and his face flushed with excitement. Then, she removed the thin cotton barrier, and gripped his hot arousal in both hands. Her delicate hands reached around its girth.

"Ah, damn!" he muttered feverishly.

She stroked up to the tip, circled the silky head, and slid back down. And again. Chad widened his thighs and groaned loudly. And again.

"Yeah, yeah! Oh yeah," he urged.

Rebecca licked her lips at the delicious sight in front of her. She felt so powerful and aroused by his reaction. He was like a vision out of a forbidden fantasy. Big, strong, ripped, and rock hard under her control. Masculine perfection. Her vagina was pulsing with excitement.

"I need you, Rebecca. Badly!" he whispered, still watching her with feverish eyes.

Chad reached out a hand to hold one breast, rubbing against the distended nipple. The other went between her legs. Feeling her readiness, he drove his index finger into her moist sheath.

She moaned, flexing her hips. He slowly added his middle finger, using his thumb to massage her clit.

"Chad," she mumbled, almost trembling from how good it felt.

"Are you ready for me?" he asked.

She nodded, unable to find the words.

Chad took a quick moment to take a condom out of his pants pocket, and slid the barrier over his glistening shaft. He then took hold of her slender hips, slipping aside the thin strip of her thong.

"Hold on to me," he instructed in a thick voice.

Rebecca did as told, gripping the top of his shoulders. He stroked into her quivering flesh, patiently inching into her tightness with short thrusts. Neither of them could breathe properly as they shared the sweet agony of his penetration. When he reached her core, they both froze, savoring the connection. Rebecca felt impaled, devoured, complete.

"You're okay?" he asked, clearly concerned that he could hurt her.

She smiled softly and nodded before leaning down to kiss him. Her mouth opened his and she stroked his tongue with hers, sucking and teasing with hot intensity. Then she moved her hips, lifting them a couple of inches and stroking back down. Chad gripped her bottom, cupping her roundness in his big hands, but didn't stop her. She slid on him again, higher and harder. He hit a wickedly intense spot deep in her body, and Rebecca nearly screamed from the sweet pleasure. She gripped his head, buried her face in the crook of his neck, and rode him at a rhythmic pace that had them both panting with readiness. Chad gave her complete control, still cupping, massaging, and occasionally slapping the cheeks of her bottom.

Rebecca climaxed first, falling apart with earth-shattering shudders that slammed through her body. She could hear Chad moaning her name as her juices flowed over his pulsating penis. His arms wrapped around her back, securing her in a blanket of his warmth, and he took over, thrusting into her quivering well with increased speed, but careful measure. He came just as her body was stilling and Rebecca savored the raw strength of his ecstasy.

They remained in each other's arms for long minutes after, occasionally stroking each other's skin with hands and lips. Finally, Rebecca started to think about where they were, what the night would bring, and the inevitability of tomorrow.

"Do you ever have sex in a bed?" she asked in a teasing voice.

Chad laughed lightly. "I do, usually. But for some reason, with you, I can't seem to make it there," he replied ruefully. "This time, I didn't even make it out of my clothes."

The both laughed a little, welcoming the lightened mood.

"Come, let me tuck you in and make up for my impolite behavior so far."

He easily picked her up and carried her to the bedroom.

Chapter 9

"So, why a tattoo that says *Assassin*?" Rebecca asked.

They were lying in his bed the next morning, spooning under the covers. Chad had her pulled up against his body with her back to his front. Her head was cushioned against his chest, her breasts coddled in his hands.

"Or do you work for some sort of secret government agency?" she teased.

Chad smiled. "In college, I was a linebacker. I had a pretty good record for sacking the quarterback, so the team gave me the nickname of Assassin."

"That's in American football, right?" she asked.

He grinned harder, puller her closer. She had no clue what he was talking about. "Yeah, that's right."

"And the dragon? What was the inspiration for that?"

He kissed the top of her head. "A dare. My friends thought I was too straight-laced and bet me that I wouldn't do it. I decided to make it worth the effort. It took me six visits to the shop to finish it."

"Yikes! Didn't it hurt?" she asked.

"Not too bad. It was just boring," Chad explained, laughing at the memory. "It was so hard to sit still for hours at a time."

"Do you regret it?"

"Nah. It reminds me that I don't always have to follow the rules."

The words came out easily, but immediately after, Chad wondered why he had said them. It was something he had recognized when he was most self-reflective, but had never verbalized to anyone, not even his mother or closest friends.

Rebecca didn't respond, and they lay there in casual comfort until she finally sat up. The alarm clock on the nightstand read nine thirty-three, less than an hour before she was leaving for the Myrtle Beach airport. They were out of time.

"Thanks again for breakfast," she stated, looking down at him serenely.

The remnants of the room service order were scattered on the dressing table across from the bed.

Chad nodded, propping up his torso on his elbow as she hopped off the bed and walked into the bathroom naked. He watched her leaving, admiring her body and the confident grace of her walk. She was perfection in a tiny package, completely natural and uninhibited in her nudity. Chad lay back on the pillow when she closed the door. He listened to the water run for a few seconds, holding on to her image in his mind. Finally accepting reality, he rolled off the bed and pulled on a pair of boxer shorts.

In the sitting room, he picked up their discarded

clothing and Rebecca's purse, bringing them back into the bedroom. He had her dress and underwear folded neatly on the bed when she returned, now wearing a towel around her body. Neither of them said anything as Chad took his turn in the bathroom, giving her some privacy to get dressed.

About ten minutes later, they were both dressed, and he was escorting her back to her room. Rebecca had stated it wasn't necessary, but Chad insisted. It didn't sit well with him that she would close his hotel room door and he would never see her again. He wanted to be a gentleman, and he needed a few more minutes before he could say good-bye.

They reached her door way too quickly.

"I really enjoyed meeting you, Chad Irvine," she stated teasingly as they faced each other.

"As did I, Rebecca Isles," he replied with mock seriousness.

Chad leaned down and pressed his lips on hers sweetly, like it was the end of their first date. She tasted so warm, sweet, and familiar. His stomach clenched with a spark of desire, and a knot formed in his throat. "Have a safe trip," he added thickly.

"You too," Rebecca replied before she unlocked her door and slipped inside.

Their eyes met again before she was gone.

He stood there for several seconds wondering if that's all there was. Should they have made promises to call or text? Should he have told her how much he wanted to see her again? But his practical nature knew the way they'd just parted was better. Their few hours together would be pure and untainted by unreasonable promises or expectations. Chad let out a deep breath and walked away.

Back in his room, he stood under the hot spray of the shower far longer than normal, trying to come to terms with his mix of emotions. It was hard for him to comprehend how he could feel so close to a woman so quickly. Particularly one he had only met a couple of days ago, and would never have been on his radar in Chicago.

Rebecca Isles was the opposite of what he had preferred for the women in his life. She was physical perfection, but not in the voluptuous, manicured style he was usually drawn to. She was sharp, witty, and streetwise, but without any interest in corporate success. Also, she was living the life of a gypsy, without a permanent residence or a plan to get one. Chad was looking for someone to build a life with in Chicago, raise a family on a tree-lined, kid-friendly street. Despite how perfect she had felt in his arms, and how natural their connection, Rebecca was not that woman.

With his head now straight, he went about the rest of his day.

The Sheppard Networks final event on the agenda was the annual presentation given by the founder and CEO, Norman Sheppard, over lunch, and several awards were distributed for top performances. Chad and his team, including William and Todd, each got a crystal paperweight for their project delivery achievements. An hour later, they were on several shuttles to the airport, and back in Chicago for a 7:30 pm landing, local time.

Chad called his mom during the cab ride back to

his apartment. "Hey, Mom, I'm back," he said when she answered.

"Hi, sweetheart. How was the rest of your weekend?" Denise asked. "Did you have fun?"

"It was interesting."

"Good, but I'm glad you're back. I went to see some houses yesterday with Susan, and I think I found one that is perfect," she explained. "Did you see the pictures I sent you?"

"The one in Oak Park?"

"No, this one is in Hyde Park. I sent the e-mail last night."

"No, I haven't gone through my e-mails today," Chad replied. "Hyde Park? I wasn't really looking there."

"Me either, Chad. But Susan recommended the property and it really is perfect. It's on a beautiful street east of the rail track. It's only a couple of blocks from South Lake Shore and all the parks," his mom outlined. "It needs some work, but the price is good, so you'd have the budget to get everything done."

"How much work?" Chad wasn't a skilled carpenter, but he didn't mind small projects. A big renovation wasn't really what he had in mind.

"Well, the house is sound, late eighteen-hundreds original construction, but it looks like there was some renovation work from the midseventies. So it really only needs some cosmetic work. The kitchen and bathrooms need a full overhaul though."

He rubbed a finger over his brow in consideration. This was not at all what he was looking for, but his mom sounded so excited about the property.

The least he could do was have a look at it. If it wasn't worth considering, she would understand.

"Okay, Mom. It sounds interesting. I'll call Susan tomorrow and set up a time this week to see it."

"Great, great. I know you'll see the potential."

"How are things with you?" Chad asked to change the subject. "How is Samuel doing?"

She spent the rest of his cab ride filling him in on the latest gossip on Samuel's daughter, Elaine. The flighty university student was often the subject of his mother's chatter. Chad didn't think her many antics were all that bad, but Denise Crothers had a low tolerance for silly behavior, and when her husband spoiled his youngest child, it drove her nuts.

Their call ended as the taxi pulled up to his condo. Once in his apartment, Chad turned on the television in the living room, then headed into the bathroom for a quick shower. While the water heated up, he checked his phone for any messages. There were several from work, one from William, and he found the e-mail his mother had sent the night before. But no new text messages. He put down the phone, ignoring the twinge of disappointment he felt.

By Monday afternoon, his life was back in its regular rhythm. He was up at six o'clock that morning to work out at the gym in his building, in the shower by seven-thirty, and out the door by a few minutes after eight o'clock. The train ride to his office took about twenty-five minutes, so Chad was at his desk well before nine o'clock.

His assistant arrived shortly after him, chatty as always about her very busy weekend. Natasha Carter was fresh out of university, and still brimming with youthful energy, drive, and optimism. She started at Sheppard Networks as a summer intern, then took the full-time position with Chad almost a year ago. They made a good team most of the time, with Natasha adding a certain liveliness to his finance team.

After work, Chad stopped at a local market to pick up a steak for dinner and a few other staples. He quickly cooked up his meal while listening to the news in the background, then spent the evening watching television, and was in bed by eleven o'clock. It was the typical rhythm of his life through the week and he fell back into it like Myrtle Beach had never happened.

On Thursday evening, he met his agent at the property in Hyde Park. Chad had driven to work, so he headed directly to the South Side of Chicago after work. He arrived at the house a little early, so he drove around the neighborhood to get a feel for the amenities and the general vibe. It was really nice. The architecture included a mix of late nineteenth-century mansions, twentieth-century brownstones, and new buildings. There also seemed to be a good mix of cultures represented. As he headed back to the property, Chad passed Lake Shore and the parks that lined it. Suddenly, he was pretty excited.

He pulled his car into the driveway beside the house just behind Susan Davis.

"Hi, Chad," she said brightly as they met each other on the front walkway. "How are you doing?"

They shook hands. Susan was a petite woman around his mom's age, with a liking for rainbow colors. Today, she had on a bright fuchsia-colored suit complete with matching pumps.

"I'm doing great, Susan."

"So, what do you think so far?" she asked, waving her arm at the house.

"It's okay so far," he stated, looking over the structure. "Not quite what I expected, to be honest. My mom said it was over one hundred and twenty years old, but it looks much more modern."

"Yes, you're right. At some point in the seventies, the owners remodeled it, including the front facade. They also removed some of the smaller rooms that were original, so it's much more open-concept than you would normally find. But there are still lots of original features.

"Come on. Let's go in and have a look," she urged.

Once inside, Chad knew immediately why his mother had recommended the place. There was no doubt it was in rough shape, with peeling wallpaper and out of date finishes, but it had great bones. The earlier renovations had created a modern loft feel in a traditional home, but left some of the original period features, like beautiful crown moldings, several wood-burning fireplaces, and graceful built-ins and woodwork.

"Well, what's the verdict?" Susan asked after they had toured the whole house.

"I can definitely see the potential, Susan. But there's a lot of work here. And it's really big. I was thinking about around twenty-five-hundred square feet, but this has to be over three thousand, right?"

"Yes, it's just over thirty-two hundred, not including the basement. But the price per square foot is really good. So you get more space for your money, and enough left in your budget to really create something special here."

Chad knew she made sense. It was pretty much what his mom had said. But he wasn't convinced this was what he wanted to do. He had to think about it, do some research on potential contractors who could be trusted to take on a project like this.

"Let me think about it," he suggested.

"No problem, Chad. You're the boss. I might have a couple more viewings for the weekend if you're available."

"Sounds good."

They parted ways soon after, with Chad heading up Lake Shore to the other end of the city. His mind was filled with all of the variables. By the time he got home, he had a mental list of things to research over the weekend. On Monday, he would make a decision to either jump into fairly major renovation or move on.

Thanks to his mom and stepdad and their network, Chad was able to interview an architect and a general contractor by Saturday, and both went with him to see the Hyde Park house a second time. Both professionals were excited about the potential and effectively shared their vision of what was possible. Like his mom suggested, the kitchen and bathrooms were in need of refurbishing, but the floor plan was solid and the overall structure was in good shape. The architect, Tyler North, recommended cleaning up the historical features, but going ultramodern for the new spaces. Chad wasn't sold on the specifics, but by Monday, his decision was made and he put an offer on the house.

The fall months flew by as Chad jumped into the renovation project. It proved to be an effective distraction from his memories of an afternoon spent naked with a fiery nomad. It didn't stop the images from invading his dreams and leaving him feeling hungry for her in the morning, but it was a start. He assumed with enough time she would be a faint memory.

While the sale was in escrow, Chad spent hours with Tyler to land on the design. While he liked modern, clean spaces, and was interested in the combination of old and new, Chad didn't want anything trendy that could go out of style very quickly. The compromise was to go with a timeless cabinetry in the kitchen with modern fixtures and state of the art appliances. The bathrooms would get a spalike feel with warm, neutral colors. While the design was conservative and the finishes would be reasonably priced for the quality, Chad made one splurge at the recommendation of his mom. The bathrooms upstairs were quite tight, particularly for someone his size. So, he agreed to remove one of the three smaller bedrooms in order to increase the size of the en suite bath connected to the master bedroom. There was an added bonus of space for a good-sized dressing room in the master suite. Apparently, that would be very important to any woman who lived there, adding to the resale value.

The sale closed without any issues, and demolition work was underway by mid-October.

"Well, the work is coming along nicely, isn't it?"

Denise asked her son as they sat in the living room of her home after the family Christmas dinner. "I really think it will be done on schedule."

According to his contractor, Hector Sanchez, the house would be completely ready for him to move in by mid-March.

"I think so. It seems to be okay," Chad replied, sipping a cup of coffee. "Susan thinks I should list the condo just after New Year's. It may take a couple of months to sell for the best price. And I don't want to have to carry both mortgages for any longer than I have to."

"Why don't you keep it and rent it out?" Denise suggested. "It's in a great neighborhood with a nice view of the river and close to the transit."

Chad was shaking his head to say no before she finished the idea. "I don't want to be a landlord," he stated simply. "The Hyde Park house will be enough work as it is. I mean, I'm really glad that I bought it, but I've done nothing outside of work but deal with the reno. Come spring, I just want to move in and relax for a bit."

"What you need is to meet someone nice," his mom stated with a teasing smile.

"Yeah, yeah. I know, Mom. I go out, I see people," Chad explained defensively. "I'm just not serious about anyone in particular."

"All I'm saying is that you have plenty of options to choose from, my dear. I can't tell you how many of my friends are on me every week to set you up with their daughters, or nieces or neighbors. If you don't get yourself a wife soon, I'm going to start setting you up."

"Come on, Dee. Leave the man alone," Samuel Crothers urged as he entered the kitchen where his wife and stepson were sitting. "Let him enjoy being single for as long as he likes." He leaned down and kissed her head affectionately, his green eyes twinkling.

"Thanks, Sam," Chad stated with a grin.

"Plus, you're too young to have a bunch of kids calling you 'Grandma,'" Sam added with a wink.

They all laughed at his smooth charm.

"Are you guys coming? Elaine has the movie all ready to go," Ethan Crothers stated from the doorway. At twenty-six years old, he was a striking younger version of his father, with the same olive-toned skin, dark brown hair, and bottle green eyes.

"We're coming, we're coming," Denise replied, shepherding the other men out of the kitchen. "I'll bring the coffee and dessert and we'll be all set."

Chapter 10

The months also went by swiftly for Rebecca. The Florida project was very successful. As promised, her uncle let her stay at his place outside Orlando for most of the trip. She then rented a car to go between locations and attractions with more freedom. Being in a true home for the duration of the assignment rather than a hotel really put her in a different frame of mind. Rather than spending all of her free time adding more pictures to her portfolio, Rebecca focused on taking stock of what she already had. And there was a ton of really good stuff. By the time her next project was confirmed, Rebecca was ready to start marketing her photos to other clients.

The next stop was New York City for the rest of the winter. She arrived in Manhattan just before Christmas for three weeks, and ended up staying through to March. The original objective was to capture the launch of a new Dunegan luxury hotel right off

Fifth Avenue. It was positioned to be the flagship property in the United States, with a marketing plan to attract the appropriate clientele. Those first few weeks were such a whirlwind of high profile events and corporate parties that Rebecca barely left the two-block radius of the hotel. So once the project was finished, and there was nothing confirmed for the next location, she decided to stay in the city for a few more weeks.

To her surprise and delight, Uncle Devon came to town for work in February and stayed for a whole week. It was an unexpected opportunity for Rebecca to feel reconnected to Jamaica and all the very good friends and family she had left behind. Though he was in meetings all day, they managed to meet for dinner each evening.

"Are you still enjoying it?" Uncle Devon asked while they shared a chocolate cake for dessert at an Italian restaurant near Central Park. They were discussing all the projects she'd worked on in the past year.

Rebecca shrugged, thinking about the most honest answer. It was a question she had asked herself several times over the last few weeks.

"Be honest, Becca. You don't pretend with me," he encouraged, using the nickname that her mom had always used.

"I love the photography," she stated with complete clarity. "There is no doubt that's what I want to do. I like the travel and the opportunity to visit cities all over the world. What's not to like? I still have to pinch myself sometimes," she explained with a girlish grin.

"Like now, hanging out in Manhattan?" he teased.

"It's pretty spectacular, even for the middle of winter."

"So good, you're enjoying yourself. Yet I still sense a *but* coming."

She shrugged again, really struggling to put her thoughts into words. It had been so long since she had someone to talk to about stuff like this.

"But . . . it's been almost four years and it still doesn't seem real," she told him.

"Becca, you are a truly talented photographer. It's a really competitive business, but our marketing department still considers you their go-to resource for anything important," he assured her, his voice filled with pride. "And it has nothing to do with me anymore. I may have pulled some strings to get you that first gig, but the rest is all you, little lady."

Rebecca smiled with gratitude at his words. They meant a lot to her, but she wasn't surprised by them. One of the things she'd learned in this career was that everyone thought they were a photographer, and with the quality and capabilities of the most basic digital camera now, anyone could pull together a portfolio. So her consistent work with Royal Dunegan wasn't a fluke or a favor to her uncle. Rebecca knew deep in her bones that she was good. It was her ability to recognize a winning shot, but also the time she took to understand what the client was trying to sell with each project, and giving them a collection of shots that hit the mark.

"No, it's not that I don't feel like a professional. I mean, it doesn't feel like a real life," she explained. "It's like I'm on a vacation with no end, or a sabbatical with no real job to return to. Ridiculous, huh? I'm complaining about being able to spend weeks in New York City doing whatever I please. I'm loving it, really. But it's not real."

Devon looked at her intently. "Maybe it's time to think about settling down somewhere. Or coming back to Jamaica," he suggested softly.

She shook her head to say no. "I'll go back to visit, for sure, but I don't want to live there again."

"Okay. But you still need a home."

Rebecca looked at him, considering his statement.

"I think it's time for you to put down some roots. Somewhere you can return to between assignments, where you have friends and other relationships. All of that is very important in life."

"I have friends," she retorted defensively.

"You know what I mean," Devon countered. "Which brings me to my other concern. We need to talk about your inheritance. You're turning twenty-six next month, and it's time for you to make some decisions."

Rebecca looked into her coffee cup, pondering his statement. It wasn't a surprise; she had been thinking about it more and more over the last year. Uncle Devon was only doing his duty as executor of her mom's will.

"I understand why you wanted to take some time to think about your options, but you can't just leave it in a savings account forever," he continued in a fatherly tone. "The interest is minimal and it's not working for you. If you want to leave it untouched for some time, then there are lots of long-term, low risk investment opportunities. They would be much more profitable than the account you have the money in now."

She nodded, still looking into space, thinking.

"Rebecca, what is your hesitation?"

When she looked up at him, her eyes started to swim. "I know it's ridiculous, but whenever I think of touching that money, I feel sick, like I'm profiting off Mom's death. Crazy, right? I know she would slap me in the head for being so silly. Not touching it isn't going to bring her back. But I just can't be happy about buying something or investing. It feels like being happy she's dead so I can have the money." Her voice was very quiet and deeply anguished.

Devon reached out and gripped her hand. "You're right, my dear. Rose would have slapped you silly."

Rebecca blinked and started to giggle. Soon they were both laughing at the truth of his words.

"Listen, Becca. The one thing that made your mother happy in the end was that you and your sister would be all right financially once she was gone. That's what you need to think about. You can't do anything about your mother's death, but you can make her wish come true. Use the money to make your life more secure."

She nodded again, wiping away the trickle of tears that laced her cheeks. "You're right, I know."

"Good girl. So let's talk about your options."

They spent another hour or so discussing various possibilities. Rebecca tried to put her girlish feelings aside to make some practical decisions. By the time she got back to her hotel room that evening, she started to feel optimistic, maybe even a little excited. She thought back to Devon's suggestion that she could be missing a place to call home. Maybe she should buy a small apartment somewhere, a place to relax between projects? Somewhere simple and quaint, in one of her favorite cities. Bali, Paris, or maybe even Madrid? They were all great places for very different reasons, and while she had acquaintances in each of those locations, they were quite far from her family and very close friends. Nadine was in California while everyone else was in Jamaica. The states were certainly an option and New York was growing on her even though the price of property there was incredibly expensive. She would have to think about it some more.

By the time Devon returned to Jamaica, Rebecca had a plan for her inheritance with a budget for a property purchase, and a short-term investment portfolio. It felt like a load had been lifted off her shoulders. Now, she only had to decide where to lay down permanent roots.

Rebecca spent the next month in New York visiting several marketable attractions and working on her portfolio. She spent hours at various local cafés and restaurants categorizing her photo files by location and subject, quickly realizing that it was a very sizable collection. It was also very good. There were hundreds of pictures that were visually stunning, capturing natural or unique cultural subjects. And there were a few that were personal, snapshots taken in various casual and fun environments of people she had become friends with on her many trips.

One in particular made Rebecca pause, bringing to surface many thoughts and sensations she had tried to bury. It was a photo of Chad Irvine, taken in a stolen moment while he slept after they had spent the night together.

She remembered waking up at dawn, like she always did. They were still cuddled together with her head resting on the pad of his chest. Rebecca had lay there for several moments, breathing in the faint musky scent of his aftershave, wondering if he would also wake up. Eventually, she slowly uncurled herself to use the bathroom, surprised that he didn't stir. When she returned to the bedroom she could not help staring down at this impressive form, naked except for where the sheets covered his hips.

Rebecca had instinctively grabbed her iPhone from her purse in the living room, and captured the image forever before crawling back into the bed and into his arms. Now, she tried not to look at his picture too often. She was happy with the memories, but refused to torture herself with what couldn't be.

The end of March brought warmer weather to the northeast. While Rebecca was itching to capture the city in spring, she resisted the urge to go out exploring. Instead, she began to develop a marketing and sales plan for her portfolio. If she was going to establish a permanent home, it would make sense to increase her stability and earning potential by selling her work through as many other outlets as possible. With three weeks of dedicated focus, she had several promising options, including a publishing company that focused on cultural travel and cookbooks. They were very interested in several of her photos from Jamaica and other Caribbean countries.

The most exciting opportunity was a permanent position with a national news agency as a staff photographer based in the New York office. Rebecca had applied for the position on a whim, convinced she didn't have a chance without formal photography or journalism training. But two interviews later, she was biting her fingers with anticipation of their decision.

Right at the beginning of April, she got an e-mail from Richard Kent at Dunegan that stated there was a new project assignment for her. He called her directly to discuss the details. "I hope you've enjoyed your time off," he said in a friendly voice.

"I have, Richard. It's a little colder than I would like though," Rebecca replied in a humorous tone.

He laughed lightly. "Yes, well it's definitely not Thailand, right? Unfortunately, the next project isn't much warmer, I'm afraid. But spring is here and summer's not far behind, so you'll have plenty of heat soon enough."

"I'm going to hold you to it," she shot back. "Where to this time?"

"It's a little last minute, but we recently acquired a new property, and we'll be launching it officially in about two months. It's in really good shape, so we'd like you to pull together some marketing shots."

"Okay," Rebecca acknowledged as she made notes.

"They also have several large functions pre-booked for this weekend, so it would be great for you to capture some of those events. We could use them for the property Web site and corporate advertising."

She nodded. "Where is it?"

"Chicago," Richard stated.

Rebecca stilled, not sure she had heard correctly. "Chicago?"

"Yeah, downtown on Michigan Avenue."

She shook her head, gathering her thoughts after this sudden turn of events.

"Any chance you could be there for Thursday?" he continued.

"Ahh, sure." It was Monday afternoon. "Sure, that's fine."

"Good. I will send you an e-mail with all the logistics."

They ended the call a few minutes later. Rebecca sat in the desk chair in her hotel room for a long moment biting on her bottom lip, her mind running in several different directions. Chicago? Of all the places in the world, she was going to Chicago. Slowly, the surprise wore off, and she started to think about the prep required. One of the outstanding issues was the opportunity with the news agency. The recruiter had promised an answer early that week. So Rebecca was going to have to be patient, hoping there was a response before she left the city. If she got the job, she would ask to start after the Chicago project.

The call came on Wednesday morning, and it wasn't what she had hoped. According to the recruiter, it was a very close race and they would have gladly hired her if there were two positions open. Crushed, Rebecca finished her packing and tried to refocus her energy on some of the other freelance options she was pursuing. Thursday morning, she went for a relaxing walk in Central Park, had lunch at her favorite deli, then headed to the airport for her flight to the Windy City.

Chapter 11

Despite a few setbacks and unplanned complications, Chad moved into his new house by the end of March. The construction went fairly smoothly except for some electrical issues. The real challenge came from selling his condo. He had set a realistic price, but the real estate market was still very depressed. It took nearly three months, many open houses and two price drops before he got an offer he could live with. When it was all said and done, Chad was pretty happy with the way things turned out. Though he had to compromise on his sale price, he had bought the Hyde Park house at a reasonable price, so even with the renovation, he was not much over his budget. Now he owned a completely finished property worth much more than he'd originally paid for it.

By the first week in April, he was almost settled in except for several empty rooms that would need furniture.

"I'm telling you, Chad, my decorator would have this place completely finished in about two weeks,"

Denise told her son as they walked through the bedrooms upstairs. It was Thursday night, and she had stopped by to bring Chad some of her lasagna for dinner.

"Mom, I don't need a decorator. My bedroom and the den are done, that's all I need right now. I even have a spare bed set up. I'll get furniture for the other rooms when I can. There's no rush," he told her.

His mom shook her head in disapproval. "Look at how wonderful the remodeling is," she continued, using a sweeping arm to indicate the space. "You now have one of the best houses on the street, baby. It's such a shame that it's so bare inside. Why not just have her come by to give you some ideas? It will be my housewarming gift."

Chad knew his mother wasn't going to stop until she got her way. Sometimes, it was better to give in early on issues that were inconsequential.

"Fine, Mom. Just a consultation. I'm not going to hire her to do any work. Make sure she's clear on that."

"Yes, yes, I'll make sure," Denise responded dismissively.

They made their way downstairs, Denise throwing out ideas and solutions for every space she went through. They landed in the kitchen, and Chad put on the kettle to make some coffee.

"I'm so excited about tomorrow night," she told him as he poured them each a hot drink from his coffee press. They both stirred in cream and sugar.

"We're expecting over four hundred guests. Let's hope they all bring their wallets filled with cash."

"What time should we be there?" Chad asked, taking a small sip from his cup.

"Cocktails start at six, so anytime between six and seven will be fine. I've seated you at a table right up front. You don't know how difficult that was. The annual Spring Bash is now one of the hottest charity events in the city, certainly the most profitable for the Chicago Kids Camp organization. And front row seats are a hot commodity for anyone who has any credentials. I almost got into a fist fight with Margaret Archer for your spot, so you best appreciate my efforts."

Chad only nodded tolerantly. He didn't have the heart to tell her he could not care less where he sat for the event. Chad was only going because his mom hadn't made it an option. He was as charitable as the next guy, but wasn't looking forward to a whole evening with a room full of self-important socialites. But his mom didn't ask much of him, and this was the most important event on her social calendar ever since she joined the board of the kids' charity five years ago.

"Maybe I can scalp my seats outside," he mused. "Trade them in for a Bulls game."

"Tsk!" His mom was both annoyed and amused by his teasing. "Anyway, I'm looking forward to meeting your date. Even though you have told me very little about her."

"Mom, it's just a date, nothing more. I only met her a couple of weeks ago. So don't get too excited. She's not having my baby yet."

"Don't be crude," she chastised.

They talked for another few minutes until their

coffees were finished, then Chad walked her out to her car. As he watched her drive away, he looked down the street of his new neighborhood. It was good to see kids outside, and people running or walking their dogs. It had a nice, established suburban feel right in the city. The neighbor on his right drove up at that point. Chad waved to him before heading back into the house, vowing to introduce himself sometime soon.

The next day, he left work early to get dressed for the charity event. His date lived nearby in Kenwood. Chad had met Nora Simmons at the gym he had just joined up the street from the house. He noticed her on his second visit, as she was heading into an aerobics class. There was a spark of interest in her eyes as they passed each other, and she was cute enough to make him take a second look and remember her the next time she was there. Tonight would be their third date.

Chad left the house at five forty-five that evening wearing a navy blue suit with a light blue shirt. His belt was a warm cognac brown to match his polished shoes. Nora lived about ten minutes away, and she came outside about a minute after he pulled up, wearing a spring trench coat and high black stilettos. They exchanged warm hellos before Chad pulled his car away from the curb and headed into the city's downtown core.

"Do you go to these things often?" Nora asked along the way.

"No, not really," Chad replied.

"Me either, but I'm really looking forward to it.

Thanks again for the invite," she stated with a happy smile.

"No problem. I'm glad you could make it, otherwise I would spend a very long evening by myself."

"Oh, I doubt that," she replied with a light laugh. "My friend Elizabeth went to the Kids Camp's annual party last year, and she couldn't stop talking about it. She said the performances and prizes were unbelievable. I kept thinking they would have to be at seven hundred dollars a plate. Then I saw the pictures in the paper the next day. So many famous people at one event. And here I am going to the party just a year later."

Chad let her chat on without interruption. She was a bit of talker, but he didn't mind. It saved him from thinking about what to say or feeling the need to fill in awkward silences. They arrived at the swanky Isis Hotel on Michigan Avenue at about twenty minutes after six. There was a line of cars for the valet parking, and they finally made it inside the lobby about fifteen minutes later. There were several young women at the front entrance to escort the event participants to the banquet rooms.

Chad spotted his mom standing beside the entrance to the main ballroom, greeting each guest personally. She looked like a queen in her copper gold floor length satin dress. He escorted Nora to the lengthy line for a coat check, leaving her there as he went over to his mother.

"Hey, baby, such perfect timing," Denise exclaimed with a beaming smile. "And don't you look handsome."

"Hi, Mom," Chad replied with a neutral tone, trying not to encourage her fawning.

She looked around dramatically, and Chad resisted the urge to roll his eyes.

"And where is she?" his mom quizzed.

"Her name is Nora, Mom. She's in line at the coat check."

"All right. Well, I'll have to meet her a little later then. We're going to start the show in ten minutes, so I have to head backstage." Denise squeezed his arm lovingly before turning to enter the ballroom.

"Oh!" she exclaimed, wheeling around. "We have some fabulous prizes in the silent auction. I'm sure you'll find something there you like. There are several golf packages to choose from." Then she was off to continue her hosting activities, waving at familiar faces every few steps.

Chad shook his head, unable to hold back a smile. She really was in her element at events like this. He remembered when he was a child, even though they lived a very meager lifestyle, his mom always managed to dress and behave like a socialite. They never had money for expensive furniture, restaurants, or costly trips, but with Denise's savvy shopping skills, their clothes were always of the best quality. She also made an effort to build a network and develop friends way above her income level, wanting to expose Chad to another way of life than what he saw every day in their economically depressed Englewood neighborhood. It was as though she knew exactly who she wanted to be one day, and plotted the journey to get there.

To see her now, a successful, respected businesswoman in a happy, supportive relationship, made his heart swell with pride. Even if her behavior could sometimes be a little over the top.

Chad turned back to the coat check area to find Nora all done and looking for him within the crowd. He waved slightly to catch her attention, then they both went into the hall to find their seats. The room was decorated in rich shades of green to reflect the foliage of the summer forest.

Nora looked around at the space, her mouth hanging slightly open. "This is just spectacular," she gushed. "Look, over there! Is that really Michael Jordan . . ."

"Yes, it is," Chad interrupted, taking hold of her hand to urge her through the crowd and tables. "Come, I think they're going to start dinner soon."

As Denise promised, they were seated very close to the front with six other people, and had a great view of the stage. The appetizers were served just as the show started. The next hour and a half was very entertaining, with three of the city's well-known comedians performing their most popular acts. The crowd roared with laugher at their outrageous and sometimes racy routines. Chad found himself laughing so hard his cheeks hurt. Nora was clearly enjoying herself, though obviously distracted by star-gazing.

There was a twenty-minute intermission in the program, where the guests could network, grab a drink, or take a bathroom break. While Nora went to the washroom, Chad went over to the silent auction items displayed around the perimeter of the room. His mom was right—there were several golf packages that looked worthwhile, and he put his name down for three using a pen provided. He was about to put it back down for the next bidder, when

he noticed the name printed along its length—
Royal Dunegan Luxury Hotels and Resorts.

He stood there staring at the writing instrument
for long seconds, his perplexity clearly visible on his
face. Chad looked further along the table, and
found that all the provided pens were the same.
The obvious answer was there in some part of his
brain. The Isis Hotel must be owned by Royal
Dunegan, probably newly acquired. But he seemed
frozen in the possibilities it created. Instinctively, he
started looking around the room, seeking a glimpse
of the shapely, petite frame that was never far from
his dreams. Then he was walking through the
crowd without any particular direction, his heart
beating a little faster.

"Hey, there you are."

Chad whipped around at the voice and gentle
touch to his arm.

"Did you bid on anything?" Nora asked, her face
bright with enjoyment.

He could not help one more look around the
room.

"What's wrong?" she asked, following his glance.
"Are you looking for someone?"

"No, no . . ." he replied faintly before looking
squarely back at her. "Come, I think the rest of the
show is about to start."

They weaved their way back to their table. The
second half of the night was equally entertaining,
but Chad could not stay focused. His thoughts were
flooded with bits of memories and scrambled with
what-ifs. *Could she be here, in Chicago? At this event?*
There was a tickle at the nape of his neck, like he

was being watched, that had him constantly looking around.

Nora occasionally looked at him, puzzled by his change in mood, but she didn't question him again. Finally, the formal schedule of events ended, and music came on in the background, encouraging people to stay and socialize, maybe spend some more on the donated items.

"Would you like something to drink?" Chad asked Nora as they walked together toward the doors of the ballroom.

"Yes, that would be great. Maybe a rum and coke?" she asked.

"Okay, I'll be right back."

"I'll be over there looking at the paintings," she told him, pointing to the mounted collection of abstract artwork near the back of the room.

He nodded and headed out into the hallway of the banquet rooms where the cash bar was set up. Something caught his eye on his right as soon as he exited the large double doors. It was the back of a woman, wearing a cranberry-colored dress that hugged her body like a silk wrap down to her knees. Her hair was a cloud of curls that brushed the top of her shoulders. Chad was walking toward her before he knew what he was doing. She was talking with two men, both mature, maybe in their mid-fifties, and they were hanging on her every word. One of the men looked up at Chad, perhaps alarmed by his large frame approaching the small group with some urgency and determination.

Chad nodded at the older man politely, but stopped about a yard from the woman, her back still facing him. Common sense was telling him that there were plenty of women in the city with the right body to wear the hell out of that dress. And that hairstyle wasn't that unique in Chicago fashion circles. It could be anyone.

As though sensing someone behind her, the woman looked slightly over her shoulder. Chad expelled a rush of air from his lungs.

There was Rebecca Isles standing in front of him as though conjured up from his nightly dreams and daytime fantasies. He looked down into her golden eyes and over those sweet lips, fighting the urge to run his hands over her slender, sexy frame and confirm she was real.

Chapter 12

For whatever reason, Rebecca was not at all shocked to see Chad Irvine standing in front of her. From the moment she confirmed the trip to Chicago for a few weeks, something told her this was inevitable. The look on his face reminded her of the one he had when they had first met under the giant oak tree in South Carolina, a mix of surprise and focused scrutiny. It was understandable, considering he expected to never see her again, particularly in his hometown without any warning. *He could very well be at this event with his girlfriend, or worse, his wife!* she thought, something that had crossed her mind more than once over the last six months or so. While he had not been wearing a wedding band in Myrtle Beach, it wasn't as if they had discussed their personal lives in any real depth.

They stood only a step from each other for several seconds, but long enough to make the two gentlemen with whom she had been speaking a little uncomfortable. They looked between her and Chad, saw his stony expression, and slowly walked away. Rebecca was about to say something flippant to Chad, to break the ice, but instead found her arm in the vice grip of his hand as he propelled her away from the crowd mingling in front of the bar. She was too busy trying to keep up with his long strides to voice her objection. He finally stopped at the far end of the long hall near a back entrance to the rear parking lot.

"Hello, Rebecca," he stated after releasing her arm. His tone was casual, almost pleasant, but his nose flared with each breath.

"Hi, Chad. Funny meeting you here."

It was a silly statement considering the circumstances. He lifted one brow in response. "Yes, funny, considering I live in Chicago, and last I heard, you were on your way to Florida."

Rebecca shrugged.

"I assume you're still working for the hotel chain," he stated rather than asked.

"Yeah, they just took over this property."

They looked at each other, not sure what to say, what this unexpected opportunity meant.

"How long have you been in town?"

"Since last week."

Chad nodded, then let out a deep breath.

"Look, I thought about sending you a note, letting you know I was in the city, but . . ." Rebecca's voice trailed off as she struggled to articulate why she didn't.

He shook his head, suggesting an explanation wasn't necessary right now. Then, he gave her a slow, decidedly sexy smile, and took ahold of her arm again with more of a caress. "It doesn't matter," he stated softly, pulling her close.

His mouth fell on hers in a full, sweeping kiss that was completely inappropriate for where they were standing, with hundreds of people networking not ten yards away, including several of the hotel staff that she was working with. Her last rational thought was that it was a good thing that he was so big, and likely hid her from view.

The embrace was hot and intense, so familiar that Rebecca's body responded quickly. Their mouths mated deeply, with tongues entangled as they emitted soft, breathless moans. She could taste his arousal and it fueled her own. They were so wrapped in sensation that neither heard the person who approached them, though her steps were heavy with determination.

"Chad? Sweetheart, I've been looking everywhere for you."

He pulled away from Rebecca so quickly that she stumbled a little to regain her balance. Then his back was to her, shielding her from view as he addressed the intruder.

"Mom," he stated simply.

Hearing that word, Rebecca had enough sense to quickly straighten her dress and wipe the moisture of their kiss from her mouth, grateful that she had only been wearing a sheer pinkish gloss on her lips.

"What in heaven's name are you doing all the way over here? I have a few people from the board who— Oh!"

The older woman stopped suddenly in her tracks the moment she caught a glimpse of someone with her son. "I'm sorry. I didn't mean to interrupt, Chad. I thought you were alone," she stated.

Rebecca realized it was ridiculous to continue hiding behind Chad's broad back. She stepped forward on an angle until she was in full view.

"That's okay, Mom. We were just . . . talking," he finally replied with a quick glance down at Rebecca.

"And you must be Nora, right?" his mother asked with a welcoming smile. "Chad, you didn't tell me how gorgeous she was."

Rebecca blinked a few times, then looked up at the man she had just been kissing.

He didn't look back, but was instead reaching out to his mother and steering her back toward the party. "No, Mom. This isn't . . ."

"Chad?"

The call came from down the hall, and all three of them looked toward the passageway to see a tall, statuesque woman in a short black dress wave at them. Then she started walking toward them in very high heels, but her progress was slow. Chad's mom looked at her son, then at the girl who was still standing beside him. Rebecca looked at Chad, whose face was even more stiff than usual, then her eyes fell to the floor. Instinct told her this situation was becoming a train wreck, and as interesting as it would be to watch it develop, self-preservation was telling her to walk away.

"Mom," Chad finally stated, "this is Rebecca Isles, a friend of mine."

"Oh. Oh dear, I'm sorry," his mom stammered, very aware that there was something awkward about what was going on.

"Rebecca, this is my mother, Denise Crothers."
His tone was polite, but void of any clue as to what
he was thinking.

"It's very nice to meet you, Ms. Irvine," Rebecca
added with a respectful nod of her head.

"Please, call me Denise, dear. Very nice to meet
you," his mother exuded, her eyes bright with interest. "Now, do I detect a Jamaican accent?"

Before Rebecca could reply, the Amazon in black
finally reached them. She seemed confused and
more than a little annoyed.

"Chad? What happened? I thought you were getting us drinks, but that was ages ago."

It was immediately obvious that this was the mysterious Nora. She was clearly attending the event
with Chad as his date, at the very least. Rebecca
straightened her back, recognizing it was time for
her to make a graceful exit.

"I'm sorry, I have to get going," Rebecca said to
no one in particular, refusing to look at Chad
though she felt the heat of his gaze burning into
the top of her head. "Excuse me."

Rebecca walked away from the small group with
smooth measured steps. Instead of rejoining the
party, she turned down an adjacent hall that led to
several smaller rooms. From there, she weaved her
way back to the hotel lobby, managing to avoid running into anyone she knew. Finally, she reached an
empty sitting area next to the bar. It had a big, wing-
back chair that allowed her to sink into its depths
and disappear from view.

There was no way to process her feelings quickly.

She had gone from exciting passion in one moment, wrapped in Chad's strong arms, to crushing embarrassment in the next in front of his woman and mother. Rebecca couldn't even begin to figure out how it had all happened so quickly. She didn't even have the right to be angry or outraged that Chad was with someone. It's not like he lied to her or had led her to believe otherwise. They met while he was on a business trip and never discussed availability for a relationship. It was a classic scenario for promiscuity and cheating, and she was a naive idiot to think their connection was any different.

She let out a deep sigh. *This is exactly why I didn't call to let Chad know I was in Chicago,* she reflected. The hard truth was that if he wanted to stay in touch, he could have reached out at any point in the last six months, even to say a casual hello. To Rebecca, that meant he didn't want to, and now she knew exactly why. All that kiss had proved was that they still had a physical connection. And that he was a bit of a dog to act on it while his woman was in the vicinity.

It took a few long minutes of reflection, but finally Rebecca started to think rationally. Maybe this was a good thing. Chad Irvine was great as a stranger. He was calm, sexy, smart, the personification of strong masculinity. His body was mouthwatering perfection. But he was just a man like any other, with much of the same ethical flaws. His behavior tonight proved that. It was time for her to recognize the Myrtle Beach incident for what it was—a really, really good one-night stand. And now she had to move on.

That shouldn't be too hard to do since the direction of her future had so many options. While she still planned to do projects for the hotel chain, the interest in her portfolio was growing every week. She was submitting work to all forms of travel marketing publications, from magazines to books, blogs, and brochures. Earlier this week, she finalized the deal to sell twenty-five photos to the publisher of an ethnic cookbook. It was her first big sale of her work outside the contract with Royal Dunegan.

The most exciting news was from a well-known publisher of travel magazines. They had expressed interest in her pictures taken from some rural parts of the Far East, untouched by tourism. It was early in the discussion, but seemed very promising. Above all, Rebecca was still intrigued by the idea of a staff photographer position, like the one in New York. It didn't have to be for a big news company, just something permanent and stable.

Her personal life also held some promise. Last Friday, when Rebecca introduced herself at the management office of the Isis Hotel, she met John McConaughey, the general manager. He would be handling the marketing campaign on-site as her prime contact for the project. They spent most of her first day reviewing the plan and touring the hotel property. John was a complete gentleman and very professional. So Rebecca was a little surprised when he had offered to take her to dinner on Saturday night.

It turned out to be a pleasant evening with decent conversation. He took her to a really impressive steak house overlooking the river and spent most of the time telling her all about the city. John was a pretty good-looking guy, average height and a trim build, with jet black hair, mossy green eyes, and an interesting Irish accent. Rebecca was flattered by his attention, though not sure there was really anything there to get excited about. They could definitely be friends, but he didn't inspire any feelings that would warrant breaking her rule not to get involved with anyone while traveling. Certainly not like Chad Irvine had.

Through the past week, she and John spent quite a bit of time together, and he took her out for dinner two more times, including the night before. They had walked to a nearby restaurant, and he held her hand on the way back. Rebecca let him, thinking it was harmless and actually quite pleasant. When he walked her up to her hotel room, they ended the evening with a light kiss. It was sweet and undemanding.

Today, as she worked the charity function and captured a variety of pictures for the corporate events page of the Web site, John's behavior toward her was markedly different. While he remained professional, there was also an attentive, almost possessive quality to their interaction. It started with her dress.

Rebecca had been taking pictures of the decorated banquet room when he approached her.

"Hi, John," she said warmly, looking up from her camera viewfinder.

"Hello."

She was about to tell him how nice he looked in his dark gray suit, but something on his face made her pause. "What's wrong?" she asked instead.

He looked her up and down with his lips a little pursed. "Nothing," he replied briefly, but his tone was not convincing.

Rebecca gave him one more glance, a little puzzled, but went back to reviewing the pictures taken so far.

"That dress is a little tight, isn't it?" he finally stated.

Rebecca looked at him, then down the length of her body. The warm red sheath did fit her body very closely, but it was completely appropriate. She had worn it to many similar events over the last year or so.

"It's fine," she replied with a teasing smile. "You don't like it?"

"You look great, but I think it's inappropriate for an event like this. You are working, after all."

That statement made her lower the camera and turn toward him. She couldn't tell if John was saying this as her client or because of the burgeoning relationship. Either way, Rebecca was not pleased with his statement. She was about to tell him so, when one of the hotel staff members called out to John with a question.

"You should change," he told Rebecca quietly before walking away.

Of course, she didn't. Instead, she kissed her teeth

loudly—a very Jamaican expression of annoyance—
and went back to work.

Rebecca had not spoken to John since then, but
had caught a few glimpses of him through the night.
But now that the night was over and very successful,
she was sure that he would be over whatever had
really been bothering him. Surely, whatever she
chose to wear could not be that important in the
scope of things.

She looked at her watch, noting that it had been
about twenty minutes since that fiasco with Chad.
She couldn't hide out in a corner of the lobby forever. It was quarter to eleven, and the charity event
should be almost over. Rebecca finally uncurled
from the chair and set out to find John to let him
know she was done for the night.

First, she stopped in the bathroom to freshen up
a bit, make sure there was no trace of Chad's kiss on
her face. Looking in the vanity mirror, she noted
that her lips looked dry and swollen, a result of her
habit of nibbling on them while in thought. Rebecca reapplied a little lip gloss kept in a small
wristlet purse she wore, just big enough to also hold
her room key, her cell phone, and some money.
Satisfied that she looked calm and contained, she
made her way back to the banquet hall, taking the
service path through the kitchens.

Rebecca found John in a meeting with the custodial staff to organize the cleanup. She waited in the
back until he was finished.

He dismissed the workers and walked up to her.
"I was looking for you earlier," he stated.

"Yeah, I wasn't feeling great so I went for a walk

to get some air," Rebecca replied. "So, it looks like things went well."

"Seems so," John stated with ambivalence.

"Well, it's been a long day. So, if you don't mind, I'm going to head up for the night. I'll send you the files in the morning, then we can meet on Monday to review."

He nodded. "I'll walk you up."

Rebecca shook her head, suddenly feeling exhausted. "No, that's okay. I'm sure you have lots to do down here."

"Come on, let's go," John persisted, dismissing her objection.

It wasn't worth arguing about, so Rebecca nodded and they walked together toward the elevators. If she were in a clearer frame of mind, perhaps she would have sensed his agitation. But Rebecca was tired of thinking and was content with their silence on the way to her room. She opened her door and they both walked into the small space.

As she turned to face him, with the intention of thanking him for seeing her to her room, Rebecca found him standing quite close to her.

"Who was the man that you went off with, Rebecca?"

She was so surprised by his question, and even more so by his tone, that she could only blink.

"I asked you a question and I expect an answer."

Chapter 13

Rebecca took a step back, completely unprepared for John's demand. "What?" she stammered, still not sure she had heard him correctly.

"Who was he!"

"Where is *this* coming from, John?"

He eyed her up and down with scorn on his face. "Look at you, dressed like a common slut. Is that what you are, Rebecca? A slut?"

"What?!" she demanded. Shocked at his nasty words, her voice was sharp and direct.

"And here I was, being a gentleman, treating you with respect," he spat. "But that's not what you want, is it?"

"I don't know what you're talking about. I would like you to leave."

Rebecca walked around him toward the door, but he grabbed her arm hard and pulled her up to him.

"This is my hotel. I'll leave when I'm good and ready."

Up to that point, she was confused and annoyed

by his bizarre behavior. Now Rebecca was smart enough to be scared. Her heart started beating like a drum in her ears. "Let go of me, John," she demanded in a quiet but firm voice.

He barked out a laugh. "Or what? It's a little late to pretend this isn't how you like things, Rebecca. Half the hotel saw that guy drag you off. You didn't protest then. Did you think I didn't see you, kissing him in plain sight?" he spat, his fingers tightening on her flesh as the venom in his voice rose. "I read you completely wrong, with your sweet voice and innocent face. But now I know what you like and I'm more than happy to give it to you."

He was clearly unhinged, and Rebecca immediately gave up any plan of reasoning with him. Self-preservation kicked in, and her only plan was to get away. As he pulled her closer to force her into a kiss, she stomped down on his foot with her shoe heel. He emitted a low curse and his grip on her weakened slightly, enough for her to pull away. She reached for the door, frantic to get away from him as quickly as possible.

"Oh, you like the chase!" she heard him say with another nasty laugh. "Where are you going to go, Rebecca?"

She didn't stop running to take the elevator, instead rushing down seven flights of stairs as fast as her high-heeled sandals would allow. By the time she reached the third floor, Rebecca was pretty sure he wasn't following her, so she stopped on the landing to think. She took a minute to catch her breath, think about what to do. There was no way to know what John was up to in his crazy state of mind.

By now, he could be on his way downstairs in the elevator, or even still standing in her room waiting for her return. The one thing Rebecca knew for sure was that she wasn't going to wait around to find out.

She slowly opened the door to the third floor. Finding it empty and quiet, she quickly dashed across the length of the hall to the staircase on the other side. If he knew she took the stairs and was waiting for her downstairs, she could avoid him by using one of the other exits.

Rebecca had no idea what she would do after that. It was almost midnight, and all she had was her camera, her cell phone, and about thirty dollars cash in her wristlet purse, but she had no intention of staying at the Isis that night. Even if she was able to avoid John and return to her room, there was no way she could sleep. She thought about going to the front desk and requesting another room, but it wouldn't make her any more safe. As the hotel manager, John could easily find her with the reservation system, and with his master passkey, could enter any room in the hotel. Staying here was not an option.

Once she was downstairs and hiding in a women's bathroom, Rebecca weighed her options while chewing on her bottom lip. One was to call the police, but she wasn't sure what the complaint would be. Yes, he had grabbed her arm and had made enough suggestive comments to scare the hell out of her, but that didn't exactly rise to the level of assault. She didn't know much about the American justice system, but she seriously doubted they would waste much time on what was nothing more than a lovers' quarrel. Never mind the damage it would do to her relationship with Royal Dunegan.

Her only other option was to call Uncle Devon and ask for his help to check into another hotel for the night. Then he could help her figure out what to do next. Rebecca quickly dialed his numbers, first the cell phone, then home. He didn't answer either, so she left him a brief message and asked him to call her back as soon as possible. After waiting another ten minutes, it was clear she needed another option, and there was only one left.

She called the cell phone number programmed for Chad Irvine. He answered after the third ring.

"Hello?" he asked.

Rebecca closed her eyes with a mix of relief and dread. "Hi, Chad. It's Rebecca. Sorry to call you so late."

There was a short pause.

"Hey, no worries. I was still up."

"Okay. Umm . . ." Now that she had him on the phone, she didn't really know what to say without sounding a little nuts. "Listen, I need your help."

"Why, what's wrong? Are you okay?" he demanded, clearly concerned.

"I'm fine, really. But something's happened and I can't stay at the Isis tonight."

"What happened?"

"It's . . . it's hard to explain. The problem is that I've left everything in my room and I can't go back there."

"What do you mean? Have you lost your key? I'm sure if—"

"No, it's not that. I'm sorry; I really don't want to go into it. I was just hoping you could help me check into another hotel nearby. I don't have my credit card or ID with me."

"Where are you now?" he asked.

"I'm still at the Isis."

"Okay. Can you go outside and grab a cab?"

"I think so."

The hotel had one entrance on Michigan Avenue, and she shouldn't have to wait too long for an available taxi to drive by.

"Good. Get a taxi going south and tell the driver to take you to Hyde Park. I live only about twenty minutes away."

Rebecca immediately shook her head at the idea. She wasn't ready to see him again, or address what had happened earlier that night. She just wanted another hotel room for the night.

"That's not necessary, Chad. I will be fine by the morning, honestly."

"Rebecca, you're obviously scared, so either you get in a taxi or I'm coming to get you. Either way, I'm not leaving you in the city by yourself for the night."

His voice made it clear she had no choice. After a deep breath, she gave in and accepted his offer. How much worse could the night get, anyway? "All right."

"Good. Call me when you're in the cab and I'll give you the address."

"Thank you, Chad," she finally declared, suddenly feeling close to tears.

"It's no problem, Rebecca. But call me as soon as you're in the car, okay?"

"Okay," she agreed.

They hung up, and she took a few minutes to collect herself before cautiously leaving the bathroom. There was no one in sight, and she made her way to the closest exit on the north side of the building. Once outside, Rebecca realized how cool the spring night air was, and how inadequate her sleeveless dress was against the strong breeze. She wrapped her arms around herself and sped up her steps as she made her way along the perimeter of the property.

On Michigan Avenue, relieved to see that the street was still quite busy, she went to the curb to hail a taxi. It was a short wait. As she opened the passenger door, Rebecca thought she heard her name called out above the traffic noise. When she turned toward the hotel, it was to see John running out of the main exit about five yards away, his face set with determination. Panicking, she practically threw herself into the car, slamming the door behind her.

"Drive, please!" she demanded urgently to the driver.

Late night escapes must have been fairly common in the city because the cabbie didn't hesitate, peeling off with quick acceleration. Two seconds later and John would have had a hand on the car door. Rebecca slumped into the backseat, breathing in deep inhalations as she tried to regain her composure.

"Where to, ma'am?" the driver asked after a few minutes.

She met his eyes through the rearview mirror. "To Hyde Park, please."

He nodded, looking at her again.

"I'll have the address for you in a moment."

Rebecca took out her cell phone and called Chad briefly for his address as instructed, repeating the details to the driver. She then laid her head back against the rear seat headrest to think through what the hell had happened. Now that she was away from the hotel and feeling less desperate, Rebecca started to wonder if she had completely over-reacted to John's behavior. Yes, he had been angry and irrational, but was he really dangerous?

She reached out to touch the spot on her arm that he had grabbed so hard. It felt a little tender to the touch, likely the effect of a developing bruise. It grounded her back to reality. Regardless of his ultimate intentions, John McConaughey's behavior was completely unacceptable for someone she had only gone out with a few times, never mind the fact that he was acting as her client in this project.

One thing she knew for sure was that she could not show up on Monday morning to work with him as though nothing had happened. First thing tomorrow, Rebecca was going to call Uncle Devon again to get his guidance on what to do.

The taxi eventually turned onto a tree-lined street. It came to a stop in front of a modern house, and Chad immediately stepped out the front door. He had changed out of the suit worn earlier and was now in a white T-shirt and dark warm-up track pants. He opened the car door for her, then went around to the driver's side to settle the fare.

"Are you okay?" Chad asked while they stood on the sidewalk and the taxi drove away.

Rebecca nodded, gripping her purse in one hand and her camera with the other as it hung from the straps over her shoulder. She felt emotion welling up in her throat again.

"Come inside," he urged with a gentle palm against the base of her spine. "You must be freezing."

"Sorry," she said with a hint of sarcasm. "I didn't really prepare for a trip in the middle of the night, did I?"

He led the way into his front foyer, a wide spacious area with a high ceiling and wall to wall oversized stone tiles. It was beautiful, but strangely empty. Chad walked ahead into the house, leading her through a big, open space with a large kitchen in the back. The floors looked like original wide-plank oak, but were finished in a modern and unique grayish taupe color. The whole first level had obviously gone through a major renovation, but there were still several nice remnants of the original architecture, like the carved molding and a wood-burning fireplace with a beautifully carved wood mantel. But other than a sectional sofa and a very large flat-screen television mounted to the wall, the whole floor was also strangely void of furniture.

"Would you like something hot to drink? Maybe some tea?" he asked, entering the kitchen.

"Sure, tea would be fine," Rebecca replied, stopping in front of a large island that ran the length of the kitchen. It was lined with four padded stools.

Chad filled up the kettle and set it on the stove. They were both quiet as he got a cup and tea bag out of the cupboard. He must have noticed her looking around.

"It's pretty empty, isn't it?" he stated, his tone humorous.

Rebecca could not help smiling since it was exactly what she had been thinking. "Well . . . now that you mention it . . ."

They both laughed a little, and she welcomed the levity.

"I just moved in about three weeks ago, and the stuff from my apartment is now lost in this house," he explained. He was leaning casually against the kitchen counter with his arms crossed at his chest.

"It's a beautiful space," she told him, looking around again.

"Thanks."

The kettle started whistling. Chad turned away to make her tea.

"Here you go," he told her, setting the cup on the breakfast bar. "Are you cold? Do you need a sweater or something?"

Rebecca shook her head as she sat on one of the stools. "No, thanks. I'll be okay. The tea will help."

"Do you want anything in it? Sugar or honey?"

"Some honey would be nice."

He took a bottle out of the cupboard, squeezed

in a generous dollop, then handed her a spoon. Rebecca slowly stirred the steaming brew for several seconds, already dreading the conversation that was sure to come next. The seconds dragged into minutes, until she finally looked up. He was relaxed against the counter again, his arms crossed tightly across his chest. His intense gaze was fixed on her.

"Are you going to tell me what happened?"

Chapter 14

Chad could hardly believe that Rebecca Isles was sitting in his kitchen brooding over a cup of tea. In fact, the whole evening was pretty surreal, even though the details were still very fresh in his mind. What on earth had he been thinking to start making out with her right there in the hallway of the hotel in plain sight of anyone who cared to look, including his mom and Nora? He had spent the rest of the night in a fog.

Of course, his mom knew something was fishy the minute Nora had arrived at the scene, but she had done a good job of handling the situation. Chad had introduced her to Nora and they had made polite conversation about the event for an appropriate amount of time before his mom went back to the hall. Her last words were a reminder to Chad that they had lunch plans for Saturday afternoon. The expression in her eyes said she was looking forward to his explanation of what she had witnessed.

The party had been quickly winding down at that

point. Chad sent Nora to get her jacket while he
checked on his auction bids. While he'd been pleas-
antly surprised to be the winner of one of the golf
packages, he was also distracted, looking around
the room wondering where Rebecca had gone and
if he would see her before they left. But there was
no sight of her even as he and Nora headed out of
the hotel to get his car from the valet. Thankfully,
his date was fairly quiet during the drive back to her
house, occasionally making small talk and seem-
ingly content with his vague responses. Even as he
dropped Nora home with an escort to her door and
ended the evening with a short kiss on the lips,
Chad was thinking about how and when he would
call Rebecca. He felt pretty callous about it, but still
powerless to control his thoughts.

He was in his bedroom changing out of his suit
when Rebecca called him, then spent the next twenty
minutes pacing around the house until her cab
pulled up outside.

Now, as he listened silently to her soft voice,
telling him about what had happened to her after
she left the party, Chad felt his heart rate increase
while his stomach dropped. Rage started to shoot
up his spine. Of the various scenarios that had
crossed his mind, this wasn't one of them.

"I thought about calling the police, but I'm not
sure what I would say. That he scared me? It sounds
ridiculous, right?" she asked, looking up at him for
an answer.

He shrugged. "If he threatened you, then you

should report it," he replied, keeping his voice calm and trying to be rational.

"I don't know if he did. Not really. He was rambling, talking about being rough and all that nonsense. He wanted me to be scared, but he didn't actually say he would hurt me."

Chad stepped forward until he was leaning against the breakfast bar. "Still, Rebecca, the man refused to leave your hotel room and insinuated that he would enter it anytime he wanted. He can't get away with that."

"I agree, Chad. But it's really his word against mine at this point. And God knows what his story will be. What if I call the police and they decide there's no basis for a complaint? It's not likely that my relationship with Royal Dunegan will survive intact. Then where will I be?"

Chad lowered his head and let out a deep sigh. There was some logic to her words, and it made him even angrier. "Well, you can't just go back to work on Monday like nothing happened. He's clearly a little crazy, so you're not safe."

"I know," she replied, rubbing her eyes with a mix of frustration and exhaustion. "I'll speak to my uncle in the morning and he'll know what to do."

She sounded so forlorn that it tore at his heart.

"There's another option," Chad said in a quiet voice.

"Really? What's that?"

"I could pay your friend a visit. Let him know you're not alone, and remind him how to treat a woman with respect."

Rebecca looked up at him with big, bright eyes.

"What's his name?" he probed in a gentle cajoling tone.

She smiled, then giggled, her eyes tearing up a little before she looked down at her now empty cup. "Are you going to fight for my honor, Chad Irvine?" she teased when she glanced back up at him. "Protect my virtue?"

"Trust me, I won't need to fight the bastard. He just needs a good talking to, that's all. Men like him are cowards, preying on women they think are vulnerable or alone."

"Well, he picked the wrong woman, that's for sure," she spat with a frown.

That made him smile. Chad instinctively knew he didn't want to be on her bad side, small as she was.

"Come on, it's late. Get a good night's sleep, then we'll decide what to do in the morning," he told her, realizing that the word "we" had rolled pretty easily off his tongue.

He put her cup in the dishwasher, then walked across the room to turn out the lights, explaining, "There is a spare bedroom upstairs. It's nothing fancy, but should be comfortable enough."

"Chad."

He turned to find her still standing in the kitchen, looking like a cold, lost kitten.

"I really don't know what to say," she added with a shrug. "This is really—"

"Rebecca, there is no need to say anything. I'm glad you called," he told her.

"Well, your girlfriend probably doesn't feel the same way. She's probably upstairs right now—"

"Rebecca," he repeated, unable to contain his amusement, "there's no one here but us. And I don't have a girlfriend."

Her mouth formed a surprised O while she looked up at him with wide unblinking eyes. "I just assumed. You know, because of the woman at the party," she stammered.

"Nora's not my girlfriend. We've gone out on a couple of dates; that's it."

There was a long pause where neither of them knew exactly what to say, making the moment even more awkward.

"Okay, let me get you into bed before you fall asleep on your feet."

Chad knew the minute the words came out of his mouth that they were inappropriately suggestive. Though he was itching to pull her close, it was only to give her comfort and warmth with no sexual intent. He knew she had been through enough for the night and certainly would not be open to anything intimate. To his relief, Rebecca was unfazed by his comment and quietly went up the stairs ahead of him.

On the second floor, he guided her to his guest bedroom, starkly decorated with a queen bed and a chest of drawers. Chad also showed Rebecca the attached bathroom, which had a spare toothbrush and some basic toiletries, then left her there to grab something from his room that she could sleep in. The only T-shirt suitable was from his first year of college when he was several pounds lighter, but it was still extralarge and likely to fit her like an oversized dress. She was still in the washroom with the water running when he returned, so Chad left the top on the bed for her.

Back in his bedroom, he climbed into bed and tried his best to go to sleep. It was after two o'clock in the morning, but while his body was tired, his mind was sharp and wired. Ninety minutes later, the night was starting to feel like the longest of his life. His mind would not stop running in a dozen directions, yet without accomplishing anything consequential. He must have fallen asleep at some point because next thing he knew, it was eight forty-five in the morning with the sun filtering through the window shades.

Chad rolled over with a big stretch, looking up at the ceiling while the fog over his brain cleared. It took a couple of minutes, but the details from the night before came back to him. Immediately, he wondered if Rebecca was awake and in need of anything. He stretched again, and got up to use the bathroom, brush his teeth, and pull on jeans and a shirt before checking up on her.

The door to the spare bedroom was closed. Chad listened for a moment for any movement inside, just in case she was still sleeping. After a moment, he knocked lightly and waited.

Rebecca opened it within a few seconds. "Hi," she said simply.

Chad tried not to notice, but she looked so cute drowned in his T-shirt that he could not help looking her up and down. Her eyes followed his, then Rebecca looked back at him with a grin. "I'm surprised I'm not stepping on it," she said.

"That one doesn't fit me anymore, otherwise I

think you would be," Chad replied. "Did you sleep okay?"

She shrugged. "I'm all right. I slept until after seven, which is rare for me."

"Good. Are you hungry?" he asked.

"A little," she admitted with an impish smile.

"Okay. Well, come downstairs for breakfast when you're ready."

"Thanks, Chad. Unfortunately, I won't be dressed appropriately."

Chad laughed. "Under the circumstances, I'll forgive you."

Twenty minutes later, he had thick ham and cheese omelettes laid out on the breakfast bar and fresh coffee ready. Rebecca arrived looking fresh faced and very youthful in the makeshift night-dress. It reminded him of the first time he saw her in the brush of the golf course wearing an orange sweatshirt and purple rain boots.

"I hope you brought a full appetite," Chad stated as he pulled out a stool for her.

"Wow, this is quite a spread," she replied, looking genuinely surprised.

"What? You didn't think I could cook?"

"No, it's not that. It's just been a long time since I've had a home-cooked breakfast, that's all. Any home-cooked meal, actually," Rebecca explained with a light laugh. "I was thinking toast or cereal. But this really looks good."

"Well, it may not be as fancy as you'll get in your five-star hotels, but you'll be satisfied, trust me," he told her.

"I have no doubt."

He sat beside her and they dug into the meal.

"I'm going to call my uncle shortly," Rebecca said some moments later. "I left him a message last night, but he probably hasn't gotten it yet."

"Where is your uncle?" Chad asked.

"He's in Jamaica. Well, he's not my real uncle, but he was very close to my mother and I've known him my whole life. So he's like family."

Chad nodded as he ate the last bite of his meal.

"He runs the Caribbean operations for Dunegan, so I'm sure he'll know the best thing to do," Rebecca added. "You were right, though. I can't just show up on Monday to continue the project like nothing happened."

"Well, you're not going anywhere without some clothes. You make your phone call, and I'll run out to the store to pick up a few things," he outlined, standing up. "What size shoe do you wear?"

"Chad, that's not necessary," she protested. "I'll go back to the hotel later this morning, to at least grab some of my things."

"It's nothing. As good as you looked in that dress last night, I'm sure I can find something more appropriate. What size?"

She let out a long sigh. "Size seven. But honestly, it's not necessary—"

"Uh-uh! No more protests," Chad interjected. "I'm just going to the nearest clothing store, not Barneys or anything fancy. Then I'll take you to the hotel for your things."

He didn't allow time for any more debate as he made a quick exit from the house, grabbing his jacket, keys, and wallet from the front table. There was a sports store just a few blocks away from his street, so Chad hopped into his car for the five-minute drive. Once he was there, it was easy to pick out a couple of pairs of small cotton fleece pants and tops, then a pack of gym socks. With some help from the salesperson, he also got a pair of athletic walking shoes. At the last minute, Chad also grabbed a light track jacket as well.

He was on his way back to the house within about thirty minutes, but also stopped at the drugstore for some basics that he knew she would need. Feeling a little silly and out of his depth, Chad grabbed a pack of pretty underwear, assuming she would need a fresh pair. He was back home a few moments later.

As he walked into the house, he could hear Rebecca talking on the phone. She was sitting on the couch in the living room, and only smiled back at Chad as he walked by. The tense expression on her face told him that it wasn't good news. He continued upstairs to give her some privacy and left her purchases on the bed in the spare bedroom before heading into the shower.

Freshened up and dressed in jeans and a light gray sweater, Chad went back down to the living room around twenty minutes later to check on her. Rebecca was sitting on the sofa again, no longer in conversation, but using the other features of her mobile phone. She was also wearing one of the outfits he had bought for her, including the jacket, with her dress and shoes from the night before piled neatly beside her. The new items seemed to fit pretty well, and Chad couldn't help smiling at how cute she looked.

"So, how did it go?" he asked as he approached the sitting area. "Did your uncle have any suggestions?"

She looked up and let out a deep sigh. "Well, he wasn't happy about the situation, that's for sure. I had to talk him out of jumping on the first plane to Chicago. He expects that once the VP of North American operations gets involved, John will likely be fired. The chain has a very low tolerance for any inappropriate or abusive behavior. The problem is that the VP is currently en route from Asia and isn't due to return to the states until tomorrow. So there's not much more we can do today."

Chad nodded. "Okay, well, that's something. You can stay here until tomorrow, or as long as it takes to have the situation resolved and they fire the guy."

"That's very generous, Chad, really. But I think you've done more than enough to help me," she replied, looking down at the clothes she was wearing. "Once I get my wallet and other things, I'll just check in to another hotel for a couple of days. There are several good ones in walking distance of the Isis, including a small Dunegan property a couple of blocks away."

He didn't argue, sensing that there was stubborn pride at play. Instead he said, "Well, I'm heading downtown to meet my mother for lunch at one o'clock. So I'm happy to give you a ride down and help to get you settled somewhere else."

Rebecca nodded as she stood up. They were several feet apart, but Chad could feel an awkward tension between them. He would give her a ride, and then what? Would they just go their separate ways?

"I can't thank you enough, Chad, for your help—" she began.

He cut her off. "Rebecca, it's nothing, really. I told you last night that I'm glad I was here to help."

"Well, I'm grateful. Just let me know how much I owe you for the clothes."

"Not necessary," he stated gruffly. "I'll get you a bag for your stuff, and we'll head out."

Her suggestion that he would need to be recompensed for a few items of clothing was almost insulting. It suggested that they were strangers instead of a man and woman who had shared hours of deep, intense intimacy. It made him think that she had moved on, and it wasn't a nice feeling.

Chapter 15

The drive back to the Isis hotel was fairly quiet,
though Chad tried to make small talk, occasionally
asking Rebecca about her time in Chicago so far
and the work she was here to do. She tried to respond with an equally casual tone, to give no indication that she was struggling to come to terms with
this bizarre situation. But it was a challenge. The
last twelve hours had turned her life upside-down,
and Rebecca had no clue what would happen next,
or what she wanted from the situation. Her mind
was reeling from it all.

Last night, as she lay down in Chad's spare bed,
she had spent several hours pondering the situation with him. Though since Myrtle Beach, her
memories of him were often the last thing lingering
in her mind before falling asleep, this time it was
very different. It made her cringe that after six
months without any contact, the minute she saw
him in a crowded room, she lost all dignity and
decorum. He only had to look at her with those intense dark eyes and she had stepped into his arms

without any regard for the consequences. Before she finally fell asleep, she concluded that to get involved with him in a casual fling now would be a painful mistake. Chad Irvine had a life in Chicago, including a woman he was dating, so it was in Rebecca's best interest to put their time together behind her, regardless of how nice and supportive he was being.

Now, as she headed closer to the hotel, Rebecca tried to understand the bizarre encounter with John. How had things gone so badly, why had he behaved so inappropriately, and what had she done to contribute to the situation? Yes, she had liked him and was entertaining the possibility of a relationship with him, but they had only gone out a few times, shared a couple of kisses. Certainly nothing had happened that would suggest they were committed to each other, or to spark the type of jealous rage he had demonstrated in her hotel room.

Rebecca recognized that the incident with Chad in the hallway was inappropriate and unprofessional. After witnessing her behavior, she could understand if John was upset and questioned her motives. She would even expect that he would not be interested in dating her any longer. But it did not give him the right to insult her or frighten her with threats of physical violence. He was clearly a little unstable, and Rebecca was glad she discovered his abusive nature before their relationship had developed any further.

But it certainly left her in a difficult situation. Despite Uncle Devon's assurance this morning that everything would be fine, and her professional reputation would not be impacted, Rebecca was not so certain. Based on what Devon knew about the purchase of the Isis property, John McConaughey's position as general manager was secured as part of the deal. So either he was essential to the success of the hotel or he was connected. Uncle Devon tried to make it sound like a minor factor, but Rebecca knew business well enough to understand it could be a major complication.

It was almost noon when they pulled into a parking spot a couple of blocks from the hotel. The late April weather was mild and sunny, and Michigan Avenue was busy with Saturday shoppers, tourists, and sightseers. The street was lined with high-end designer stores and smaller boutiques with a beautiful mix of early to mid-century architecture and sleek new ultramodern design. Rebecca was itching to turn on her camera and start taking pictures. Maybe after the situation with John and the Isis was resolved, she would spend some time exploring the city.

She and Chad entered the hotel and headed for the elevators. Rebecca could not help checking around them, wondering if John was somewhere nearby.

"Are you okay?" Chad asked, noting her agitation.

"I'm okay. I know he's off for the weekend, but he could still be here somewhere. He's aware that I have to return here eventually, right? What if he's just waiting for me to come back?" she stated softly.

"I hope he is here," he replied in a hard tone.

Rebecca's room was on the tenth floor and they were the last to get off. She cautiously stepped onto the landing, immediately remembering the last time she was here and her desperate run down the stairs to get away from John and the possessive rage in his eyes.

She felt Chad take her hand in his large grasp, and she tried to relax.

"Come on," he urged. "Everything's going to be fine. No one is going to hurt you."

Silently, Rebecca led him to her door. Once there, she slid the key card in the slot. The light indicator flashed red. She frowned while turning the handle, but the door didn't budge. Rebecca took out the key and slid it in again. The light was still red.

"What's wrong?" Chad asked from behind her.

"I don't know. My key isn't working."

"Here, let me try."

She stepped aside and gave him the plastic card to see if he would have better luck. Chad inspected it for a few moments, then slid it in the lock as she had done. The indicator flashed red again.

"There's something wrong with your card," he finally said.

Rebecca could feel her pulse quickening. "No," she uttered, running a hand over her forehead. "It's John. He's locked me out of the room."

They looked at each other for several seconds.

"Okay," Chad said slowly. "Well, let's go back to the front desk and get a new one."

"What is he trying to do, Chad? What's the point?"

"I don't know. But whatever it is, he's not going to get away with it."

Back in the lobby, they tried to explain the problem to the girl behind the reservation counter.

"I'm sorry, ma'am. I do have that room booked, but to another guest. Your name is not on the reservation. If you are also staying in that room, then I can only reissue a key to the guest on file."

"No, you don't understand," Rebecca stated, trying her best to stay calm. "That is my room, and I'm the only one staying in it. I checked in over a week ago. All of my things are in there. So there is some sort of mix-up with your system."

The young girl barely looked up from the computer screen. It was clear that she had heard every kind of explanation for situations like this and was unfazed by Rebecca's forceful insistence.

"Are you sure you have the right number? Do you have your card sleeve?"

"No, I don't, but I'm positive that's my room. I'm telling you, your computer is wrong."

"Well, I'm sorry. There is clearly an error somewhere," the clerk stated. "What's your full name, ma'am? I'll see if I can locate your correct room number."

Rebecca tried to be patient and gave the information. But she was pretty sure this situation was only going to get worse, and the look of intensity on Chad's face suggested he wasn't optimistic either.

"I'm very sorry, Ms. Isles, but there is no record of your reservation at this time. However we do have rooms available and I can secure one for you," she finally replied after a couple minutes of fruitless searching.

"You don't understand. Everything I own is in my

room. I don't even have my identification!" Rebecca shot back.

She bit her tongue to stop the tirade that was building in her chest as Chad reached out to wrap a comforting arm around her shoulders.

"I don't know what to say, ma'am," the girl replied, clearly baffled.

"The error is in your system," Chad insisted in a firm voice. "If you allow us access to that room, then we can get her things."

The poor clerk stared at them with wide, blinking eyes, clearly out of her depth.

"I can't do that, sir. As I've stated, I can only reissue a key to the registered occupant of the room," she explained. "We take the privacy and security of our guests very seriously."

"There must be someone in the hotel who can give us access to the room," Chad persisted. "Can we speak with your supervisor or someone from maintenance?"

"My manager is not in over the weekend, and our custodial staff can't enter rooms for anything other than housekeeping and maintenance calls without consent of the guest."

"Okay, fine," he replied. "When is the maid scheduled?"

"That floor was already cleaned this morning," they were told flatly.

Rebecca was so frustrated that she wanted to pull out her hair.

"Look, we're not going to get anywhere today, Rebecca," Chad said in a soft voice. "He's sewn it up pretty tight."

She nodded, clenching her teeth to hold on to her composure.

"Thank you for your help," he said politely to the girl behind the desk before guiding Rebecca away.

"I can't believe this," Rebecca mumbled. "I don't get it. Why would he do this to me? What does he hope to gain?"

"He's on a power trip, obviously," Chad shot back as he took a soft hold of her arm, and used his other hand to nudge her chin up until she was looking into his eyes. "He wants you to feel like he's in charge, right? Remind you that this is his hotel. But it doesn't matter, Rebecca. We'll get you whatever you need until you can straighten this whole thing out."

"But everything's in that room, Chad, including by wallet, my laptop, and iPad. What am I going to do?"

"You'll stay at my place. No argument," he insisted when she opened her mouth to protest. "I'll walk you over to Water Tower Place so you can do some shopping, get whatever you need while I'm at lunch with my mom. Okay?"

Rebecca watched speechlessly as he took out his wallet, counted out a bunch of twenty-dollar bills, and handed them to her. "Chad," she stammered, very uncomfortable with his offer.

"Look, consider it a loan if you have to."

She let out a deep sigh and took the funds. As much as she hated the situation, until she got back her wallet or arranged for funds to be transferred from Jamaica, Rebecca really had no other choice. When things were resolved, Chad would get back every penny he had dished out, including what he spent on the clothes she was wearing.

They left the Isis to walk south on Michigan Avenue toward Water Tower Place, a large shopping complex in the heart of the city's historic Magnificent Mile district. The street was lined with every exclusive designer store imaginable, and peppered with elegant restaurants and cafés. Chad explained that he was meeting his mother for lunch only a few streets away, so he would leave her at the shopping mall with about an hour and a half to wander around. They agreed to meet at one of the main entrances at two-thirty. Before leaving her, he gave her shoulder a reassuring squeeze, insisting that everything was going to be okay, and the situation would be resolved in a few days. Rebecca nodded with a tight smile. As much as she wanted to believe it, things had only gone from bad to worse so far, and it seemed unlikely they were going to turn around anytime soon.

Once alone, Rebecca started a slow exploration of the mall. It was a beautifully modern glass and chrome building. There were seven floors of shopping wrapped around an elevator shaft made of glass prisms that ran up the center of the space. She spent half of her allotted time admiring the design and architecture, taking several dozen pictures with her iPhone. It was past one-thirty before Rebecca remembered that her main objective was to get some clothes.

It did not take her long to get a pair of snug skinny jeans and a couple of tops. At the lingerie store, she bought a bra with a few matching panties, and a comfortable sleep set in a soft cotton. With almost half of Chad's money still in her pocket, Rebecca also purchased a less practical pair of wedge sandals in dark cream leather.

With about twenty minutes to spare, she stopped at a coffee shop for a brew and a sandwich. Her phone rang while she sat eating and watching other shoppers pass by. It was an unlisted number.

"Hello?"

"Hi, Rebecca."

It took her a couple of seconds before she recognized the voice, mostly because it was so unexpected.

"I saw you at the hotel earlier. You seemed upset. I hope you weren't having any difficulties."

She let out a sharp gasp, and quickly looked around the eatery and surrounding area, suddenly feeling vulnerable and exposed.

"What do you want, John?" she finally demanded.

"I'm only concerned, Rebecca."

He almost sounded sincere! It made her nauseous.

"Well, you have nothing to be concerned about. Everything is just fine." Her voice dripped with sarcasm.

"Really? It didn't look that way to me," he stated. "If you need my help, you only have to ask."

"You must be even crazier than I thought, John," she muttered.

"Look, I know I got a little angry last night. But it was only because you hurt me, Rebecca. The sight of you with another man had me seeing red, that's all."

"Are you serious? That's your excuse?" she sputtered, unable to believe what she was hearing.

"I'm just saying that I may have overreacted. Why don't you come back to the hotel, alone this time, and I'm sure we can work it all out."

"Listen to me and listen good," Rebecca spat, her Jamaican accent now thick with anger. "Don't call me or come anywhere near me again. Do you understand?"

"Now you're the one overreacting, don't you think? We had a little disagreement, that's all. No harm done, right?"

"If you call me again, or if I see you anywhere near me, I'm going to call the police and have you charged with harassment."

Rebecca quickly hung up the phone before he could add anything else.

Chapter 16

Though Chad arrived at the restaurant right on time, Denise Crothers was already at their table, sipping a cup of tea. She stood to greet her son with a big hug, then they made small talk while ordering their lunch. Chad wondered how long it would take for her to bring up the elephant in the room. It took about ten minutes.

"Did you have a good time last night?" she asked.

"Yeah, it wasn't too bad," he replied. "I got a golf package for a pretty good price in the auction."

"Good! I figured you'd see something there you liked. We had some excellent sponsors this year. Everyone I've spoken to so far was quite impressed. And your date—Nora is it? Did she enjoy herself?" Denise added once Chad nodded.

"I think so. She was pretty starstruck most of the night."

His mom smiled with satisfaction and said, "She seems very nice, attractive and well spoken."

Chad nodded as he drank his iced sweet tea, waiting for more comments.

"But I didn't really spend much time with her. Only a few minutes at the end of the night," she continued. "Who was that other woman you were with? The one with the accent."

Chad put down his drink. "Her name is Rebecca. She's a photographer working for the hotel," he replied as casually as possible while his mother read his every expression.

"She was quite stunning," Denise stated. "Have you known her for long?"

"Not really. We met when I was in South Carolina last fall."

"Well, there's definitely more to that story, but I won't pry. It was hard to miss the chemistry between the two of you."

"There's no story, Mom," Chad stated. "I was just surprised to see her, that's all. I didn't know she was in Chicago."

"Oh."

Their waitress brought their meals at that point, a grilled T-bone steak with vegetables for him and Cobb salad for his mom.

"So where is she from? Rebecca, right?"

Chad knew the questions would continue until her curiosity was completely satisfied. Any hesitancy or evasiveness on his part would only make the interrogation worse.

"She's Jamaican," he replied.

Denise smiled wide with a sparkle in her eyes. "I

thought so. I could tell by her beautiful skin and straight white teeth."

Chad rolled his eyes.

"I may not have been back home in over twenty-five years, but I know a girl from home when I see one. I can also tell that she's well educated. Probably at a private boarding school."

"Mom, I think she said two sentences to you."

"It doesn't matter. It was obvious in her posture and politeness."

He just shook his head.

Denise Crothers had left Jamaica as a young girl, and though she'd returned only a few times and no longer had her accent, she still held everything about the island close to her heart.

"Does she live in Chicago?"

Chad knew Rebecca was still the focus of her attention. "No, she doesn't live anywhere apparently," he explained. "She's been traveling around the world taking pictures for hotels and tourism companies. So she's only in town to do a project," he replied.

"She must call somewhere home," Denise insisted.

"Apparently not. She's been living in hotels out of a suitcase for several years now."

"That's unusual, isn't it? Especially for a young woman? Sounds a little lonely, if you ask me."

Chad agreed, but only shrugged dismissively in response.

"Will you be seeing her again while she's in town?" Denise continued.

Chad let out a big sigh, not for his mom's

questions—he was used to them—but because he had been asking himself the same thing and didn't have any answers. "Mom, I have no idea what her plans are or how long she'll be in the city. Like I said, she's just a friend."

"All right, all right," she ceded with a laugh. "I'll leave it alone. You can tell me all about Nora instead."

He laughed with her. "Sorry to disappoint you, but there's not much to share there either. We've only been out a few times. You'll have to give me a little more time to get you some real information."

"Oh, so that means you plan to continue seeing her?"

Another question Chad did not have an answer to, so he only raised an eyebrow sardonically. His mom smiled innocently, but let the subject drop.

"I spoke to my decorator, Naomi, this morning. She's available to do your house," Denise told him as they were finishing their meals.

"Okay, but as long as you told her I want a consultation to start. I'm not convinced I need to hire someone or do it all at once. There's no rush."

"She's fine with that," she confirmed. "I'll arrange for her to come by sometime this week to have a look around and discuss what you would want."

Chad nodded in agreement and they talked for a little while longer about what furniture and other finishes could work in his house. Then, conscious of the time, he called for their check at around ten minutes after two. They left the restaurant together and Chad walked his mother to her car parked in a garage about a block away before waving her off.

He was back at the shopping center at the time arranged and quickly spotted Rebecca standing near the entrance where they had parted. She was staring off into space, completely wrapped up in her thoughts, and it took several moments for him to get her attention. Though she smiled to say hello, the shadows in her eyes suggested she was worried and preoccupied.

"So, how was the shopping? Did you get everything you need?" he asked when standing in front of her.

"I think so," she replied, looking down at the bags by her feet. "Hopefully, this situation will last only a couple of days anyway. Can we stop at a drugstore on the way back to your place? I still need a few supplies."

"Sure. We'll go to the grocery store near my house. I'm going to pick up some food," he told her as they headed out of the building. "What did you think of the mall?"

The question managed to shake Rebecca out of her gloom. Her eyes came to life as she talked at length about all the pictures she took of the design and architecture. Chad didn't understand or appreciate everything she tried to explain, but really enjoyed listening to her talk with such passion and enthusiasm. He found himself thinking about all of the beautiful and historic places he could show her in Chicago, including several in Hyde Park, walking distance of his house.

As planned, Chad took them to a large food market on their way home. Rebecca immediately made a beeline for the pharmacy area while he

slowly wandered through the produce and meat
sections, planning a meal for dinner and groceries
for the week. He bagged apples and oranges, potatoes, carrots, and green beans, then perused
through packages of steaks and chicken. Even as he
filled up the grocery cart with his usual staples,
Chad realized he had no clue what Rebecca would
eat and if his choices would work for her. The sober-
ing fact was that they had spent maybe two days
together—that was it. So, even though the strong at-
traction between them may have created an odd
sense of comfortable familiarity, he really did not
know much about her.

Chad continued his shopping through the dairy
and packaged food aisles, then headed to the
checkout, looking for a glimpse of Rebecca along
the way. He finally found her at the front of the
store in the wine section.

"I was thinking that if you're making dinner, the
least I could do would be to contribute a bottle of
wine," she stated as he approached. "Do you like
red or white?"

He rolled his eyes dramatically. "I told you, Rebecca, don't worry about it. It's nothing, all right? I
would be cooking for myself anyway, so I'm hardly
going out of my way here."

She still looked skeptical and uncomfortable. "I
doubt you would be home on a Saturday night,
doing nothing," she countered.

"Honestly, I didn't have any plans for tonight."

Rebecca picked up a bottle of Gewürztraminer.
"Not even with your date from last night—Nora?"

Chad lowered his head for a moment. It was a

fair question. He didn't have any plans with Nora, but he probably would if Rebecca had not turned up on his doorstep last night, cold and desperately scared.

"No plans with Nora," he told her solemnly. "And she's not my girlfriend."

"Well, I'll buy us something to drink anyway. I definitely need it," she told him, tucking the slender bottle under her arm.

It was late in the afternoon when they got back to his house. Rebecca headed upstairs while Chad put his groceries away. He was on the couch watching a Chicago Bulls game when she came back downstairs to join him, and they spent a couple hours in comfortable silence until early in the evening when he was ready to start dinner.

"I hope you're getting hungry," Chad said as he stood up. "I'm going to grill up a couple of steaks."

"Sure. Anything I can do to help?" She got up as well and followed him into the kitchen.

"Can you cook?" he asked with a teasing grin.

"Yes!" Rebecca insisted, clearly offended at the suggestion. "I haven't done much of it recently, but I'm a pretty good cook, actually."

"All right, all right. How about I barbecue and you can make some veggies? Maybe some potatoes?" he suggested as he took the meat out of the fridge. "Take whatever you need."

She nodded.

"I wasn't sure what you would like, so I just picked up a variety of things," Chad admitted.

"No worries, anything is fine. I'm not a picky eater," she told him.

"Okay, good. I'll go light up the grill."

He went out the French doors behind the kitchen, which opened onto a small patio area in a decent-sized backyard. Next to the doors was a brand new gas barbecue. Chad had bought it soon after moving in, anticipating christening it in warmer weather for a house-warming party or some other opportunity to entertain his family and friends. But now seemed like as good a time as any to test it out. It fired up beautifully, and he spent a few minutes setting the right temperature before heading back inside for the meat.

"Okay, we're all set," he told Rebecca. "How do you like your steak?"

She looked up from in front of the sink where she was washing a bowl of produce. There was a large skillet heating up on the stove. "Medium, if you can do it."

"Good, that's how I like it too."

With the meat and seasoning on a tray, Chad went back outside. He stood over the smoking, sizzling grill, tending to the thick slabs of tenderloin while his mind was elsewhere. The conversation with his mother played itself in his mind, including the questions she asked that he didn't have answers to. He was normally a pretty patient guy, content to see things develop in due course in both his personal and professional life. In fact, the bigger the reward, the bigger the time and investment required. So it was very odd for Chad to deal with this sudden and urgent need to understand this situation with Rebecca.

He had enough self-awareness to recognize that

the way they had met and hooked up had been unusual and exciting. What man had not fantasized about a night of hot sex with a beautiful stranger? Chad would be foolish not to see that it was partly to blame for the awkward anxiety he felt in his belly whenever she was around him. Yet, that rational thinking didn't prevent him from hoping she planned to stay in Chicago for a while.

"Okay, the veggies are ready."

Rebecca's announcement suddenly pulled him out of his thoughts. He turned around to find her standing in the open door frame, arms folded across her chest against the cool evening air.

"Great. The steaks are almost done," he told her.

"I'll go ahead and set us up on the counter. Unless you just want to eat in front of the television?" she asked.

"No, the counter's fine. You should be able to find everything easy enough. I'll be there shortly."

She smiled and closed the door. He let out a deep breath and gave the beef cuts a final turn on the fire.

They ate the meal while enjoying the wine that Rebecca had purchased. Chad took the opportunity to ask her more about her travels over the last few years. Like every discussion about photography, she lit up, talking at length about all of the cities visited and projects completed since she left Jamaica. He learned about her favorite café in France, a secret garden she discovered in Naples, and the most beautiful, untouched beach in Bali. He also rediscovered her sharp and quirky sense of humor.

After the dishes were washed and leftovers put

away, Rebecca offered to show Chad her newly developed Web site and online portfolio. They spent the rest of the evening back on the couch going through her pictures on his laptop. It was after eleven o'clock when she started to yawn.

"You must be exhausted," he said softly as he closed the computer and put it on the coffee table. "It's been a crazy day for you, I'm sure."

"I was fine a moment ago, but I suddenly can't keep my eyes open," she replied. "I think I'll head up and take a shower before getting to bed."

Chad nodded as she stood up.

"Listen, Chad . . ."

He cut her off before she could continue her sentence. "Okay, if you thank me one more time, I'm going to be insulted," he stated in a slow, firm voice.

Rebecca blinked a few times with her mouth still open. Then she grinned, proving to him that he had correctly guessed at her intentions.

"All right. But can I tell you that I had fun?"

"Yes, that's okay," he conceded with a chuckle.

"Good night," she told him as she turned and walked toward the staircase.

"Good night, Rebecca."

Feeling wired, Chad turned on the television, hoping to find something interesting on to keep his brain occupied. But after over thirty minutes flipping channels and searching through the program guide, he gave up and turned it off. Though he wasn't really sleepy, there was nothing else to do but go to bed. He rose and began turning off the lights behind him on the way to the stairs.

Suddenly, Chad stepped back as the light near the kitchen came on. There was Rebecca, looking even more surprised than he was.

"Oh, sorry! I didn't realize you were still awake," she said.

"I was just heading up. Are you okay?" he asked.

She was dressed in a tank top and loose cotton shorts, her hair pulled into a fluffy puff at the top of her head and her face fresh and dewy. "Yeah, I was just going to get a glass of water."

The scent from her bath products was soft and sweet. Chad stepped forward until she was close enough to touch. "Do you have everything you need?" he asked softly.

"Yes . . ."

He knew she had more to say, but he didn't care. It was impossible to have her in his house again for another night and not touch her, to continue pretending that he didn't want her. Chad bent down and pressed his lips on hers. He felt her surprise and hesitance, but also the incredible charge of electricity that passed between them. Then her lips softened as she opened to him, kissing him back with sweet, soft brushes.

"Ahh, Rebecca," he moaned, pulling her up into his arms until she had to be on the tips of her toes.

The taste of her was like a fiery drug, burning him up from the inside, but so intoxicating that he only wanted more. Chad was so wrapped up in his arousal that it took him a few minutes to notice how still she had become. He pulled back and loosened his arms so she lowered back onto her feet. Then he rested his forehead on hers, and let out a deep, calming breath.

"I'm sorry," Rebecca whispered, and he felt her warm breath as it brushed lightly against his arm.

She sounded so shaky and vulnerable. Chad felt like an ass. He dropped his arms from around her shoulders and stepped back.

"No, Rebecca. I'm the one who's sorry," he told her with the shadow of a smile. "Get a good night's rest."

Then he headed up the stairs to his room. Sleep took a long time coming.

Chapter 17

On Sunday morning, after that surprising kiss with Chad in the kitchen and a restless night's sleep, Rebecca woke up just before dawn. With nothing on the agenda for the day, and an instinct to avoid Chad and any reference to the night before, she decided to spend the day exploring. Dressed warmly in her new jeans, a T-shirt, and a fleece jacket Chad had given her, she was out the door before seven o'clock with her camera hung across her shoulders, and a note left for Chad to say she would be gone for the day.

According to the browser search she did on her phone, Hyde Park was a treasure trove of historic and cultural attractions right outside Chad's front door. The neighborhood was in an area of just over one and a half square miles, with a high concentration of significant landmarks, including the University of Chicago.

Rebecca spent the next fourteen hours fully immersed in her art, talking to residents and taking pictures of everything from homes to local shops, to gardens and parks. There was something interesting at every turn, and she was almost able to forget her questions about Chad and problems with work for the whole day.

The one thing she could not completely shake was the feeling of being watched, and the need to look over her shoulder. Obviously, that was the intent of John's phone call on Saturday afternoon at the mall, to make her feel scared and vulnerable, maybe force her to back down or leave the city altogether. As Rebecca had told him on the phone, she refused to let someone control her through empty threats. While she was not going to hide out in fear, it was hard not to feel shaken and cautious. By the evening, there was no sign of anyone resembling John lurking in the shadows, and she was able to relax her guard a little.

Once the sun went down, she found a Thai restaurant for dinner, then walked back to the house with a list of places to visit on the next available opportunity. Chad had not given her a key, but he had sent her a text message in the afternoon that he was going out also, and provided the security code for his garage door opener in case he wasn't back when she returned. After ringing the doorbell with no response, Rebecca let herself in to the empty house as instructed. She spent the rest of the evening in her room and fell asleep before any sound of Chad's return.

Monday morning, after a few phone calls to Devon and her contacts at Royal Dunegan, she went downstairs to find Chad finishing a bowl of cereal in the kitchen. She was still in her night clothes while he looked polished and professional in a dark gray wool suit and a crisp white shirt. The sight of him sucked the breath out of her.

"Good morning," he stated with a nod of his head.

"Hi," she said, walking slowly into the kitchen area.

"I've made a pot of coffee if you want some."

"Thanks."

"How was your day yesterday?" Chad asked.

Rebecca brushed by him to pour a cup of coffee. He smelled like clean soap and light aftershave.

"It was good. Productive," she told him, trying to keep her tone light and casual. "I spent the whole time in the neighborhood, and still have a long list of places I want to visit. I never even made it onto the university campus."

"Did you go to the lake shore?"

"Mmm-hmm. I did. You're lucky to be so close to the trails." She sipped at her coffee.

"Yeah. I'll definitely be taking advantage of it in the warmer weather," he told her.

There were a few moments of silence as Chad finished his breakfast and washed up his bowl and spoon. She watched his actions furtively over the rim of her cup.

"Any news about that manager or your stuff?" he eventually asked.

"Not really. I spoke with my uncle this morning, but we'll have to wait until the VP, Paul Smithers, is back in the office. But I'm hoping to know more later today. I also called my client in marketing about the pictures from Friday's event and bought some time. They're fine as long as they have them by tomorrow."

"Feel free to use my laptop to work if needed."

Rebecca closed her eyes briefly. Her fragile pride hated to be so dependent on someone else's generosity. "I'm praying I'll have my stuff back by then, but if not, I may have to take you up on that offer," she finally admitted.

Chad nodded, then checked his watch. "I have to get going. Call me on my cell phone if you need anything, but I'll touch base with you later in the afternoon."

"Okay," Rebecca replied. "Bye."

He was gone a few minutes later.

She indulged in some time to brood over toast and a second cup of coffee before heading into the shower. Since it was pointless not to take advantage of Chad's offer, Rebecca used his laptop to work on the photos for the charity event, and sent off the finished file to her client. Next, she spoke with her uncle to get an update on the situation at the Isis. It wasn't good news.

By the time Devon was able to arrange corporate direction to the front desk staff to check suite 1015 for her stuff, the report back from the assistant manager was that the room really had been given to another guest and her stuff was nowhere to be found. Clearly, John had one of his staff members take care of it over the weekend, but there was no way to prove it.

She and Devon considered getting the police

involved, but agreed that it would only complicate things further at this point. He assured her that the company would compensate her for the inconvenience and anything that was not safely returned. Thank God she had held on to her camera and cell phone through the mad dash out of the hotel the night John attacked her. Other than her wallet and identification, the only items of real value that were missing were her iPad and laptop, but since all of her photo files were safely stored on an Internet-based data warehouse, they too were replaceable if needed.

Next, Rebecca spent some time with her bank to make the arrangements necessary to have funds transferred to a local branch. Once satisfied that she would have money by the next day, she headed out for the afternoon to continue the exploration of Hyde Park, starting with the university.

Chad did reach out to her a few times through the day by text message. He seemed genuinely concerned and supportive, so Rebecca started to think she had overreacted to the kiss on Saturday night. Perhaps while she was confused and conflicted about what it meant and what she wanted between them, he was unaffected. And if that was the case, it was a good thing that she had stopped the kiss when she did, because the one clear fact in all the chaos was that she had real feelings for Chad Irvine. Rekindling a casual sexual relationship with him could only end in heartache and humiliation.

By the end of the day Monday, she decided to take his lead and maintain a casual friendship. It was the least she could do to thank him for his very generous help over the last few days. To that end, Rebecca stopped at a local market on the way back to his house and picked up food to make them dinner. Chad was not home when she arrived, so she let herself in and spent the next hour and a half cooking curry chicken with rice. When he still did not arrive by seven-thirty, she ate on her own while watching television in his living room.

She eventually fell asleep on the couch, waking when she sensed she was being carried in Chad's arms, her face buried in the curve of his neck.

"What happened?" she asked, disoriented by the weightless feeling of being in his arms.

"You fell asleep," he whispered.

"What time is it?"

"Around nine-thirty. You must be exhausted," Chad added.

"Hmmm. I'm okay. I'm awake now. You can put me down," Rebecca protested, now awash with embarrassment.

"Relax, you're as light as a pillow."

"Really, I'm okay. Please put me down."

Chad stopped at the foot of the stairs, and slowly released her legs so she could stand on her own feet. Rebecca slid down his chest, but somehow her arms remained around his neck. It seemed so hard to let go and step away from his warmth. The moment lingered far longer than was natural.

"Rebecca," Chad whispered.

She quickly stepped back, blinking to clear her head. He was still in his work clothes, minus the suit jacket, so she assumed he had just gotten home.

"Sorry, I'm . . . I'm just a little fuzzy."

"Come up to bed," he encouraged, while adding a supportive arm across her back to help her up the stairs.

"Wait," she interrupted, looking up at his face in the dim light. "I want to explain. About the kiss."

She felt him go very still.

"There's no need to explain anything, Rebecca."

"Yes, there is," she whispered, unable to stop her wayward, sleep-addled mouth. "I don't want you to think I didn't want it or enjoy it. We had such a great time in Myrtle Beach and while I would love the idea of continuing what we started, things are different now. I've already made such a mess of things here. . . ."

"Hey, shhh," he urged, cupping her cheek with a gentle hand. "You don't need to explain anything, Rebecca. I'm here for you, that's all. No expectations."

She closed her eyes with a deep sigh. *Maybe this thing between us should be embraced rather than avoided?* she asked herself. The feel of his hand was so warm and comfortable that Rebecca felt drawn toward him like a beacon. His scent, his touch, his voice all felt so right, so familiar, that she just wanted to melt into the moment.

True, it would not be smart to give him her heart, expect a future together. But right now, he was the only one who could help her feel safe and secure. That was enough.

Rebecca placed both her hands on the firm slab of his chest covered with fine cotton. The muscles jumped under her touch. She looked up into Chad's eyes and felt the heat from their dark depths. Then he lowered his mouth to hers.

They spent a few, long moments enjoying the kiss, allowing the heat and passion to build slowly until they both craved more. Feeling greedy and empowered, Rebecca fumbled for the buttons of his shirt, popping each open as swiftly as possible until the naked flesh underneath was revealed. She ran her hand over the warm skin, reacquainting herself with the thick, hard ripples and folds. Chad reached down and pulled her T-shirt up, ending their kiss only to pull it over her head, leaving her with only a bra on top. Then they both made quick work of removing all outer clothing until they both stood in their underwear under the shadows of the hall light. The only sounds around them were of heavy breathing, soft moans, the rustle of discarded clothing, and the fumbling of limbs as they tried to make their way blindly up the stairs.

They made it halfway up before abandoning the effort. Chad sat on one of the steps and pulled her down into his lap to straddle him. It was quickly becoming her favorite position, with the feel of his strong thighs supporting her, and the power of his arousal nestled between her legs. Rebecca quickly undid her bra, tossing it somewhere below. She then leaned forward to wrap her arms around his neck, fusing their torsos together. Chad gripped the curves of her bottom and squeezed gently.

"Why can't I ever make it to the bedroom with you?" he mumbled between deep hot kisses.

Rebecca giggled as his hands moved up to roam over her back. "We'll have to get there eventually, unless you have protection on you," she teased in a whisper before gently biting his earlobe. "You do have something, don't you?"

She took that moment to work her hands down between their bodies and ran them over the thick extension of his penis.

"Mmmm! Yeah, yeah, I think so."

Rebecca stroked him again from tip to base, causing Chad to throw his head back with a deep moan. She ran her mouth along the exposed length of his neck and continued a wet trail down his chest. Then, slipping off his lap, she went on her knees on the lower step and continued the journey over his stomach with her lips.

Chad straightened his neck to look down at her, his eyes hot with the knowledge of her intention. "Rebecca!" he growled.

She gave him a slow, seductive smile before freeing his arousal from his underwear and brushing her lips over the sensitive head. It was like liquid steel, hot and silky to her touch. She opened her mouth and sucked it in, using her tongue to tease and stroke the tip. Then she swallowed him deeper, encasing his generous length to her full abilities. Chad let out a deep guttural moan and gently ran his hands through her hair. Over and over, Rebecca stroked down on him with her mouth, teased him with her tongue until his body was vibrating with tension.

"Jesus, Rebecca!"

Suddenly, he gently reached down and pulled her back up his body until he could place a deep kiss on her lips. Chad then stood up while lifting her in his arms, and climbed the rest of the stairs two at a time. They were in his bedroom before she had a chance to do anything but hold on to his shoulders. Under the moonlight streaming in from the window, he placed her gently on the edge of his bed. It took him seconds to step out of his underwear and slip on a condom found in his nightstand, and he was next to her before she had a chance to miss his warmth.

Rebecca lay back on the bed with her legs hanging over the edge and watched with wide-eyed anticipation as he slowly worked her underwear from her hips and down her legs before dropping them on the floor. Their eyes met and there was no need for words. He slipped between her thighs and stroked deep into her ready sheath, filling her completely. They both froze for a moment, thoroughly savoring the reunion.

She reached out a hand and gripped his fingers between hers. Chad slipped a hand under her hip and pulled her closer to him, thrusting even deeper into the wetness. It was so good that she groaned deep in her throat in abandon. He pulled back to stroke hard again, and again, long and deep until they were both moaning and panting uncontrollably. Their passion was so hot and urgent that Rebecca was unprepared for the intensity of the orgasm that crashed down on her body and stole the air from her lungs. It seemed to go on forever, wracking through her in hard, shuddering waves until she finally stilled, completely spent of energy and slick with perspiration.

When she eventually opened her eyes Chad was

looking down at her with eyes feverish with want, and bright with accomplishment. He was still hard and pulsing inside her, and with a few deep thrusts, soon dissolved into his own powerful climax.

Tuesday morning, Chad was gone to work before she woke up. She spent a few minutes stretching under the sheets, trying to control the tingly feeling of excitement that was tickling her stomach. She was back in Chad's bed and it was every bit as intense and fulfilling as she imagined it would be.

After she finally got up and showered, Rebecca spent the morning dealing with the situation John McConaughey had created in her life. According to Devon, the VP, Paul Smithers, was now aware of her allegation against John, including the disappearance of her personal belongings. But until they were able to hear his side of the story, there was not much they could do. That meeting was now arranged for Thursday morning.

Until then, Rebecca's assignment was on hold since she was not willing to work on the property, even with repeated assurances that they could have a security guard with her at all times. They had also offered her another room in the hotel or one of their other properties in the downtown core, but John had proven himself to be cunning as well as unhinged, and she wasn't going to feel safe anywhere near his sphere of influence until he was made accountable for his actions in some way.

Tuesday afternoon, she walked out of the bank with a replacement bank card and enough cash to

cover living expenses for a couple of weeks. She also
needed to make some decisions about what to do
next. Despite Chad's generosity so far, the smart
thing to do was to find a more suitable place to stay
while in the city and until she could go back to work.
But after sleeping in Chad's arms through the night,
it was really easy to leave things as they were.

Chapter 18

"Chad? Are you still there?"

Chad looked at the phone in his office and blinked a few times. "Yes, sorry about that. I was talking on mute," he replied with a little white lie.

"No worries," stated his boss, Ivan Black. "What do you think about the revised forecast? Is it realistic based on the current sales numbers?"

Chad sat forward in his chair and tried to get his head in the game. He was on a conference call with his boss, and several other department heads. It was definitely not the right time to be daydreaming.

"I think the numbers are conservative. We've revised the forecast several times to minimize the risk, so I think it's as accurate a picture as we're going to get at this time," he told the other meeting participants.

"Okay, then let's submit it up to the executive office," Ivan replied. "Chad, let's meet tomorrow and we'll work on our presentation for the quarterly review on Friday. Two days should be enough time."

Chad nodded though the others couldn't see

him. Then he pressed the mute button as the conversation went on to another topic. As much as he would like to daydream for the rest of the hour, he had some work to get done before he left the office. His mom was supposed to meet him at the house with the designer. Though they had not yet confirmed what time they would meet, Chad wanted to be home as early as possible to straighten up a bit. And decide how to explain Rebecca's presence.

Rebecca. The reason for his daydreaming all day.

That morning, he woke up with her warm naked body spooned in front of his. After months of sleeping alone, it had been a foreign feeling, and unexpectedly nice. He had gently swept a hand along her waist until it rested under the softness of her breast. Her lips curved into a teasing smile and her hips twitched against the heat of his. Chad's regular morning erection needed little encouragement, and he was aching for her within seconds. There were no words necessary. He slid deep into her hot, moist cocoon from behind with ease, and they made love with lazy abandon.

Rebecca had fallen back asleep right after, and he gently tucked the sheets around her again before heading to the shower. It was hard to walk away, but he did so with a satisfied grin on his face.

Now, as the conference call finally ended and he started to pack up for the day, Chad's thoughts were filled with anticipation for the evening. If his mother was still stopping by, it wouldn't take too long. Then perhaps he and Rebecca could walk to one of the many small restaurants in Hyde Park for dinner, and she could tell him about her exploration of the city so far, as well as any updates from the hotel and her project.

But before all that, he had to decide on how to explain their living arrangements to his mom, particularly since he had insisted they were just friends only four day earlier.

"Hey, are you headed out?"

Chad turned to his office door and found Sandra leaning against the frame. She had a cubicle in the same area of the floor.

"Yeah," he replied as he logged off his computer. "What's up?"

"So early? You're usually the last to leave, making the rest of us look bad," she teased.

It was true. Chad rarely left the office before six o'clock, and it was only a few minutes after four. He shrugged dismissively. "My mom's trying to convince me that I need a decorator to help furnish the house. I'm supposed to meet them there this evening."

"Oh, that sounds like a great idea. Then maybe we'll get an invite over to see the finished project."

"Maybe," he chuckled. "But you and Eddie have been in your new house for months now, right? I think you should be planning your own open house."

Sandra laughed. "Touché. It *has* been almost a year and a half. All right, I'll plan something soon. Maybe in a few weeks, at the beginning of June?"

"Works for me," Chad replied.

"Okay, I'll send a note to William and a few others and confirm the details."

He nodded.

"Great!" Sandra continued. "I'm glad you suggested it. It's going to be fun!"

They both laughed before saying good night. Chad left the office soon after and was home before five o'clock. On the way there, he decided to tell his mom that Rebecca was staying in the spare room only for a few days. There was no need to go into more detail and create confusion, especially since things between him and Rebecca were undefined.

His cell phone rang as he turned onto his street. Chad answered it using his headset, without checking the caller.

"Hi, Chad," said the soft, bubbly voice.

"Hi, Nora. How's it going?"

"I'm good. How are you doing?"

"I'm okay. Just on the road on the way home."

"Okay," she said. "I won't keep you then. Give me a call later this evening. I had so much fun last weekend and I wondered if you were free on Friday. You mentioned on Sunday that you hadn't been to a movie in a while, and there are a few new releases this weekend."

Chad closed his eyes briefly. He had not thought about Nora since their date on Sunday. On Saturday night, when Rebecca had pulled away from his advances, Chad had made a decision to respect her wishes and do his best to be platonic friends. He then woke up on Sunday to find her gone from the house with only a note to say she would be out for the day. Feeling disappointed and frustrated, Chad had made every effort to get her out of his head and return to his life before she showed up in the city.

He went to the gym, did some errands, then

called Nora and asked her out to dinner. The date
went fine, just like the ones before. Nora was nice,
talkative, and laughed at all his jokes, suggesting
she enjoyed his company. They'd gone to a seafood
restaurant in Edgewood and went for a long walk
after. It was during their stroll that Chad mentioned
it had been months since he had gone to the the-
aters and admitted he was an action junky, with a
preference for movies with high speed chases, violence, and shooting. She didn't seem impressed,
but suggested they go to a show for their next date.
He may have agreed—Chad wasn't sure—but by
the time he dropped her off at her house and
kissed her on the lips, it didn't really matter.

He had walked away from Nora's door with the
certainty that they did not have a future together.
The kiss was fine, similar to others they had shared
since they met. It was stirring enough to encourage
more intimacy, but lacked any of the explosive
sparks he felt just thinking about Rebecca's lips. It
was crystal clear to him that no other woman was
going to do anything for him right now, even if he
and Rebecca were never intimate again.

Chad had intended to call Nora and let her know
that things wouldn't work out, but now with her on
the phone, sounding cheerful about weekend plans
together, he felt like an ass. The last thing he
wanted to do was hurt or mislead her.

"Let me give you a call later," he suggested as he
got to his block.

"Sure," Nora agreed. "I'm going to the gym in a
bit. Will you be there?"

Chad was about to answer, but became distracted

by a car parked along the curb about three driveways away from his house. There was nothing remarkable about the dark blue Ford sedan, except he seemed to remember seeing it there yesterday with the driver sitting in it with a baseball cap and dark sunglasses, as he was now.

"Chad?" Nora prompted when he did not respond to her after a few seconds.

"No, I can't make it today," he finally told her. "But I'll call you tonight."

They quickly said good-bye and hung up. Chad slowed down and glanced into his rearview mirror to note the blue car again, trying to decide if his memory was accurate or if it was just his imagination. That debate ended abruptly when he got home to find his mother's car parked out front. He pulled into the driveway beside it, but she was nowhere in sight.

"What the hell!" he muttered.

Chad walked through the house, and there was his mother and a much younger woman sitting at the breakfast bar with Rebecca, and the kettle whistling on the stove. All three looked at him with various degrees of surprise on their faces. His eyes locked with Rebecca's first as he tried to silently express an apology. He should have known his mother well enough to realize she might just let herself inside, and could have given Rebecca some warning.

"Chad, you're home early," Denise stated as she stepped down off her chair. "Your friend Rebecca just offered to make us some tea."

He finally looked down at his mother, trying to

contain his annoyance. To be fair, she had always held a key to his place and was usually welcome to enter whenever she needed.

"Hi, Mom," he mumbled as he bent down and kissed her on the cheek. "I thought you were going to call me to confirm what time we would meet."

"I know, but Naomi was available early, and knowing how busy you are, I thought we could get started before you got home," his mom explained innocently. "As I just told your friend Rebecca I didn't mean to intrude."

"Please, Ms. Crothers, it's no intrusion at all," Rebecca insisted.

Chad could tell from Rebecca's voice that she was embarrassed, and unsure of how to explain her presence to his mother. He wanted to kick himself for not planning better.

"Mom, it's fine. Rebecca needed a place to crash for a couple of days, that's all. There was a problem with her hotel room so I suggested she stay here until it's sorted out," he interjected.

His mom nodded, looking between the two of them speculatively.

"Well, you certainly have the room," said the third woman, who Chad assumed was the decorator. "Hi, Chad, I'm Naomi Cuthbert. Your mother has told me so much about you and this wonderful renovation."

She stood and stepped over to Chad with her hand extended and a bright smile on her very pretty face. Naomi was a tall, slim woman no more than thirty years old, with skin the color of warm honey and long light brown hair that fell around her shoulders in soft waves. She was dressed in an expensive light blue skirt suit that draped over her lean body perfectly. Chad was momentarily frozen by her stunning appearance and bright personality.

There was a lengthy silence until the moment was broken by the sound of a glass landing on the granite counter.

"Would either of you like anything in your tea?" Rebecca asked with an innocent smile. "Chad has sugar and honey if you'd like."

"Thank you, dear," his mom replied.

"No problem at all. I'll leave you to it then. Excuse me," Rebecca said softly before quickly walking out of the room and up the stairs.

Chad looked after her with his brows lowered. Something in the stillness of her face made him concerned, and he was almost certain her Jamaican accent was more pronounced than usual.

"So, where should we get started, Chad?" Naomi inquired. "Do you want to finish down here and also upstairs?"

He blinked to refocus on his mom and her decorator friend. Both ladies were sipping at their steaming brews and looking at him patiently.

"Downstairs is fine."

"All right. Well, let's start at the front hallway and work our way through," Naomi suggested. "Open concept designs like this are wonderful, but they can sometimes feel cold and empty. I'll give you some options on how to create a cozy feel with the right furniture and placement."

"Oh, that sounds perfect, Naomi. Right, Chad?" his mom added.

He smiled in agreement and followed the women. Though the next forty-five minutes were mind-numbingly annoying, Chad tried to listen politely and provide some feedback whenever asked. But he wasn't really listening. His thoughts were on Rebecca, wondering what she was doing and thinking. He was anticipating their evening together once the distractions were gone.

"So, what do you think, Chad? Should we move forward? I can have some designs drawn up for you by this weekend," Naomi offered. She looked up into his eyes, blinking at him with anticipation, her pretty pink lips spread wide to show her brilliant white teeth.

"No, I don't think so," he stated.

Her smile faded, and she looked at his mom with uncertainty.

"Chad, what Naomi is suggesting would be just beautiful," Denise added with her best coercive tone.

He looked back firmly. "I'm sure it would be great," he told them both with a pleasant smile. "But I think I'll take my time and finish it off slowly myself."

"But, Chad!" his mom objected.

"Thank you for your time, Naomi. It was nice to meet you," he said to the younger woman.

"Oh, ahh . . . It was nice to meet you too. Please, take my card. Give me a call if you change your mind. Or for any reason."

Her smile was a little less bright as she took a card out of her notebook and handed it to him. He nodded and walked them both to the front door.

"Chad . . ."

"Mom, I'll give you a call tomorrow, okay?"

She pinched her lips tight and gave him a look of disapproval, but followed her friend out the door.

Chad quickly made his way up the stairs, tossing the business card on the kitchen counter on the way. The door to the spare bedroom was closed, so he softly knocked. "Rebecca?"

She opened it within a few seconds.

"Okay, they're gone. I'm really sorry about that. I should have called you to tell you my mom wanted to stop by. But we hadn't confirmed, and I assumed she would wait until I got home . . ." he tried to explain as she walked through the room and into the bathroom.

Chad's gaze landed on the large bag on the bed with a small pile of clothes next to it. "What's going on? Rebecca, what are you doing?" he asked again when she came back a moment later.

"I can't thank you enough for your help, Chad. But it's not fair of me to intrude in your life like this," she told him, her eyes not quite lifting to meet his.

"Rebecca, I told you, it's nothing."

"I know, but your mother must be—"

"Don't worry about my mother."

"I finally got funds from my bank today, so I'll just go to a hotel until—"

"Rebecca, stop!" he insisted, putting a gentle hand on her arm. "You don't have any identification. What sort of place are you going to be able to check in to?"

She finally stopped moving around, but still

wouldn't look up at him. Somehow, seeing her packing her things made him feel like he would never see her again. He wasn't ready to deal with that.

"I'm sorry about my mom."

"Don't be sorry, Chad. It's your home," she quickly insisted.

"I mean, I didn't want to make you uncomfortable. So stay as long as you need to. Why not wait until you get all your stuff back, then make a decision on where to go?" he suggested. "Don't go."

Rebecca finally looked into his face. He could see she was still uncertain of what to do, so he waited patiently as she thought through the options.

Finally, she sighed. "Okay, I'll stay, at least until I get my things from the hotel."

He smiled broadly, flooded with a sense of relief. "Now that we've settled that, what do you want to do for dinner?" he asked.

Chapter 19

Chad made it very easy for Rebecca to let down her guard, set aside her pride, and enjoy the rest of the evening. His visible disappointment in seeing her packing took her by surprise, as did his earnest request that she stay. It did funny things to her stomach and was impossible to refuse.

It was about quarter to seven, so Rebecca suggested they go out to eat rather than make dinner. Chad quickly obliged, taking her to a neighborhood buffet restaurant about four blocks away that was an interesting mix of southern home cooking and authentic Indian cuisine. She loved spicy beef vindaloo and rich butter chicken, but also sampled some of the soul food options. Chad tried everything that could fit on his plate.

"Hmmm, this corn bread is almost as good as my mom's Jamaican recipe," she stated with a satisfied smile. "She used to add just the right mix of sweet and spicy."

"You look like you really miss her cooking," he

replied, laughing. "That should be enough of a reason to go home for a visit."

Her smile didn't fade. Other than Uncle Devon, there had been very few people to talk to about her mom over the last few years; it felt good to share her memories.

"I would, but she died several years ago in a car accident," she told him simply. "But she taught me almost all of her recipes, so not all is lost."

Though she tried to keep her voice light, Chad's face fell with a mix of surprise and dismay. "Rebecca, I'm so sorry. I had no idea," he stammered awkwardly. He put down his fork and covered her hand with his.

"Don't apologize. How could you know?" she suggested. "Anyway, it was a long time ago, over seven years. I've come to terms with it."

"God, that must have been hard for you. Were you close?"

She laughed dryly. "My mom was my whole world. Of course I didn't realize it at the time. I was nineteen and thought I knew everything about the world. Life was all about possibilities and adventure. I just took everything else for granted. Then one day, she didn't come home from work. A truck ran her off the road and she died in the hospital a week later."

"Oh, Rebecca."

There was such compassion and sympathy in his eyes that she felt embraced. But she didn't want to be sad anymore. All she had left were the many memories of a wonderful childhood. That's what she wanted to share.

"It was rough, I won't lie. All I could think about

was all the things I didn't do for her, thank her for. Even laughing made me feel guilty. All my dreams suddenly seemed frivolous and unimportant. I quit school, got a job to pay the bills, and stayed close to our home, thinking it would keep her spirit near to me. Photography was the only thing that helped. My mom used to love to see the pictures I took. She would print them all off, and e-mail copies to all her friends. So that's what I did with all my free time.

"But the guilt just wouldn't go away and I pretty much cut myself off from everyone I knew. How could I enjoy life when she was dead? Then Uncle Devon put his foot down. He was in Montego Bay, about forty-five minutes from where we lived. But when I stopped answering the phone and replying to his e-mails, he showed up at the house. He said my mom would beat me if she could. She gave me a life to live, not to hide away bitter at the world about things that were out of everyone's control. And if I didn't stop sulking, he would beat me for her."

Chad chuckled at that.

"It didn't stick right away, but eventually I realized that I *was* angry," she continued, expressing those thoughts and feelings out loud for the first time. "And that my mom would never have wanted that. She was the happiest, most content person I knew and I was turning into someone she wouldn't like. I also realized that I couldn't stay in our town. It was a lonely place without her. So I took my first travel assignment."

He looked at her hard, his food still untouched. "And you haven't stopped since."

Rebecca smiled, shrugging. "I didn't plan it that way. Things just . . . evolved."

"Were you less lonely, traveling around the world by yourself?" he asked.

"No, not really," she told him, snorting at the irony. "But I felt better. I was living the adventure that I wanted, and that my mom encouraged me to do. If she were still alive, she would be bursting with pride. Me, a simple country Jamaican girl, taking pictures in Paris, Rome, Monte Carlo, Thailand, Beijing, Dubai. . . ."

"She would be very proud of you. You *should* be proud," Chad insisted.

Rebecca smiled at him, then went back to eating the rest of her corn bread. He resumed eating his meal also, as a comfortable silence developed between them.

"You mentioned that Devon is a family friend, not really your uncle. Do you have any other immediate family?" he eventually asked.

Rebecca paused, unsure if she wanted to burden him with another heavy discussion. But it felt good to open up and reveal her life to him.

"I have a sister," she stated.

"Really? Where? In Jamaica?"

"She's in California right now."

He looked at her thoughtfully while chewing his food.

She shrugged, unsure of exactly how to label their relationship. "Nadine is older so . . . you know . . . We were never at the same stage in life."

"Was she around when your mom died?" he asked gently.

Rebecca nodded, understanding what he meant. The question in his eyes reminded her of the conversation with Uncle Devon a couple of months ago when they met in New York. For a long time, her conflicted feelings for Nadine made sense, felt justified. But the more that she thought about it over the last few weeks, the more it made no sense at all. When their mom died, Nadine was not much older than Rebecca was now, yet she had seemed so mature and adult to Rebecca at the time. It seemed completely reasonable that her big sister should step in and help calm the chaos. Instead, Nadine got married and moved to the United States within six months, taking her portion of the life insurance to get settled in America. At the time, it felt like disrespect to their mother, and abandonment of Rebecca. Now, it seemed more like a young woman trying to deal with her own tragedy, and grasping at a chance for love and a new family.

It also revealed how selfish and self-centered Rebecca was at that time—unable or unwilling to understand her sister's perspective—a realization that felt awful.

"She was in Jamaica at the time, but then moved here soon after."

"I take it you're not very close to her."

"We talk regularly. She has a little boy named Aaron and sends me pictures all the time. He just turned six."

"That's nice. Now that you're in the same country again, you'll be able to visit, right?"

Rebecca nodded, agreeing to herself that it was long overdue and something to look forward to.

"Enough about me, Chad. Tell me about your life in Chicago. I already know that you and your mom are very close since she has a key to your house." They grinned at each other. "Do you have a large family?"

He spent the remainder of their dinner and the walk back to his house telling her more about his mother and his stepfamily. It was easy to see that he had the utmost respect for his mother and a healthy fondness for his stepdad and the other kids.

It was close to nine-thirty when they arrived back home. While Chad stayed downstairs to make a phone call, Rebecca changed out of her jeans into comfy clothes. She then joined him on the couch intending to watch television together before bed. Innocent snuggling quickly evolved to stimulating strokes, then frantic petting. There was little time before Chad had her draped over the back of the sofa, her slender hips gripped firmly in his big hands while he stroked deep into her quivering body from behind. When they finally made it to his room, it was to sleep naked in each other's arms.

On Thursday, Rebecca got the news that John McConaughey had been suspended from his position as manager of the Isis pending additional investigation of her allegations. He had not shown up for the meeting with his boss and the VP of operations for the hotel, nor had he provided his explanation or version of what had happened that fateful night with Rebecca. But, the Isis staff had finally found her property in a maintenance storage room. To compensate her for her trouble, they provided her with a suite in their more exclusive boutique property, the Dunegan Inn Chicago, a couple of blocks east of Michigan Avenue, for as long as needed to complete her current project.

Anxious to get back her things, Rebecca took a taxi into the city that afternoon while Chad was at work. It felt so good to have her wallet, passport, and identification in her hands, as well as her iPad and laptop. Back in Hyde Park, she spent several hours on the phone with Richard Kent to redefine the scope of the assignment and time lines required, then with Uncle Devon updating each other. He assured her that her reputation and value as a consultant with the company were untarnished by the recent situation with John, and there was no indication that she would not get additional projects after Chicago.

But Rebecca could not help feeling vulnerable. There was no doubt that she had been very fortunate to have consistent work with one major client for the last three-plus years, but it couldn't last forever. She was in an incredibly competitive field with thousands of eager photographers who would do the work for a lot less than she charged. This fiasco with John might make it easier for Richard and other decision makers at Dunegan to go with another person, despite her success to date and her relationship with Devon.

It was time to rethink the direction of her career, and take more advantage of the work she had done on her portfolio in recent months. The idea of a staff position was still very attractive to her, like the one she had interviewed for in New York. Rebecca made a mental note to investigate the options for similar opportunities in Chicago.

The fact that a change like that could mean something long term with Chad was something she purposely did not contemplate. The possibility was too exciting and scary to consider right now. Was it even something he wanted? They had both committed to no expectations or obligations, so even if her situation changed, it did not mean their relationship would naturally evolve as well. Chad Irvine was obviously a very eligible bachelor with lots of women to choose from, including his date from the weekend, and the stunning decorator from the day before that looked more like a runway model. Rebecca honestly didn't know the answer, and she was not ready to find out.

On Friday, she went back to the Isis for the first time to complete the photographs required for that property. Chad met her there after work for dinner and a movie, an action film recently released that they both wanted to see. On Saturday, Chad took her to a couple of other notable urban neighborhoods, such as Lincoln Park, Bucktown, and Englewood, where she was able to take a few hundred pictures. They stopped at a Jamaican restaurant on the way home for takeout.

The only blemish to the day was an ominous message that she received on her iPhone from an unlisted number:

I'm not finished with you yet.

It took Rebecca a few moments to wrap her brain around the context. Since it was sent through the phone's iMessage system, she knew right away it was from another iPhone user. That narrowed the list a bit, but still left her guessing. Against her better judgment, she sent a reply:

Who is this?

The response was fast:

You've forgotten me already, Rebecca? You won't ever again, I promise. Enjoy the sightseeing while you can.

There was no doubt in her mind that it was John McConaughey, obviously quite pissed off with his current situation and blaming her for his suspension. She wanted to believe his thinly veiled threat was about fighting his case with Royal Dunegan to get his job back, but her instincts said it was more personal. Clearly, he was watching her, and this note and the phone call were meant to scare her. Rebecca refused to give him the satisfaction of reacting to his attempts to intimidate her. She told herself that he was a pathetic coward, without the courage to take it any further, and if she ignored him, eventually he would go away.

Hopefully, she was right.

Chapter 20

"Chinese or burgers?"

The question to Rebecca came from Julie Harper, the manager of the Dunegan Inn in downtown Chicago. She was a petite blonde with a slender frame and alabaster complexion. The two women had spent lots of time together over the last four weeks after Rebecca had relocated to that property. Lunch at the various take-out restaurants nearby was now their regular routine.

"Salad?" Rebecca suggested instead. It was one-thirty on Friday afternoon. She and Chad were going to a dinner party later, so she didn't want to ruin her appetite.

"I'm game. We'll go to the deli at the corner. They have a good selection," Julie replied.

They left the hotel offices a few minutes later for the short walk to the eatery.

"We had a managers meeting this morning," Julie stated once they were seated and waiting for lunch to be prepared. "It's now official. John was terminated, effective today."

Rebecca let out a deep breath, but kept her composure. "Really?" she replied.

"Yup. My boss didn't say why exactly, but it seems from what I've heard, he's kind of disappeared since your complaint. No one from the Isis has spoken to him since, and he hasn't responded to several phone calls from the head office," Julie continued. "Have *you* heard from him at all?"

The question caught Rebecca completely by surprise and she blinked a few times. "Me? Why would I have heard from John?"

Julie shrugged. "I don't know. The whole thing is just so weird. I'll be honest with you. When I heard that he had been accused of threatening a photographer, I found it really hard to believe. I mean, I didn't know him well, but John always seemed so . . . calm and in control, you know?" Julie clarified. "Of course, now that I know you, I realize there is no way you would have exaggerated something like that. But I still assumed he would defend himself, explain his side of the story, that you had misunderstood his intentions. But for him to just completely disappear . . . It's so odd!"

Rebecca opened her mouth to reveal the truth— that John hadn't disappeared. Instead, he was lurking around in the shadows, sending her cryptic text messages meant to keep her checking over her shoulder. Five of them to be exact, not including the phone call after his assault in the hotel.

"Well, it's better for you that he's gone, right?

At least you can just put it behind you as a bad experience," Julie continued, her eyes shining with concern.

"I guess," Rebecca replied, staying quiet about the rest.

As she originally decided, ignoring him was the best approach. Once John realized that Rebecca wasn't going to react or respond to his harassment, he would eventually give up. Then he truly would be out of her life forever. Since it was already almost a week since his last message, maybe being fired was the reality check he needed. In which case, telling anyone about the harassment would only cause unnecessary concern for the people around her.

"So, what are your plans, now that you've wrapped up your project, Rebecca? Are you staying in town for a while?" Julie asked, changing the subject, her bottle green eyes wide with interest.

From the day they had met, Julie had been openly curious and inquisitive about all aspects of Rebecca's life, from her hair to her accent to her unconventional career. The blonde was born and bred in Illinois and lived the all-American life of a cheerleader, prom queen, and sorority sister. They could not have had less in common with such different life experiences, yet the two had hit it off right away.

"I'm not sure, to be honest. Relax for a few weeks, I think. Then see what comes up next," Rebecca told her as they both started eating.

"Have you heard any more from that publishing company?" Julie asked.

"Yup. They've decided on about thirty shots for

their catalogue. I think most of them will be in travel and tourism books."

"That's so cool."

Julie's enthusiasm was always infectious. Rebecca smiled back.

"What about Chad? What does he say about your plans?"

Rebecca shrugged. It took her a moment to formulate a good response. "Nothing. We haven't really talked about it," she finally replied.

"What? Why not? Your project ends today. You could be in Timbuktu by next week!" Julie shot back. "He does know that, doesn't he?"

It was impossible to eat with those green eyes staring back at her, unblinking. Rebecca eventually put down her fork. "I'm sure I've mentioned it at some point. But I told you, he and I aren't like . . . boyfriend and girlfriend. We're seeing each other while I'm in town, that's all," she explained, not at all for the first time.

"Oh, please!" her friend exclaimed. "Don't pretend it's just casual, Becca. I see the way you talk about him. You guys are together every night from what I can tell. There is no way it's just fun while it lasts. Why do you keep insisting that it's nothing more? I know married couples that spend less time together."

"It's not that simple, Julie. It's not like we met at a local bookstore, you know. Our relationship started out as temporary, in the moment. I don't know if it's supposed to be anything else."

"But it's simple. If you love him and he loves you,

then you stay together," Julie insisted. "You do love him, don't you?"

Rebecca really wished it was as easy as Julie made it out to be. But it wasn't. There was no doubt that the last few weeks with Chad had been wonderful. They had been almost inseparable outside work, spending time around the city taking advantage of all the interesting cultural things to do and see. Or relaxing in her hotel room during the week, and his place on the weekends. They had an easy rapport during the day, filled with conversation, teasing, and laughter, until something triggered the chemistry between them. Then, the hunger that was always smoldering below the surface would roar to life, all consuming until finally sated.

But none of that changed the fact that Chad had a plan for his future, and according to his mother, it did not include a flighty travel photographer with no place to call home. Denise Crothers had not told Rebecca that directly. The polished businesswoman was far too polite to ever say such a thing. Instead, Rebecca had overheard the comment in a conversation between Chad and his mother almost one month earlier.

On the Sunday after Rebecca had left his place to move into the Dunegan Inn, Chad took her to his mom's house for lunch with his family. Rebecca had been nervous about the visit, wondering what he had told everyone about their relationship. But Chad had introduced her as a friend who was in town for work, and though there was some speculation in his mom's eyes, the rest of the family seemed unfazed by the explanation.

It had been a very nice afternoon with Chad and his stepbrother, Ethan, barbecuing steaks and burgers, and everyone else sat in the kitchen sipping lemonade while Denise made a salad and finished a cake for dessert. They were a verbal, boisterous group. Rebecca had enjoyed the interaction between the different personalities, and the stories about Chad that they took great delight in telling her. She'd also been surprised at how comfortable and accepted she felt. That is until her conversion with Denise near the end of the visit.

It was a bright, sunny afternoon, warm enough to sit outside without a jacket. Chad went out on the back patio with Ethan and Ethan's sister, Elaine, while Samuel went into the den to watch a Cubs game. Rebecca excused herself to visit the bathroom, and on her way back to join Chad and the others outside, she found his mom alone in the kitchen.

"I'm about to put the kettle on for tea, Rebecca. Would you like some?" Denise asked.

Rebecca paused, not wanting to be rude. "Yes, please. That would be nice," she replied.

"Have a seat. It will be ready in a moment."

She did as asked, and Denise took the chair across from her.

"So how are you liking Chicago?"

"It's a beautiful city," Rebecca told her simply. "So many things going on all the time."

"So Chad has been showing you around, then?"

"Yes, he's been an excellent tour guide so far," Rebecca assured her with a smile.

"Good. From what he's told me, you've been all

over the world, so we certainly want you to remember our city fondly. How long will you be staying?"

It was an innocent question on the surface, but Rebecca could not help feeling there was an agenda beyond polite curiosity. "I'm not sure yet. At least another month, I think," she replied.

The kettle whistled, so Denise got up to make the tea.

"And where are you off to after?" the older woman asked with her back turned.

"I don't know that yet, either."

There were a couple of minutes of silence as Denise prepared the hot drinks and brought them back to the table along with a sugar bowl.

"That must be so strange, dear. Not knowing where you'll be next and for how long. How do you maintain relationships with your friends and family?" Denise eventually asked.

Rebecca smiled and shrugged without offense. It was a common question, particularly from older people. "I've gotten used to it. It's not as isolated as it seems. I stay in touch regularly, and I'm always reachable by phone or on my computer. And I get to make new friends everywhere I go. People that I would never have the opportunity to meet otherwise."

"Like Chad."

There was an implication there that Rebecca found hard to ignore.

"The rest of us must seem so boring to you, with our mundane jobs day in and day out," Denise continued with a laugh.

"Not at all. Nothing can replace having a home

and family around you," Rebecca countered. "It's just another kind of adventure, right?"

"Yes, that's certainly true.

That speculative look was back in Denise's eyes, but she didn't ask any more questions. Chad came inside shortly after to get a drink and Rebecca took the opportunity to excuse herself and join him and the others outside. She tried hard not to put any unintentional importance on the brief conversation with Denise, but her intuition was telling her that Chad's mom knew that there was more than just friendship between Rebecca and her son, and the older woman didn't really approve.

Thirty minutes later, Rebecca's suspicion was confirmed. She had gone to the front door of the house to get some lip balm out of her purse when she overheard Chad say her name from a hall near the entrance to the house. Not wanting to eavesdrop, she was about to turn back, but then his mom spoke, and her words stopped Rebecca cold in her tracks.

"She seems like a very nice girl, sweetheart, but she'll be gone in a few weeks. I just don't want you wasting your time on someone who can't give you what you really want."

"Mom, I'm aware of her situation."

"Good. You want a wife and a family, Chad. You can't have that with someone who's gallivanting all over the world," Denise stated with a little scorn.

"She's not a gypsy, Mom. She travels for her job. Plenty of women do that."

"Yes, they do, but then they return home. She doesn't have one from what you've told me."

"Mom, I'm not planning to marry her, okay? I know she'll be off to another city soon. So not to worry, I'll have plenty of time to find the perfect Chicago wife. You'll have a grandchild in each arm before you know it."

"Speaking of which, I saw Naomi Cuthbert a few days ago and she asked about you. . . ."

Rebecca didn't stay long enough to hear Chad's response. There was only so much truth she could handle at once. She and Chad left his parents' home not long after. Though there seemed to be a tense silence between them on the drive back to her hotel, Rebecca assumed it was from her own conflicted emotions.

Now, four weeks later, with his words still fresh in her mind, Rebecca continued to feel uncertain of what would come next for her and Chad.

"Well, do you?" Julie repeated, still waiting for Rebecca to admit her feelings. When Rebecca looked at her blankly, as if she hadn't heard the question, Julie asked again, "Do you love him?"

"I don't know how I feel, Julie. I love being with him. It's becoming hard to imagine my life without him."

"It's called love, dummy!" her friend exclaimed with a giggle. "Now all you have to do is decide to stay here, and get a real job like the rest of us."

Rebecca tried to smile back, but it was stilted. If only it were that simple.

The two women finished eating and went back to the hotel. Rebecca only had a few calls to make to wrap up the assignment, so she went up to her room to work. Chad wasn't meeting her until six o'clock, so she also used some of the free time to Skype Nadine.

As Uncle Devon had urged weeks back, Rebecca had finally called her sister a few weeks earlier, for the first time in over a month. They had spoken for a couple of hours, catching up on their lives. Though the dialogue started out a little stilted and unnatural, it quickly became a genuine and more natural conversation as soon as Nadine started to talk about her son, Aaron. Rebecca could clearly tell that her sister was happy and content in California with her new family, and any old, childish feelings of resentment seemed to be fading away. Their calls since had been fairly frequent, on a weekly basis if not more.

It was after four o'clock by that Friday afternoon when Rebecca had completed all of her outstanding tasks, and rang Nadine through Skype. Her sister answered on her own computer after a couple of rings.

"Hi, Becca. You have good timing," Nadine said with a big smile.

Rebecca smiled back at her digital image. They looked a lot alike, except that the older sibling was a couple of inches taller and had her hair permed straight and cut in a stylish bob.

"I figured Aaron would still be in school for another hour or so. How are you doing?" she asked in response.

"I'm good. We're having a bake sale for Aaron's soccer team tonight, so I've spent the whole day in the kitchen."

"What are you making?"

"Coconut drops, if you can believe it!" Nadine replied.

"No way. Are they popular in California?"

Drops were a Jamaican dessert made with fresh coconut meat cut into small chunks and mixed with melted brown sugar, cinnamon, nutmeg, and ginger, then set out to cool in individual-sized portions until they hardened.

"I made them for his birthday party a couple of months ago using Mom's old recipe and everyone loved them. Something a little different from the staple of cupcakes and cookies."

"Good choice," Rebecca added as both laughed. It felt good to talk about some of the great times with their mother.

"So? Any idea when you'll make it out to San Francisco? Adam is looking forward to seeing you again. And Aaron is so excited to finally meet his Auntie Rebecca."

"Ahhh. I'm so excited to meet him too," she replied. "I'm officially all finished up here, I think. But I'm still not sure where I'm heading next, so I don't know how long I'll be free."

"That's okay. You can stay as long as you'd like, or until your next assignment. I told you, we have plenty of room," Nadine added.

Rebecca paused, not sure how to articulate how confusing her situation suddenly felt.

"What's wrong?" Nadine finally asked, reading her sister's face.

"Nothing. It's just . . . I haven't quite figured out whether I want to stay in Chicago or just pack up and move on," Rebecca finally stated.

"Is it Chad? Have you guys finally talked about what happens next?" It seemed to be the big question of the day.

"Not really," Rebecca admitted. "I don't think we have to. As far as he's concerned, I'm here until the next project comes along, then we both move on." Saying the words out loud was so hard. She felt her throat close up with emotion.

"Becca, if you don't want it to end, just tell him," Nadine urged. "What's the worst that can happen?"

"Nadine, I know him. If I stay, we will continue to see each other, but then what? I'm still a photographer, which means I have to go where the work is and where my clients need me to be. That's what I love. It's who I am, and I'm not willing to give that up. That's not what Chad's looking for in a partner or a wife."

"But you don't know that for sure."

"I do know that. He wants a woman who'll be content to stay home and raise his kids. And trust me, he has plenty to choose from. I don't know if that's me, Nadine. And I'm afraid if I stay and we try for something long term, one of us is going to end up disappointed and resentful."

"You should still talk to him, Becca."

Rebecca sighed. "What if I do? What if I tell him that I can't bear the thought of leaving and he asks me to stay? I know deep down in my heart that I would. I would walk away from the only career I've had to stay with him. Then, what if it doesn't work? What will I have then? No, it's better that I just leave things the way they are."

"That's a whole lot of what-ifs," Nadine cautioned,

and Rebecca only shrugged. "Well, maybe a trip to Cali is exactly what you need to make your decision, right?" Nadine urged.

"Maybe," Rebecca replied with an attempt to smile. "I'll think it through over the weekend and let you know."

"Okay. Just remember that we're happy to have you stay with us as long as you'd like."

"Thanks, Nadine. That really means a lot. I have to get going. Chad will be here in a few minutes."

"Okay. But don't stress too much, Becca. It will all work itself out, I promise. Love you."

"Love you too."

After Rebecca ended the connection she sat on the bed for a few more minutes trying to get control of her thoughts and emotions. How did things get so complicated?

Eventually, she headed into the shower to get ready for the evening and to pack a small overnight bag. After dinner with his friends, she and Chad would spend the weekend at his house. Realizing it could be their last weekend together, Rebecca planned to make the most of it.

Chapter 21

It was a beautiful June night with a clear sky and bright moonlight. At nine-thirty, Chad was sitting outside on Sandra's back porch with William, Eddie, and a couple of other men, sipping on a beer while Rebecca stood in the kitchen sipping wine with a small group of women. The boys were talking sports, but Chad wasn't really listening. His thoughts were elsewhere, mostly centered on the petite figure wearing a sexy pair of figure-hugging white jeans and a silky blue shirt. As though sensing his gaze, Rebecca looked outside and smiled at him.

The last few weeks had gone by so quickly, yet Chad could remember every enjoyable moment. He tried to convince himself that their time together only felt perfect because it was temporary and fleeting. But it wasn't true. He knew himself well enough to recognize that the things that he was wanting and feeling were real. Pretending otherwise was only a way of coping with the reality of his situation.

He was completely and uncontrollably in love

with a woman who was leaving the city and his life any day now.

Every day for the last two weeks, Chad woke up with a new resolve to deal with the inevitable. It ranged from a vow to enjoy her while it lasted, to begging her not to leave. He didn't consider himself to be an indecisive or passive man. In fact, he was the opposite of those things in most aspects of his life. Yet, he was now completely frozen by a level of fear and emotion that he had never felt before. This indecisiveness and insecurity were the first clues that Rebecca Isles was the woman he had been waiting for.

She certainly did not come in the package he had envisioned in his well-outlined plan—with her slight figure, globe-trotting career, and Jamaican accent—but his plan now seemed so misguided. Rebecca fired his spirit and lit his imagination about all that their future could hold, and the possibilities were far more exciting than just a successful corporate career and a house in the city with a couple of kids. She was the essence of being alive, from the simplest pleasures, to exotic adventures, to a sexual satisfaction Chad had not thought achievable. She was what he wanted, and then some.

"Hey? What's up with you tonight?" William asked, pulling Chad out of his thoughts. "You're a million miles away with a goofy look on your face."

Chad sat back in the patio chair and let out a deep breath, his hands hanging between his knees in defeat. "I'm out of time," he replied simply.

William knew something about the situation with Rebecca, and understood exactly what Chad was referring to. "Damn, Chad! I didn't figure you to be such a punk, man! I told you; put up or shut up. Stop brooding about it and do something or she'll leave."

There was no point in refuting the statement. Chad realized William was right. It was now or never. "I hear you, bro. One way or the other, I'll know this weekend."

Both men sat silently for a long moment, looking out at Sandra's backyard in the night light.

"And I haven't been brooding," he eventually added, defensively.

"Yeah, you have. Like a punk bitch, with those puppy dog eyes all sad and love stricken . . ."

"Call me a punk again and I'll knock you out."

"Punk—"

William's words were cut short when a thick elbow landed squarely in his midsection, sucking the air out of his lungs. The slight man doubled over, moaning loudly. Chad sat relaxed in his chair feeling much better about things. Adam and the men around them had not heard their conversation, but gasped and laughed as William continued to writhe in pain from what looked like a light tap.

"Children, what's going on out here?" Sandra stated from the patio doors. "What happened to William?"

The other women gathered behind her to see what the men were up to.

"Chad . . ." William sputtered, coughing from the effort to speak.

"Nothing," Chad interjected, innocently patting his friend on the back a little harder than necessary.

"He choked on something that went down the wrong way, that's all. He'll be fine in a moment. Right, Billy?"

Adam and his friends laughed harder while Sandra rolled her eyes.

The party broke up soon after. Chad and Rebecca were among the first to leave.

"It was so good to see you again, Rebecca," Sandra stated at the front door with Adam by her side. "I'm so glad you and Chad reconnected and he brought you along."

"Thanks for having me, Sandra. It was nice to see you again also," Rebecca replied. "And I had a lot of fun tonight."

"Good," the older woman said. "Hopefully, we'll see you again before you leave."

"Thanks again for dinner, guys," Chad interjected.

"Just remember that the next one is at your place," Sandra threw in before they left.

On the drive to Chad's house, Rebecca told him the latest news about John McConaughey. While Chad was relieved about the outcome, he was still frustrated by the idea of that loser walking around free.

"I'm glad he was terminated," he replied in a quiet voice. "But I still think he should have been arrested. It's not too late to report it to the police, you know. I guarantee that you're not the only woman that he's done that kind of thing to. And he'll continue to abuse women for as long as he can get away with it."

"He didn't exactly get away with it, Chad. He's lost his job."

"Yeah, and he'll just get another one," he shot back. "Hopefully, he's smart enough to get the hell out of Chicago. 'Cause I'm telling you, he wouldn't want to come face to face with me in a dark place."

Rebecca giggled, and Chad looked at her with raised eyebrows. "You find that amusing?"

She laughed harder. "My gentle giant has an evil side," she finally replied while taking hold of his free hand. "I find it sexy."

He grinned back, his anger quickly replaced by another type of passion. They were still about ten minutes from home, and he suddenly could not wait to get her inside.

"Enough about John," she said. "What are we doing this weekend? One of Sandra's friends mentioned there's a blues festival happening."

"Yeah. I've never gone, but it's supposed to be really good," he told her. "Do you want to go?"

She shrugged, and they spent the rest of the drive weighing the options. Chad couldn't really care less what they did. All he could think about was the soft feel of her hand in his, and the escalating need that was building in his loins. Rebecca must have sensed his restless energy because she willingly stepped into his arms the moment the front door closed. They kissed with almost feverish intensity, their mouths hot and wide as their tongues entwined with long, sweeping strokes. Then they parted, frozen with their lips less than an inch apart, both gasping for a calming breath in the dark of the front hall.

Chad moved first, reaching up to stroke a thumb over her tender, silky lips. Rebecca swiped his flesh with a flick of her wet tongue and sparks from the touch streaked through his arm like an electric charge.

Christ! She's driving me out of my mind with need.

"Do you know what I couldn't get out of my head in those months after we had first met?" he whispered as she sucked his thick digit slowly into her mouth. "Our first time, in Myrtle Beach. Standing, with you naked, wrapped around me." He moaned at the memory and at the feel of her wickedly sucking on his finger.

"Taking you like that . . . pressed against the wall . . . It was so hot, I think I blacked out a little," he continued in a pained voice. "I must have dreamt about it a hundred times after . . . wishing I could have you again, but half convinced I had imagined the whole thing. No one, *no one* could feel so good, I told myself."

Chad wrapped his arms around her slender back and pulled her body flush against his. With one quick move, he took hold of both mounds of her bottom, lifting her until her legs were wrapped around his waist. They kissed deeply again.

"Jesus, Rebecca. You . . . this . . . It's even better than I dreamt," he groaned.

"Do you want me again, like this? Right now?" she whispered in his ear, sending erotic shivers down his spine.

"Sweetheart, I don't have any preference. Every time, every way is better than the last." He started walking through the house, gently and effortlessly carrying her weight on his hips.

"Hmmm, I like the sound of that," Rebecca teased, moving her lips down the taut tendons of his neck.

"Good. 'Cause I would much rather focus on what you want. What do you want, Rebecca?"

Chad stopped in the living room, unable to go any farther as her hand reached between their bodies toward the base of his stomach. He couldn't walk and breathe at the same time.

"Tell me what you want," he almost begged.

"I want this," she whispered into his ear, and reaching her goal, stroked a hand over the rigid arousal that strained against the confines of his clothes.

"Take it any way you want, sweetheart. It's yours. I'm all yours," he confessed, trying hard to stay in control.

Rebecca used his shoulders to climb down from his hold. Silently, they stripped off their clothes until they were both completely bare. The lights were still off, but filtered moonlight cast a dim glow in the room. Chad's eyes feasted on her nakedness from the delicate curves of her shoulder, over the plump curves of breasts, to the sweet mound between her legs, and down the firm length of her legs. Her creamy brown body was perfect.

Her eyes traced over his body in a similar fashion, stopping at the erection that now stood hard and strong, thick with rushing blood. She licked at her bottom lip, her cheeks flushed from the sight of him. The look in her eyes made Chad feel like a god, powerful and invincible.

"How do you want it, Rebecca?" he asked softly, too excited to be polite.

Rebecca looked up at him, her eyes bright with need, but clearly hesitant to say the words. Then, to his delight, she slowly turned away from him and walked to the sofa to kneel on the ground with her back to him, thighs spread apart and her arms braced on the top of the seat. She looked back at him over her shoulder with her delicious, round bottom presented like a precious, delicate gift. Words weren't necessary and Chad certainly did not need a clearer invitation. He took a moment to grab a condom from a discreet storage bag in one of the side tables. A stash that had become a necessary convenience since they hardly ever made it up to the bed once things got heated.

As he joined her on the ground to kneel behind her sweet body, Chad marveled at the power of the excitement she aroused in him. They had done almost nothing so far, but he was already panting to press his cock deep into her tight, slick sheath and lose his mind while she milked him dry. But as he wrapped his arms around her slender frame to cup the smooth silky curve of her breasts, Rebecca expelled a throaty moan of pure pleasure and anticipation. The thrill of her response went straight to his head, and ensured her pleasure became the most important thing, even if it killed him.

It quite nearly did. His vow to be slow and patient, using his fingers and mouth to stroke her tender crevices, was tested almost immediately. Rebecca was already plump and wet, ready for him from the start. It would have been so easy to grab her hips and drive into her taut body until he came hard and fast. But he didn't. Chad still took his time, experiencing immense satisfaction from every moan and quiver of her body as he licked over her swollen clit. He savored her sweet nectar on his tongue while sinking his fingers into the tight heat of her hot, wet core. And when she finally came with frantic, uninhibited urgency, he paused to watch, certain he had never seen anything so beautiful or breathtaking. When her quivering body began to still, with her torso lying on the top of the couch, spent for the experience, her eyes looked back at him with wonder and satisfaction. Only then did he give up his control, gripping her hips with a firm hold, and penetrate her with one deep stroke from behind.

Maybe he did die for a while, with his soul sucked out of his body by an orgasm so intense, it defied nature. When his consciousness returned and his heart rate slowed, the echo of the words uttered unchecked as he climaxed still hung in the quiet night air:

"Rebecca, Becca, my Becca. I love you, I love you. . . . I love you so much, it hurts. . . ."

As they both stilled in the aftermath, the silence became deafening. How the hell had those words come out of his mouth? They were honest, and he had wanted to say them for some time, but not like this. Now Rebecca was likely to think it was just the sex talking, not the truth torn from his heart at his weakest moment.

Unable to find the right words at that moment, Chad gently picked her up and carried her upstairs to his bed. When they were wrapped in each other's arms under the covers and on the edge of sleep, he whispered the other words he needed her to hear.

"I've fallen in love with you, Rebecca. I know that wasn't the plan. We agreed to no expectations. I get that. But I've fallen in love with you and I can't stand the thought of you leaving. I want you to stay in Chicago, with me."

Rebecca stirred, moving to sit up. "Chad . . ." she started.

"Shhh," he urged, tightening his arms around her, unwilling to let go yet. "It's okay. You don't have to respond. Just think about it, okay?"

She settled back down with her head against his chest. Chad squeezed her again and pressed a light kiss on the top of her head. He closed his eyes and prayed for sleep.

There was no going back now.

Chapter 22

Rebecca barely slept that night. Her mind was racing with the impact of Chad's words. It was exactly what she hoped for, that he would feel the same way she did. Hearing those words said out loud should have been the answer to her dreams, quelling any concerns about the possibility of their future together.

Yet now, on Saturday morning at the crack of dawn, one doubt was replaced by another.

Did he mean it? Was it real or just the sex talking?

Rebecca wasn't naturally a suspicious or jaded person. It was her nature to take people at their word. And Chad had never given her any reason to question his motives before. Neither had John McConaughey, until the night he attacked her and threatened to rape her. By no means did she think Chad was anything like John, for that she was certain. But she now acknowledged that what motivated people was not always clear or simple, and to blindly accept their words alone was naive and childish. It was a hard lesson to learn, but also a bell that was impossible to unring.

By the time Chad woke up later that morning, Rebecca had made a decision. She decided to be cautiously optimistic about his late night sex-drugged declaration. If she gave in to her heart and accepted his offer, there were big decisions to make about her inheritance, her current work and long-term career as a travel photographer. Decisions that could be irreversible once made. They were options she was already weighing, and should be decided upon for her own objectives, not for the love of a man.

While Chad might risk his heart by asking her to stay, she could lose hers as well plus everything else of value in her life. It was too big a risk to take without more time. So she would take all the time she needed until she was sure.

"Hey," he said sleepily, pulling her close under the sheets.

"Hey," she replied with a shy smile.

They kissed tenderly.

"Did we ever decide what we were doing today?" he asked.

Rebecca giggled. "I think we got distracted."

"Hmm. I remember now."

They kissed again.

"Well, let's start with breakfast. I'm starving. Let's go to that breakfast place near the university."

She willingly agreed, suddenly hungry herself.

They spent Saturday close to home, walking

around Hyde Park, visiting Promontory Point and the Japanese garden in Jackson Park's Wooded Island so Rebecca could take a ton of pictures. Chad grilled steaks for dinner and Rebecca made potato salad and corn bread. They settled into the couch to watch a movie for the evening and went to bed before midnight.

On Sunday, Rebecca talked him into going to the blues festival, taking along her camera and iPad. They found a central spot to spread a blanket and hung out there for the day, listening to music and eating more street food than was healthy. Chad was content to play games on her tablet or flip through her portfolio while she roamed freely, capturing pictures of the venue, artists, vendors, and the crowd. They got back to Chad's place late in the evening, but had plenty of energy to make love in the shower before heading to bed naked.

The bed was empty when she woke up the next morning. The clock on the nightstand read eight-fifteen, so she knew Chad had already left for work. Rebecca rolled over and stretched, taking a moment to decide what to do for the day. Without anything urgent to get done, it was the perfect opportunity to update her Web site and do some marketing of her portfolio. A few more deals like the purchase from the publishing company would allow her to be less dependent on travel jobs.

Rebecca quickly showered and dressed, then called a taxi before packing up her weekend bag. When her ride arrived, she locked up the house using the security code in the garage. She was looking out the window when her phone beeped indicating a message. There was a moment of hesitation before she turned on the mobile and looked at the message. With relief, she realized it was from Chad.

> Morning, sunshine. Call me at the office when you wake up.

She smiled while dialing the phone number, feeling silly to think it could be another annoying threat from John.

"Hi, Chad," she said when he answered.

"Good morning. Did you just get up?" he asked, sounding cheery.

"No, I've been up for a while. I'm on my way back to the hotel."

"Oh. You don't have to leave, you know."

"Thanks, but I have some work to do, and it's just easier on my laptop."

"Okay. If I had known, I would have driven you in on my way to work. But you looked so peaceful, I didn't want to wake you."

"I guess I was really tired. It was a busy weekend," she replied.

There was a pregnant pause.

"Rebecca, we should discuss what happened," he finally stated.

"I know," she acknowledged, her heart immediately beating faster.

"Okay." He cleared his throat. "I can't talk now—I have to go to a meeting. But how about this evening? I'll come by the hotel after work."

"Okay," Rebecca agreed.

"Okay."

She smiled, sensing that he was as nervous and excited as she was.

"Bye, Rebecca."

"Bye, Chad."

The remainder of the ride into downtown was spent in a dreamy fog. At the Dunegan Inn, she stopped by Julie's office to say hi for a few minutes and made plans to meet for lunch, before heading up to her room to make a plan of action.

Her morning went by fast as Rebecca started working through her list of things to get done. One of the first things she did was to call a recruiter from a national news agency in New York and ask if they had any photojournalism opportunities based in Chicago, permanent or freelance. Surprisingly, the recruiter remembered her, and promised to check with her colleagues to see if there were any positions available.

Close to noon, Rebecca was ready to upload her pictures from the weekend onto her Web site. When she took her camera out of her weekend bag to remove the SD memory card, she saw the slot was empty. Then she remembered transferring the card to her iPad on Sunday on the way home from the festival. Rebecca checked the bag again, but the tablet wasn't there. She stopped for a moment, unable to remember packing it, or even seeing it that morning before leaving Chad's house. Which meant she must have left it in his car.

With a sigh, she went back to her laptop. Her

iPad had been set up to automatically copy any new files to an online data storage site as a backup. Rebecca logged in to the secure database and was relieved to find all the pictures there. Content to work with what she had, she made a mental note to call Chad later in the afternoon so he could check his car for the tablet, and bring it with him if it was there.

A few moments later, her iPhone beeped again with another text message. Rebecca smiled with anticipation, assuming it was Chad. Maybe he had already found the iPad? She clicked on the messaging app, but instead of finding text, it contained a picture file. Frowning with confusion, she clicked on an image.

It was a snapshot of Chad leaving his house. Rebecca blinked a few times, still bewildered by the message.

The phone beeped again as another picture came through, this time of Chad backing out of the driveway. Then a third, now with the two of them walking hand in hand at the festival. Then a fourth, her exiting Chad's house that morning through the garage.

Rebecca froze as she realized two things: the sender had an unlisted number, and the messages got to her phone by iMessage from another Apple user. It was John, and he was still following her. The hairs on the back of her neck rose quickly, and a shiver went down her spine. She held her breath, praying that there was no more.

The fifth message sent pure fear through her body:

How romantic ... Will you mourn him when he's dead?

She almost dropped the phone in panic, her heart beating so hard and fast that it sounded deafening in her ear. *This can't be happening,* she thought. *This can't be happening!* Fingers trembling, Rebecca replied to him for the first time:

I'm calling the police, John.

Too bad it will be too late for your lover.

Rebecca almost screamed with fear.

What do you want?

The response seemed to take forever.

I told you, sweetheart. I want you to remember me. When you've lost your precious lover, you won't forget how you betrayed me.

Oh God, oh God! This was all her fault. She should have told someone about him following her, harassing her. At the very least, she should have reported his assault to the police like Chad had urged. Now if anything happened to Chad, it would be all her fault. She had to do something, anything to make sure he was safe.

He means nothing to me, John. I'm leaving Chicago today, but it's you I'll remember.

Don't lie to me, Rebecca. I'm watching you.

Then watch and you'll see. I'm leaving and not coming back.

She waited over five minutes, staring at the phone for a response, but there wasn't one. In that time, it became so clear that leaving was the only option. John was targeting Chad to hurt her, but if she left the city and walked away from their relationship, he would be safe. He had to be safe!

Feeling sick with dread and regret, Rebecca frantically packed up everything she owned within fifteen minutes. Then she did a quick search online and made a series of phone calls. The first was to Chad at work. His assistant answered his line.

"Chad Irvine's office, Natasha speaking."

It took a moment for Rebecca to find her voice.

"Hello?" the young woman repeated.

"Hi, sorry about that. Is Chad still in the office?" she asked.

"Yes, but he's in an all day meeting. Can I take a message?"

"No, no. That's okay. Thank you."

Rebecca hung up before she changed her mind. She had to assume Chad was safe at work for now. It was smarter to call him later, after she was gone and the police were notified. He would realize that she'd had no choice, and had to stay away for as long as John was out there. It was the only way.

She called her sister next.

"Hi, sis. What's up?" Nadine greeted.

"Hey, Nadine. I've decided to come to California for a visit."

"Really? That's great, Becca. When?"

"Today."

There was stunned silence.

"What? Today? Rebecca . . ."

"I know it's very last minute, but I hope that's okay."

"Of course it's okay, but I don't understand what happened. Is it Chad? Did you guys finally talk?"

"Sorry, Nadine. I have to run if I'm going to get to the airport on time. I promise to fill you in later."

"Okay. Give me your flight information."

"I'll send you a text message with the details after I've checked in. But if all works out, I should land in San Francisco by around four-thirty your time."

"All right," Nadine replied, clearly confused by the urgency in her sister's voice.

"One more thing," Rebecca added. "I don't think I should stay with you after all."

"What? Why not?"

"I'll explain later. But can I ask you to book a room for me at a hotel nearby, in your name?"

"Rebecca, what the hell is going on? Are you in trouble? You're scaring me," Nadine insisted.

"Please, Nadine. I'll be there in a few hours and I promise I'll tell you everything."

"Okay, okay!"

"Thank you," Rebecca replied, almost in tears. "I'll get the details from you at the airport."

"Be safe, Rebecca."

"I will."

Rebecca hung up and almost fell apart. *How on earth did things get so crazy so fast?* she wondered. But she didn't have time to indulge in emotions. There was a flight to San Francisco leaving O'Hare at two o'clock and she was determined to be on it. Once in California, maybe, just maybe the nightmare would be over. But if John was crazy enough to stalk her around the city and threaten Chad, he might be unhinged enough to follow her halfway across the country. For that reason, Rebecca couldn't lead him directly to her sister and her family by staying with them right away. She needed to stay distant and take every precaution to protect everyone she loved.

After a few deep breaths, she made the final phone call.

"Hey, Rebecca. Are we still on for lunch?" Julie asked.

"Hey, Julie. I've had a change of plans. I need to check out right away," she explained.

"What? Why? Did you get another assignment?" her friend asked, perplexed.

"I'll explain when I get downstairs. But I'll be in a rush to get to the airport, so do you mind checking me out? You can put any outstanding charges on my credit card."

"Okay, no problem."

"Thanks so much. I'll be down in a few minutes."

Rebecca hung up and let out a deep calming breath. That call had gone more smoothly than she expected, but their final good-byes were going to be much more tricky. Once she smelled a fishy situation, Julie Harper was not easily put off or appeased.

Finally, just minutes after noon, she left her suite at the Dunegan Inn, ready to leave Chicago, Chad Irvine, and a madman behind.

As Rebecca walked down the hall toward the elevator with her luggage in tow, her thoughts were completely occupied with all the things she still had to do. Calling the Chicago police was at the top of her list, and would be done on the drive to the airport. She only hoped that they would take the threats seriously and act quickly to find John. The alternative was too scary to worry about right now.

She pressed the elevator button going down, and one of the three units arrived quickly. Rebecca stepped into the empty space and pressed the button for the lobby as the door closed. Noticing that the button didn't light up, she pressed it again, impatiently. It remained unlit. Then the lift started to move, but going up instead, passing all the floors above hers, heading to the top of the building. She kissed her teeth with annoyance. Whatever the problem, there was no choice but to patiently continue the ride, and try the lobby button once the doors opened again.

It finally stopped on the top floor and the doors slid open slowly. There was no one there. Rebecca kissed her teeth again, quickly losing patience, and tried the lobby button once more, but it still didn't work. Giving up, she stepped out into the hallway to wait for one of the other two elevators.

The arm that wrapped around her neck came from nowhere, taking her completely by surprise, and overpowering her slight frame with little effort. Rebecca had no time to react or fight before a foul-smelling cloth covered her nose and mouth. She could only blink in terror, trying desperately to resist the feeling that she was passing out. She tried to move her head or kick her legs, to struggle against the strange sensation. But it was useless. Darkness quickly encroached on her vision until there was only nothingness.

Chapter 23

When Rebecca regained consciousness, it took her a few moments to remember what had happened. She tossed her head gently while blinking, trying to shake off the feeling of dizziness and disorientation. The movement increased the ringing in her ears, so she stopped, staying as still as possible with her eyes closed tight while breathing deeply.

It took a couple of minutes for her to feel close to normal. Rebecca cautiously opened her eyes again only to find herself lying on the floor in a small room. She slowly sat up and looked around. Judging from the exposed plumbing and patchy tiling, she assumed she was in a bathroom in some stage of repair or renovation with discarded building materials and debris scattered about. Her purse and luggage were not there.

Feeling better by the second, she turned onto her knees and stood up. There was a light wave of dizziness, but it was bearable. With wobbly knees, she walked a couple of steps to the door of the room and turned the handle. As she suspected, it was firmly locked. Somewhere in her practical mind, it seemed really odd for a bathroom door to be secured from the outside. But she was too busy getting panicked to care.

Rebecca banged on the door with the palm of her hand, screaming at the top of her lungs. "Hello? Hello! Can anybody hear me? Hello!"

Her cries were followed by complete silence. There was no one behind the door.

"Hello? Please! Somebody help me! I'm locked in this room!"

Banging turned to pounding with her fists, then kicking with her feet until she almost broke her big toe. Finally, exhausted and spent, Rebecca stopped to catch her breath with her back rested on the aluminum barrier. Whoever grabbed her by the elevator and put her in this room was obviously prepared enough to ensure no one would be around to find her.

Rebecca looked at her watch. It was only twenty-five minutes after twelve, less than half an hour since she left her room. There was no doubt in her mind who was responsible for this.

John McConaughey had set her up.

Chad had never been in any danger. John was too smart, too methodical to do anything so stupid. This was what he had wanted all along, to make good on his threat to her that night at the Isis. Everything else was a trick to get her to pack her things to leave Chicago. And Rebecca had walked right into it.

Now, here she was, locked up in this cubbyhole,

and it would be hours before anyone knew she was missing.

"Oh God, Chad!" she gasped.

What was he going to think when he tried to meet her later, only to find she had checked out of the hotel? Would he believe she had run off without a word to him? Surely, he would question it, right? She didn't want to think about it. At least he was safe, with no threat to his life. Now all she needed to do was get out of here. There was no doubt John was not far away and he obviously had a plan. Rebecca had no intention of standing around helplessly to find out what it was.

Feeling reenergized, she resumed her banging and screaming, praying that someone would hear her. When after ten minutes that failed, she started to look around the space for anything that could unlock the door. There were small piles of garbage scattered around, and she carefully sifted though them, hoping to find an object or tool sharp enough to use as a key. Rebecca was almost out of hope when she used her toe to poke at a rag that was wadded up in the corner. There was something hard in it. She kicked it again, then bent down and shook it loose. A dirty flathead screwdriver fell out. She was so surprised that it took her a moment to realize what it was.

"Yes, yes!" she whispered, feeling hopeful for the first time since she found herself in the dingy cell.

Grabbing the screwdriver, she quickly went back to the door and tried to insert the tip of the tool into the tiny keyhole. It was too big.

"No, no! Come on, damn it!" she muttered, trying to force it in.

But it was nowhere near being the right size. Rebecca threw down the tool with frustration, now close to tears. It was no use. There was no way out. She was stuck in here until John came back. *If* he came back! She wasn't sure which prospect would be worse. What if he left her here? Judging by how abandoned the space was, it could be days, maybe weeks before any workers came back. She could die in this little room!

Rebecca began to hyperventilate as crippling panic and fear started to overtake her. She slowly slid down the wall until she was sitting on the floor, taking in deep, laborious breaths, willing herself not to fall apart. There had to be something she could do!

She must have sat there for about ten minutes, thinking through everything that had happened that day, all the bizarre details that had led to this moment. John had gone through a lot of trouble to get her here. He had to have known that she had finished her project for the hotel, making it easy for her to willingly leave Chicago. Then, there was the business with the elevator. He must have put it on service mode, ensuring it would take her to this floor. And of course, he needed to know about the work being done on the rooms up here, so he could leave her locked in here without anyone seeing or hearing.

He still had access to the company's systems or information, or he was getting help from someone on staff at Dunegan Inn. And she also knew in her gut that this whole elaborate risky plot wasn't so that she could rot away up here. John McConaughey felt betrayed by her, and he wanted his pound of flesh. Her flesh to be exact.

As Rebecca speculated on all those things, her eyes fell on the doorknob. It was a typical brass, hardware store privacy lock, but a little out of place in a high end hotel. And why would there be a knob on a door for a bathroom that had no fixtures and was in the middle of a renovation? And why would it lock from the outside rather than the inside?

She eagerly got on her knees to look more closely at the hardware. Someone must have installed it there, specifically to lock her in. Rebecca leaned closer, suddenly noticing the two screws that fastened the knob to the door through a plate. They had standard Phillips heads with two slots in an X shape. If John had just put it on, then she could just as easily remove it.

With her heart beating like a drum, she turned around wildly, searching for the screwdriver she had tossed away in frustration. It was lying a few feet away. With the tool in hand, Rebecca knelt in front of the door and got to work. The head of the driver was a little bigger than the screw, but it was close enough to function. Slowly, she started to turn the small metal bolt, careful not to strip the head. It took all her effort to get it started, but once she did, it twisted off pretty easily. Then she did the same with the second. Once unsecured, the rest of the handle came apart like a jigsaw puzzle until the door finally swung open freely.

It took Rebecca a few moments to realize that she had done it. She was free. And while she wanted to run out of there like a madwoman, leaving the bathroom didn't mean she was in the clear. John could be right outside the room or somewhere nearby. She was going to have to be very careful and cautious to completely escape his clutches.

She tucked the lifesaving screwdriver into the back pocket of her jeans and covered the handle with her shirt. Then, as quietly as possible, she stepped out of the confining space and into another room. The area was quite large, with two separate rooms suggesting an executive suite. It was also completely empty and in the middle of a big renovation, with everything stripped out down to the walls, including the carpet. Rebecca took this in quickly, only looking around long enough to confirm that it was empty. With tiptoe steps, she crept over to the front door, which was closed, praying the whole time that it wasn't also locked from the outside. She slowly pressed the lever handle, and to her surprise, it easily swung open.

Rebecca inched wider until she was able to stick her head out and look down the hall. To her shock and dismay, John McConaughey was standing right there not two steps away, carrying a small paper bag. Their eyes met for a second before she stepped back inside and slammed the door back shut. But before she could turn the bolt lock, the heavy barrier blew inward with the force of John's body, knocking her backward off her feet.

She landed hard on her side, banging her head on the bare subfloor and cracking her shoulder on impact. Rebecca lay there dazed for a long while. She wanted to move, crawl away, get to her feet, but her body wouldn't cooperate. None of her limbs seemed to be working properly, no matter how hard she tried to get them going. But her hearing was sharp, almost magnified. She heard the door close and the bolt lock in place. She heard his foot-steps, approaching her in slow motion, each one getting louder and louder until they stopped near her head. Then, John crouched down until his face was right over hers.

"Hi, Rebecca. Long time no see," he stated calmly, with a pleasant smile on his lips.

"Stay away from me," she managed to whisper.

He chuckled. It sounded sick and evil. "Are you hungry?" he asked, raising the paper bag up to show her. "I brought you a sandwich from the deli across the street. It's hot corned beef, done as you like with mustard and lettuce."

She could hardly believe his words. "Go to hell, John," she spat.

"You really are an ungrateful bitch, aren't you, Rebecca?" he continued in that sadistically calm tone, his Irish brogue making the words roll off his tongue. "No matter what I do for you, you just throw it back in my face."

Rebecca tried again to move, using her feet and hips to wiggle farther away from him. Excruciating pain spread from her collarbone and down her right arm. It sucked the air out of her body and she closed her eyes tight, afraid she would pass out.

"Oh no, are you hurt?"

She felt his fingers on her arm and lost it. "Don't touch me, you sick bastard!" she screamed.

His laughter rang loudly in the room, echoing around the empty space. It sounded like something out of a bad horror film. "Oh, Rebecca. You're so feisty, just like I knew you would be. We're going to have so much fun, you and I."

"Please," she whispered. "Don't do this. You won't get away with it."

"Ahh, you're so pretty when you beg. What do you think will happen to me, Rebecca? Will I lose my job, my friends, my reputation? Will I be humiliated by a whore with no morals? It's a little late for concern, isn't it? You made sure of that, didn't you? And now you want mercy?"

Rebecca closed her eyes against the hate and ugliness reflected in his. How was it possible for John to twist everything into such a perverted reality? She couldn't understand it, but was now certain he had completely taken leave of his senses. In his mind, she deserved this and whatever else he was going to do to her, and there was nothing rational that she could say to stop him.

"Come on, enough time wasting. I've created a comfortable little nest for us back here," he continued, taking hold of her left arm near the elbow.

"UGGGH!" she screamed in pain as his grip pulled her arm away from her shoulder socket. "I can't move; it's too painful. Please!"

But he didn't listen. Rebecca could not have imagined anything hurting that much. If felt like there was a fire inside her arm burning her up from the inside out. It seemed to be never ending, with wave on top of wave of throbbing intensity, until she fainted into blessed numbness.

When she came to a short time later it was to the feel of her cheek being slapped. "Come on, wake up," she heard.

"No . . ." she mumbled, not exactly sure what she was protesting.

"That's it," the voice said. "Nap time is over. We have work to do."

She blinked and found John standing over her body, that sick smile still on his face.

"You're back. It's no fun if you're not awake to feel it, you know," he continued, clearly amused by his own sick jokes. "Too bad about your shoulder. From the way you screamed, I think it's broken. But never mind. After what I have in mind, you'll welcome the pain."

Rebecca looked around, realizing he had moved her into something like a bedroom, and had laid her on a dusty old blanket. She looked down at her body and found that her shirt had been unbuttoned and pushed aside to reveal her bra.

"Sorry, but I hope you don't mind that I got started without you. I've waited a long time to get a peek of what you have to offer and it was too hard to resist."

The sound of his zipper going down was unmistakable in the vacant space.

"Of course you don't mind. You like a man who takes charge, right? A brute who'll take what he wants instead of politely waiting for an invitation. That's where I went wrong, isn't it?"

The echoes of pain still rang through her body,

and her jaw ached from clenching it so hard. But his incoherent, nonsensical babbling was driving her insane!

"What the hell are you talking about?" she managed to say with some force.

"There she is, my little spitfire," he replied with a giggle.

"You're crazy. You are a demented little man with nothing to offer a woman." Once she started, Rebecca just couldn't stop. "Don't you get it? I didn't want you. I never wanted you. You were just a pastime, something to do until I found Chad again. So play your games. Do whatever it is you plan to do. But it won't change anything. You'll still be a crazy pathetic little boy." It took almost all of the energy she had in her bruised body, but it felt so good to say what she was really thinking.

"Shut up," he growled. "Shut your damn mouth." He wasn't smiling anymore.

It was just a little victory, but it motivated her even more. "Or what?" she baited. "What are you going to do to me, John?"

"I said shut up! It's not your time to talk."

"Or what? Are you going to rape me? Is that it?"

"Yeah, that's right!"

Rebecca laughed, mocking him. "I don't think you can. You're not man enough to do anything other than try to terrorize women with your empty threats."

He turned away and started pacing.

"That's it, isn't it? You can't do it," she stated with an attempt to smile. "Ahhh, poor Johnnie. Your wee-wee doesn't work. . . ."

He bent over and slapped her across the face, hard. "Shut your damn mouth!"

Rebecca tasted blood, but didn't care. If he was going to assault her, maybe even kill her, she wasn't going down without inflicting a few wounds herself.

Chapter 24

"What's going on? What are you doing back so soon?" Chad's assistant Natasha asked. "I thought the meeting was going all day. It's only twelve-thirty."

"Something's going on with one of our clients, so half the sales and delivery team got pulled away," Chad told her, stopping by her desk. "Ivan's going to rebook the last two presentations for later this week."

"Okay. Hey, are you still seeing that woman with the Jamaican accent?" she added as he was about to walk away.

He turned, puzzled by the question. "Rebecca? Yeah, why?"

"I think she called you not long ago," Natasha told him.

"What did she say? Did she leave a message?"

"No, and she didn't say anything. I just recognized the number. I've seen it enough times to memorize it." She grinned cheekily.

Chad was in too good a mood to take the bait.

He smiled back and replied as he walked away, "She probably left a message on my cell phone. Thanks, Natasha."

Back in his office, he checked his messages, but there was nothing from Rebecca. Chad thought he had a pretty good idea why she might have called. On his way to work that morning, he had noticed her iPad on the floor of the passenger side of the car. He remembered that she had used it on the way home last night, and was probably looking for it now. It was the reason he had sent her that text message to call him when she woke up. But once he heard her voice, it completely slipped his mind.

Chad called her cell phone and then her hotel room to let her know the iPad was safe with him, leaving messages on both when there was no answer. Then he tried to get his head to refocus onto work, happy to have a couple of hours back to get some things done. But it was difficult to concentrate, wondering if Rebecca was worried about her tablet, or needed to use it to get something done. He checked his watch. It was only twelve forty-five. Maybe he could run out of the office for a couple of hours and take it to her. With midday traffic, he could be downtown just after one o'clock. They could have lunch together if she hadn't already eaten.

Now that the idea was rooted, he moved into action.

"Natasha, I'm going out for lunch," he said from outside his office. "I'll be reachable on my cell if anyone needs me."

"Sure. No problem. Have fun at *lunch*," she replied brightly.

The cheeky smile was even brighter and she wiggled her brows suggestively. He rolled his eyes, but couldn't resist grinning as he headed out of the office. With any luck, he would have some fun.

In his car, Chad sent Rebecca a quick text message to call him. Then he drove downtown, whistling to tunes on the radio. Occasionally, he was distracted by a beeping sound somewhere in the car. Puzzled, he looked around, even checked his own phone while at a stoplight. It wasn't until he had parked near the Dunegan Inn that he thought about the iPad. He flipped open the protective cover to turn it on. As he suspected, several of the apps on her main page had red indicators beside them, suggesting new messages. Chad closed it up, tucked it under his arm, and headed into the hotel.

He was still whistling when he got to her floor and stepped out of the elevator. Rebecca's room was located around the corner from the elevator shaft. As Chad turned in that direction, he thought he heard someone call her name.

"Rebecca? Are you in there?"

A blond woman, not much bigger or taller than Rebecca, banged on the door again.

"Excuse me? Can I help you?" Chad asked as he approached her.

She jumped in surprise and turned to face him. Then she backed up two steps, clearly intimidated by his height and size so close to her.

"You're looking for Rebecca?" he asked patiently.

The young woman blinked a few times, still flustered. Then a light seemed to go on in her eyes. "Yes. She's not answering the door."

"And you are?" Chad probed politely.

"Sorry," she apologized. "I'm Julie Harper. Rebecca and I are friends."

"Julie," he stated, recognizing the name Rebecca had mentioned a couple of times in passing. "You're the manager here, right?"

"Yes, that's right. And you're Chad," she stated with certainty.

"Chad Irvine. Nice to meet you," he confirmed, extending his hand.

She accepted it, and visibly relaxed even further as though very glad to see him.

"So, Rebecca's not here?" Chad asked as he also knocked on her door.

"I don't know. She was up here about an hour ago when she called me from the room."

"Okay. Well, maybe she just went out for an errand or to get something to eat," he suggested, unconcerned.

He turned back to Julie, and noticed quickly that she seemed quite distressed, wringing her hands and biting on her lower lip.

"What's wrong?" he asked.

"Was she expecting you?" she asked.

"No. She forgot her iPad in my car, so I thought I'd bring it to her," Chad explained, taking the device out from under his arm to show it. "I called her, but I didn't get an answer. Why?"

Julie turned and banged on the door again. "Rebecca? Rebecca? Are you in there?"

There was only silence. Her obvious distress got his heart rate going.

"Julie, what's going on? Is there something wrong?"

She just looked up at him before pulling out a key card and swiping it though the lock. They both walked inside to find a spotless room that was completely empty.

"What the hell?" Chad demanded, looking around.

There was not one sign of any of Rebecca's things anywhere. It was like she was never there. He turned and walked into the bathroom. All of her toiletries were gone. *Did she change rooms since last week?* he wondered. He peered into the shower stall to see a bottle of shampoo on the floor. Chad opened the glass door and picked it up, smelling the familiar rich, fruity scent. It was definitely hers.

"She's gone."

He turned to find Julie standing in the doorway of the bathroom looking almost as shell-shocked as he felt. "What?" he demanded, sounding harsher than he intended. His heart was beating so fast he could barely think.

"She's gone," Julie repeated in almost a whisper. "But she was going to say good-bye to me. Why would she leave without saying good-bye?"

"What do you mean she's gone?" Chad growled, still clutching the shampoo bottle. "Gone where?"

Julie stepped back, her sharp green eyes open wide. "I don't know! She didn't say!"

Chad looked around, suddenly feeling the walls closing in on him in the tight space. "I need some air," he muttered, pushing past the tiny woman as he went back into the hotel room, tossing the bottle of shampoo on the TV console.

He took several deep breaths and sat on the edge

of the bed. It was a couple of minutes before he felt calm enough to talk.

"Okay, Julie. Tell me everything from the beginning."

"I don't know. I don't know what's going on," she sputtered.

"You said she called you today. When? What did she say?" he urged.

"That's right. She called at about twelve o'clock to cancel our lunch plans. Which was weird since she was the one who suggested we go out when she arrived this morning," Julie mused. "Then she called and said she was checking out of the hotel. That she was going to be in a rush and needed me to take care of it for her. Charge anything outstanding to her credit card." She pulled a hotel receipt out of her pocket to show him.

"That's it? Why was she checking out? To go where?"

"I don't know. She was going to tell me that when she got downstairs, which she said would be in a few minutes. I waited for over an hour for her to come down. I called the room and her cell phone, but she never answered. That's why I came up here."

"Okay, okay," Chad stated, his mind running in circles, trying to tie things together. "Maybe she's found somewhere else to stay? Or she's headed back to my house? I just told her this morning that she could stay there as long as she needed."

Julie looked at him, thinking through his suggestion.

"I forgot to tell her I had her iPad in the car," he

added, taking it out from under his arm again. "So maybe she's gone back to my house thinking it's there. That makes sense, right?"

They looked at each other, weighed the logic, wanting to believe there was a simple answer to explain the otherwise bizarre behavior.

"I guess," Julie added. "The company was paying for her accommodations here for as long as the project lasted, and it's pretty much completed as far as I know. It's an expensive suite, so it makes sense that she would look for something less costly."

They both nodded.

"She probably just forgot to get the receipt, right? I could easily e-mail it to her, or give it to her the next time I see her," Julie continued.

"Right," he agreed with a slight smile. His heart was still pounding, but the panic was slowly subsiding. He stood up and they both walked out of the suite.

"Okay. Well, I'm sure glad you showed up," Julie told him. "I would have gone out of my mind with worry. Rebecca is always so organized and punctual, with everything well planned out in—"

She suddenly stopped in her tracks, just steps from the elevator. Chad turned toward her, finding her expressive eyes wide with a new revelation.

"What?" he demanded, his stomach suddenly dropping with dread.

"She said she was going to the airport."

They looked at each other for a long moment.

"What?"

"I just remembered. That's why she needed me to check her out right away, before she got downstairs.

She said she was going to be in a rush to get to the airport."

"No, that's not possible," Chad stated, more to himself than Julie. *Is that why Rebecca called me at the office? To tell me she was leaving?* It was just inconceivable. What about their plans? He had told her how he felt about her, asked her to stay with him in Chicago. They were going to talk about it tonight. *But she hadn't responded to my giant declaration of love. And she certainly hadn't reciprocated to say she loved me too and wanted to be with me in a real relationship. She hadn't said anything at all.*

He was so stupid, so self-absorbed in his own fantasy of happily ever after that he never considered that she might not have wanted the same thing. After all, what did he really have to offer? A boring life in one city? She was probably on her way to Bora-Bora right now, or some other breathtaking location on the planet. Why on earth would she stay here—just because he asked her to?

"It's just not like her to leave without saying good-bye," Julie continued, unaware of the turmoil swarming through his head. "I'm going to send her a text message." She took her iPhone out and quickly tapped in a note.

The tablet under his arm beeped and vibrated. Chad took it into his hands, looking down at it with surprise.

"Did you text her phone or this?" he asked.

"I sent it to her phone, but it's probably gone to both. I used iMessage so it would go to all her Apple devices."

"So anything sent to her phone would also be here?" Chad confirmed.

"No, only messages sent from other iPhones."

He looked at her, then back down to the iPad. Maybe there was something there that would explain her sudden departure.

"Chad, I'm really worried. Maybe she got a last minute project and ran out of time to see me before going. But it's not like her to leave like this, without a word or a note to anyone, particularly you. It just doesn't make any sense. She's in love with you."

He wanted to believe those words so badly and felt a glimmer of hope that his worst fears were unfounded. But he needed to know for sure one way or the other. Chad opened the tablet cover and tapped the app called iMessage.

There were two notes that were unread, and he tapped the first, sent less than a minute ago, obviously from Julie, which read:

Where are you? I'm worried.

Chad then tapped the second, from Nadine White sent within the last twenty minutes. He recalled that Nadine was Rebecca's sister who lived in California.

I've checked you into the Dunegan on Market Street. Don't forget to send me your flight details. Look forward to seeing you soon.

He let out a deep breath. "She's gone to San Francisco," he stated, feeling an odd mix of relief

and dread. At least he knew where she was going—
but she had still left him.

"What?" Julie took the iPad from him to read the
note herself. It beeped again at that moment.

"Wait, her sister's just sent another message. It
says **Are you getting on the flight? What's the time of
arrival? Let me know so I can pick you up when you
land**," Julie read out loud. "I don't get it, Chad.
What happened between nine o'clock this morning
and lunchtime that would make her run off to California like this? Did you guys have a fight?"

"No," he replied, suddenly exhausted. "She
called my office around the same time she called
you to check out, but she didn't leave a message."
There was a giant lump in his throat that was block-
ing his ability to speak or breathe properly. He swallowed hard, repeatedly, but it was lodged firmly and
didn't budge.

"Something's not right here. I'm going to check
her e-mails," Julie said.

"I don't think we should invade her privacy—"
he protested weakly, but was cut off by Julie's announcement.

"Wait, what's this?"

"What?" he demanded.

"Rebecca sent an iMessage to someone at eleven
thirty-three this morning. It says: **Then watch and
you'll see. I'm leaving and not coming back.**"

"What? Who's it to?" Chad grabbed the device
out of her hands, too impatient to wait for her
answer.

"I don't know. There's no number or e-mail address attached to it."

"There's a whole conversation here," he stated.

Instead of reading the messages backward, he swiped the screen to the beginning of the chain of communication. The first was dated from the end of April, almost six weeks ago. Chad went stone stiff as he quickly read through the list of notes.

"What? What else is there?"

"Oh Christ!" he muttered. "Oh God! That damn bastard! That pathetic, goddamn coward!"

"Chad? Who?"

He looked down at Julie with murder in his eyes and his heart. "It's John McConaughey."

Chapter 25

"John? What does he have to do with this?" Julie demanded.

"He's been stalking her, Julie. For weeks now! And when he threatened to kill me, Rebecca told him she was leaving town," Chad explained.

Suddenly, an image flashed into her mind of a dark blue Ford repeatedly parked down the street from his house several weeks back, the driver's face hidden by a hat and dark glasses. There was no doubt in his mind that it was McConaughey.

The elevator arrived at that point, and they both entered. Julie pressed the lobby button, then took the iPad from Chad to read the messages herself.

"Oh my God. What does he want from her?"

"I don't know," Chad muttered, rubbing a hand over his forehead as the magnitude of the danger to Rebecca became fully realized. "That sick bastard was watching her this whole time and wanted her to know. He wanted to scare her."

"But why didn't Rebecca tell us?"

He let out a deep breath, feeling more helpless

than ever before in his life. "Probably for the same reason she didn't go to the police in the beginning. She didn't think anyone would take it seriously, that there was any real threat."

They exited the elevator, and Chad followed Julie as they walked across the lobby toward the management offices behind the front desk.

"I can see how she would feel that way," Chad continued. "The notes are pretty innocuous on their own, with nothing really specific or detailed enough to prove he was following her."

"And there's no proof they're actually from John, right? I mean, Rebecca obviously believed they were, but there's no ID."

They were about to go into her office when Julie suddenly stopped to talk to one of her maintenance staff as he walked by them. "Eduardo, why do we have elevator one in service?"

"We don't," the young man replied.

"I just came down in number three, and the power indicator panel shows number one in service."

"I don't know anything about that, Julie. We don't have any work going on this afternoon. What floor was it stopped on?"

"The top floor," she told him.

"Okay, I'll check it out within the hour. Weren't the renovations on hold for another week?" he asked.

"I thought so, and I haven't gotten notice of anything different," Julie confirmed before escorting Chad into her office. Then she said to him, "Chad, I haven't known Rebecca for long, but we've become pretty good friends. I just want to make sure she's okay."

He nodded, relieved to hear it. Julie may have been the last person to actually talk to Rebecca, so he was grateful for any help she could offer. "Has she replied to Nadine's note yet?" he asked, checking his watch. It was over five minutes since the last message.

"No, not yet," she confirmed. "Do you think this is what John wanted? For her to leave the city? What's the point of that? It doesn't get him anything, certainly not his job back."

"I don't know. I have no clue how a crazy mind like that works. And I don't care. I'm calling the police to report his sick ass, like I should have done from the beginning." Chad pulled out his cell phone and dialed 911.

"Hi, I would like to report a threat sent by text message," he started, then spent the next five minutes going through what he knew with the emergency representative, including a description of the car that John was probably driving. But once he admitted that the note was sent to Rebecca, not him, and Rebecca was not filing the complaint, the operator explained there was nothing she could do. His additional comments to reference John's initial assault didn't help once he confirmed those charges were never filed.

But Chad pushed further, insisting that his girlfriend was now missing and possibly in danger. Yet, she'd only been unreachable for about ninety minutes, hardly a matter for the police or emergency services.

At that point, he wanted to scream obscenities and throw his phone against the wall in helpless frustration. Sensing his breaking point coming on, Julie gestured to him for the phone.

"Hi there, my name is Julie Harper, the manager at Dunegan Inn Chicago. Mr. Irvine is calling from my office at the hotel regarding one of our guests. I too am concerned about the safety and where-abouts of Rebecca Isles. She has been a long-term resident and consultant for our hotel, and has now disappeared suspiciously. I have also seen the threats that were sent to her phone, and believe them to be from a former hotel employee who was recently fired for similar inappropriate behavior." There was a pause as she listened to the response. "Thank you. I really appreciate your help."

Chad let out a deep breath. The solid mass was back in his throat, and he blinked hard to keep his emotions in check.

"Okay, she's sending a patrolman here to speak with us."

"Thank God," he muttered.

"To be honest, what we have is pretty thin. The officer is probably going to tell us the same thing the operator did. But it's worth a shot," Julie replied.

"That's fine, I don't care. I just can't sit here doing nothing, waiting for some word from her."

"I know. There's no way the Rebecca I know would simply walk away like this, even with John's threat." Her eyes lit up like bright green lightbulbs. "Unless . . ."

"What?" Chad asked as she turned and went out the door. "Julie?"

But she was already scampering across the lobby and he had to hurry to catch up. They both stopped outside, in front of the main entrance to the hotel, where two bellhops stood dressed in sharp hotel uniforms, ready to assist any new guests that arrived.

"Hey, Gary, Nigel?" Julie raised her voice to get their attention.

"Hi, boss. What's up?"

"You guys know Rebecca, right? The photographer?" she asked, looking back and forth between the young men.

"Yeah, of course. Why?" one of them replied.

"Did you hail a cab for her this afternoon? Anytime within the last hour and a half?"

"Sorry, boss, I just started at one o'clock. But I haven't seen her since."

"What about you, Gary?" Julie added, turning to the other guy.

"Nope. I haven't seen her since this morning. She arrived in a cab at around nine o'clock, maybe quarter past," he told them.

"But not since, right? Are you sure?" Chad added, suddenly understanding what Julie was trying to confirm.

"No, sir. I'm positive."

Chad looked down at Julie, his jaw clenched hard

and his nostrils flared from the rage that was building in his gut.

"Thanks, guys," she replied politely, pulling Chad back into the building.

"She never left," he said, stating what they were already thinking. "Are you sure there isn't another exit she would have used?"

"No," Julie replied quickly. "I mean, yes. She could have used one of the other doors, but it would be hard to get a taxi in the middle of the day. And she deliberately wanted John to see her leave, right? So why would she use another door? Particularly if she were in a rush to get to the airport. We always have a cab parked outside on standby, and she would know that."

He let out a deep breath, trying to keep a lid on his mounting fury, taking a moment to think through everything they knew for sure.

"Chad, if she never left the hotel, she has to be here somewhere, right? She didn't just disappear sometime between leaving her room with bags packed and reaching the exit door!"

"No, she didn't disappear at all," he acknowledged, starting to pace back and forth with anxious energy. "That bastard has her and I'm not leaving this building until we search every square inch! And you need to have your security check the area for his car," he spat.

Julie opened the door again to yell out to the bellhops. "Guys, the police are on their way here to take a report. Can you call me on my cell phone as soon as they get here?" Back inside she turned to Chad, unflinching in the presence of his rapidly crumbling restraint. "Let's go begin searching. I think I know where to start first."

"The elevator," Chad stated with certainty.

"Yup. Someone put it in service without my knowledge or sign-off. And I don't think it's a coincidence."

They both rushed back to the front desk.

"Where's Eduardo?" Julie asked the girl behind the counter.

"He just went to the elevators," they were told.

Julie and Chad both launched into a full sprint.

"Hold the elevator!" Chad yelled as they approached the shafts.

Eduardo stuck his hand out between the two sliding doors, and the panels slowly reopened. "Hey, Julie. I'm just on my way up to check that elevator," he explained.

"We're going with you," Chad stated.

"Eduardo, this is Chad Irvine, a friend of mine," Julie quickly explained to alleviate some of the confusion on her employee's face.

Both men nodded to each other.

"It's still stuck on the top floor?" she asked, looking up at the digital indicator panel mounted near the top of the cubicle, above the buttons.

Chad had not noticed when they had headed downstairs, but now understood what Julie had been referring to. Each of the three elevators had a light that showed where it was stopped and how it was moving between floors. The light under number one was blinking rapidly at the top of the board.

"Yup," Eduardo replied. "I tried to change the status, but I couldn't get to it from the central control downstairs. I'm not sure what's wrong, so I'm going to try to take care of it by going inside the elevator."

Julie nodded. "How long have you worked for the company, Eduardo? It's been, what, two years?" she asked in a conversational tone.

"That's right," the young man replied. "Two years in July."

"Good. Do you know John McConaughey at all?" she added casually.

"No, I don't think so. Who's he?"

Chad was watching Eduardo's face, and couldn't see any signs of concern or stress.

"Nobody important. Listen, Eduardo, when we get upstairs, I want you to stay by the elevators, okay? If you see anyone or sense any problems, head back down to the lobby. Don't try to do anything or confront anyone. Do you understand?"

Her instructions were stated calmly and clearly. Eduardo looked alarmed and clearly had questions, but only nodded and said, "Yes, ma'am."

"The police have been called. I'll ask them to be escorted up as soon as they arrive."

"Yes, ma'am."

The ride seemed to take forever until the doors finally opened on the top floor. All three of them stepped out into the hallway and looked around. It was obvious that the whole floor was going through a major remodeling, but there was no sign of anyone else around.

"What now?" Julie whispered.

Frowning, Chad looked down at her. She was trying hard to present a tough front, but there was no doubt Julie was scared and out of her depth. Though the two women could not be more different on the outside, Julie's dogged spirit reminded him so much of Rebecca. He was very grateful for her help to this point, but he could not let her go any farther.

"Julie, you need to stay here with Eduardo," he stated in a stern voice that invited no argument.

"No way! I'm going with you, Chad. This is my hotel and I'm her friend. . . ."

"Julie," Chad demanded, gently taking hold of her shoulder, "I know how you feel, but it's too dangerous, all right? You've done all you can; you got us this far. But this isn't up for debate. He's a dangerous, sick man. There's no telling what he'll do when cornered."

She bit her lip, knowing Chad was right.

"Plus I need you here when the police come so you can explain everything. Okay?"

Julie finally nodded.

"Good. Eduardo, please stay with her," he told the other man.

Then Chad turned away and walked down the derelict hallway, trying to figure out where John could be holed up with Rebecca. He quickly ignored all of the rooms without doors or with doors swung open, which left six others closed up. Then it was just a process of elimination to go room by room, starting with one end of the floor.

The first door opened easily, and a quick look around confirmed it was empty with no sign of any recent visitors. The same was found for the next two. The fourth room was locked.

Taking a deep breath to steady himself, Chad pressed his ear against the cold steel and tried to listen for any movement or sign of distress. There was only eerie silence. He looked down the hall at the remaining doors, not wanting to waste any time. Every second he spent in the wrong direction was putting Rebecca in more danger. With more certainty, Chad continued on to the last two doors, but they both swung open freely.

Armed with a clear focus, he ran back to the elevators where Julie and Eduardo were still waiting, with the maintenance worker in the stuck elevator trying to undo the service status.

"I think I've found them," he declared. "Room two-two-one-six is the only one that's locked. It has to be him."

"That's great!" Julie replied. "How are you going to get in? Maybe you should wait for the police. Gary just called to say the police cruiser has pulled in and I've told him to escort them up here."

"No, I'm not waiting. God knows what he's done to her already, Julie," he choked. "Will your master key work on the lock?"

"I don't know. I don't think so. These locks would all have been disabled from the security system to allow access by the construction crew."

"Then I'm going to have to break it down."

"That might not be that easy, Mr. Irvine," Eduardo interrupted. "These doors have a one-inch throw bolt into the metal frame. It will be nearly impossible to break, even with your size."

"Well, I'm going to have to try," Chad stated, turning away.

"Wait, I have another idea," Eduardo stated, stopping him in his tracks. "Most of the rooms on this floor are larger suites with connecting doors for families with nannies. That would be a better way to break in. Those doors were quite flimsy and the locks were pretty basic."

"That's right, Eduardo," Julie confirmed. "We're upgrading all of the hardware as part of the renovation."

"Okay, that's it then," Chad said decidedly before he ran back down the hall.

As Eduardo had suggested, he quietly crept into the room before the locked one, checking for the connector door. There was one, but it was wide open and leading into the adjacent suite. Stifling a curse, he swiftly went along the hall to the room on the other side of the one he needed to get into. Chad almost wept with relief when he walked into the suite and found the frame of an entrance on the right wall.

He didn't bother to listen through the door or check the lock. In his heart, he knew Rebecca was on the other side of that wall, in the most vulnerable position possible. There wasn't any time left for precautions. So he backed up across the width of the room to create a runway, then sprinted forward with explosive force, using his shoulder as a ram. The simple dead bolt gave out with little resistance and the door flew open with a loud, splintering sound, with Chad stumbling in after.

Chapter 26

The scene that Chad discovered sent cold chills down his spine and would haunt his dreams for a long time to come.

At first he didn't see them, and thought he had been wrong about the room. It took a few seconds to gather his bearings after breaking through the door, and he swung around wildly, not wanting to lose the advantage of surprise. The space looked empty at first, except for a paper bag on the floor near the front door. Chad started to walk toward it, when something caught his eye in the adjacent space. Acting on pure instinct, he rushed forward, ready to tackle the first person he saw.

But he stopped cold in his tracks not a foot into the bedroom area.

There was Rebecca, lying awkwardly on the floor, with her clothes partially removed and terror in her eyes. And beside her was the man he assumed was John McConaughey, with his filthy hand over her mouth and a knife against her throat. No one moved for several long seconds.

"Well, this is awkward," the man said.

"Get away from her," Chad demanded in a deep growl.

"This isn't exactly the party I had planned, I'm afraid. But we can make do. Right, Rebecca?"

Chad took a step forward, but froze again as the madman pressed the knife deeper into her delicate flesh.

"Tsk! I wouldn't do that if I were you. This body won't be nearly as fun to play with if she's dead."

Rebecca closed her eyes, and Chad's heart broke into pieces. He had to do something—now, before she was hurt any more.

"You can only hide behind a tiny little woman for so long, John," he spat. "Eventually, you have to face me like a man. And I'm going to kill you, slowly."

He saw Rebecca wiggle a little, her eyes still clenched tight.

"That might be, *Chad*. But it will have to be over her dead body," he replied smoothly, smiling widely at his joke. "I'm okay with that if you are."

The stalemate lasted a few seconds, then several things happened at the same time.

There was the unmistakable sound of heavy footsteps coming from the room next-door, and as John reacted, loosening his grip on Rebecca, Chad seized that moment to rush forward in an attempt to knock him away from her. But before he reached them, John inexplicably screamed and flew forward, writhing in pain on the ground, flopping like a fish out of water. Sticking out of his neck was the handle of a screwdriver, its tip buried in his flesh.

Even as the police rushed in with guns drawn,

and John continued screaming as blood gushed out of his wound, Chad could only think of one thing. As gently as possible, he scooped up Rebecca into his arms and carried her out of the horror show. No one tried to stop him. She felt so frail and lifeless, her expression still riddled with pain, that his heart ached with anguish. Tears ran down his face unchecked.

When he reached the elevator, Julie was still there waiting and pacing. Her face lit up with immense relief at first, until he got closer and she saw the state of both of them. Her mouth opened, then shut firmly.

"Can I take her to her old room?" he asked.

"Yes, of course."

They made the journey silently. There was no doubt Julie was bursting with questions, but she didn't ask, and Chad just wasn't ready to talk. Eventually the police would get plenty of information from him.

When they got to the room, Chad laid Rebecca on the bed under the sheets, buttoning up her shirt before tucking the covers around her. She moaned deeply, and he wanted to stab John himself.

"Get some rest," he whispered, pressing his lips on her forehead.

"Chad?" she mumbled, stopping him from walking away.

"Yeah?" he asked, leaning close so she wouldn't have to strain.

"Did I kill him?" Even bruised and in pain, the fire in her eyes burned bright.

Chad's eyes filled again, but he smiled back at

her. "I certainly hope so, or I'm going to have to finish the job."

She tried to smile back, but it looked more like a grimace. Then, she closed her eyes again.

Unfortunately, John McConaughey didn't die from his neck wound. The paramedics arrived on the scene with enough time to remove the tool and patch him up. But, he was safely locked up in the city jail awaiting arraignment, and that was a very good start.

As Chad expected, the next few hours were filled with questions from the police investigators and the Dunegan security representative. They pored over every detail with both him and Julie, over and over again until he wanted to bolt. But in order to save Rebecca from a similar experience, he cooperated all the way, explaining the sequence from every possible angle until they all were satisfied that the ends were tied up.

The paramedics visited Rebecca soon after the incident, and confirmed that she had separated her shoulder in the initial fall. They quickly bundled her up on a stretcher and transported her to the hospital to have it treated. While there, the doctor also completed a full examination as requested by the police. Rebecca told them McConaughey hadn't done anything to her sexually, but still consented to the checkup. She was willing to do whatever was necessary to support and cooperate in the case against him.

It was early evening before she was discharged from the hospital, and Chad and Julie were allowed to take her back to the hotel. Chad wanted to bring her to his house, but Rebecca insisted the Dunegan was better, with plenty of people to help her if she needed anything. Julie agreed, and he didn't push the issue. The police had found all her things in a small storage room on the twenty-second floor, and her belongings were back in her suite when she arrived. The first thing she did was call Nadine, who was out of her mind with worry at that point, still expecting her to land in San Francisco at any moment. Rebecca took a few minutes to give her sister a brief description of what had happened, leaving out the more horrifying details for a more appropriate time. They hung up with a promise to talk again the next day.

Chad helped her into bed fully clothed, then stayed with her until the pain medication kicked in and she fell asleep. He was gone in the morning when she finally woke up.

She spent the next couple of days in her room, doing her best to relax and keep her shoulder still and in the sling the doctor had provided. But there was only so much sleep and television watching that she could stand. By Thursday, she was ready for some fresh air.

"Are you sure you want to do this? There's no rush, you know? Why not wait another couple of days?" Julie insisted, her brows creased with concern.

"I'm fine, Julie, really. I just want to go for a short walk, get some sunshine."

They were in her room, and her friend was sitting in the chair while Rebecca got dressed in a skirt and T-shirt. It was a very slow process, but Julie had learned from previous experience to let her do it herself.

"Okay, I'm all set," Rebecca said a few moments later with her feet in a pair of flip-flops. She wasn't ready to tackle laces as yet.

"I don't mind coming with you," Julie added.

"I know, but it's okay. I'm just going around the block. If I make it as far as the park, I might sit for a while. That's it, okay?"

"All right. I'll stop mothering you."

"Good. Though you do make a good mother."

The women smiled at each other and headed downstairs.

"How's Chad doing?" Julie asked when they reached the lobby.

"Okay, I guess. He stops by every evening and stays until I fall asleep," Rebecca told her.

"He's a good man, Rebecca. You're very lucky to have him."

Rebecca let out a dry laugh. "I don't think he's feeling so lucky," she replied.

"What do you mean?"

"Nothing. Don't worry about it."

"No, tell me. Something's eating at you," Julie insisted.

Rebecca sighed deeply. "I don't know. It's been a crazy, bizarre few days, and with everything that's happened . . . I just think it's been too much for him."

"Why would you say that?"

"I'll put it this way. He had a calm, organized life before I came along. Then I showed up, bringing chaos and disorder right along with me. I think he found it exciting at first. But after John and the . . . After that, I'm pretty sure the novelty's worn off."

"Rebecca, that's not true. You should have seen him when you were missing. He was beside himself with worry," Julie insisted.

"I know he cares about me. He might even think he loves me. But I'm not what he wants or needs in his life. And there's something in his eyes that tells me he's figured that out himself."

Julie shook her head, ready to express her disagreement, but Rebecca didn't give her a chance.

"Okay, time for my walk," she continued, putting a pleasant smile on her face. "I have my cell phone, and I'll send you a text message when I get back so you know I'm safe."

"I'll give you forty-five minutes. A minute longer and I'm calling the police."

"Yes, Mother," Rebecca replied, recognizing that her friend was only half joking. The incident with John had been very difficult for everyone involved, leaving scars on all of them.

The women parted ways and Rebecca stepped outside into the warm spring air and headed down the street. What she didn't tell Julie was that she had made a decision that morning to let Chad go. It was what he needed in order to return to the structure and routine he required in his life. She had known that about him from the day they had met, months ago in Myrtle Beach. And she was equally sure that if she didn't let him go, Chad would continue to see her, spend his evenings watching over her for as long as his conscience required. But it was out of concern and obligation, not necessarily love, and Rebecca couldn't allow that. He needed to move on and find that perfect Chicago wife he had told his mother about.

She returned from her walk feeling tired but more focused, and even more determined to follow through with her decision. And she was back before Julie had to send out the brigade. When Chad arrived to see her later that evening, Rebecca suggested that they have dinner at a restaurant nearby, claiming to be tired of the hotel food. Though he protested like Julie, insisting it was too soon and volunteering to get them some takeout, he gave up when she persisted.

Rebecca didn't waste any time once they were seated. She wasn't really hungry anyway. The restaurant was just a setting that she hoped would allow her to be less emotionally charged than if they talked in her room.

"How are you feeling?" he asked as their waiter poured them glasses of water.

"I'm better. Finally off the pain medication," she told him. "I even went for a short walk today."

"Good," Chad replied

There was a pause as they looked through the menu. Finally, Rebecca swallowed her courage and barged forward.

"Listen, Chad. I think it's time that we talked. About us," she told him.

He didn't seem at all surprised by her statement, nodding as he lowered his menu. "You're right, it is."

"I'm going to visit my sister for a while." From the look on his face, she could see it wasn't at all what he was expecting.

Chad sat back in his chair. "Okay. For how long?"

"I'm not sure. As you know, it's long overdue, and now that we're rebuilding our relationship, I want to take advantage of the opportunity," she explained.

"Of course." He cleared his throat, looked into her eyes, studying her for a long moment. "Are you coming back?" Chad finally asked.

She opened her mouth to say the words that needed to be spoken, but they wouldn't come out. The truth was that she didn't know. But still, she hesitated to tell him that, and her silence stretched to an uncomfortable length of time.

"Rebecca, you need to do what's right for you. I realize now that it was unfair of me to expect that you would abandon everything you've worked for because I want you to stay. After what McConaughey did to you, it's no wonder you're tired of this city," he added with a smile, but it didn't quite reach his eyes. "Do whatever you need to. I just want you to be safe and happy."

She tried to smile back, but her lips quivered and the tears filled her eyes before she could hold them back.

"Rebecca," he whispered, sounding tortured. "Please don't cry." He reached across the table and took hold of one of her hands.

Blinking rapidly, she tried to pull herself together, reminding herself to be grateful at how quickly it had all been resolved. There was plenty of time to cry about him later. "Sorry. I didn't mean to do that," she eventually stated.

"You've been through hell, Rebecca, so it's no

wonder you're a little emotional. A trip to California is probably exactly what you need to recuperate," he told her. "Just promise me one thing? That you won't regret anything that happened between us?"

Rebecca shook her head, unable to speak as her composure slipped again and a shaky sob escaped her throat.

"Because I won't. I'll hold every memory close to my heart," he told her, his own voice a little shaky. "Well, maybe not every memory. I'm trying to forget this week."

They both chuckled a little as their waitress arrived.

"Hi, ya'll. Can I start you off with some drinks?" she asked in a friendly voice.

Rebecca and Chad looked at each other, recognizing that dinner was the last thing either of them could stomach at that point.

"Actually, we've decided not to stay after all," he replied as he stood and helped Rebecca out of her chair.

He left ten dollars on the table and escorted her back to the hotel.

"There's no need to walk me up, Chad. I'll be fine."

"I think we've had this conversation before, remember?"

She smiled, thinking back to the first time they had said good-bye forever. It had been hard then, but it was excruciatingly painful now.

They walked together at a leisurely pace, neither in a rush for the end. But it inevitably came as they stopped in front of her suite. She took out her key and unlocked the door before turning back to him. He pulled her into his arms for a long, hard hug.

"When are you leaving?" he asked against the top of her head.

"Saturday."

"Can you do me one last favor? Can you let me know when you arrive in California safely?"

"I will," she promised.

They slowly pulled apart, but before he let her go, Chad lowered his mouth to hers, stroking her lips with tender, sweet caresses. It was an achingly familiar kiss that made her knees go weak, and threatened to stir up all the fire and passion that remained between them and probably always would. When it ended, they were both breathless. He rested his forehead on hers for a few more seconds.

"Good-bye, Rebecca Isles."

Then she watched him walk away and out of her life for the second time.

Chapter 27

Chad was surprised at how quickly he managed to return to his life before Rebecca and the routine he had. He woke up each morning at six o'clock during the week to get to the gym before work, and was in his office before nine. He was there until at least six o'clock, then headed home to watch television or sports, sometimes stopping to do an errand along the way. On the weekends, he visited his mom and the family, hung out with a few friends, and occasionally went on a date. It all fell back into place with almost no effort.

There were a few things that he changed. He finally gave in to his mother and hired Naomi to finish decorating the main floor of the house. It took a little effort on his part to decide what he really wanted, but otherwise it was pretty painless. The results were exactly what he hoped for, with an open space that was comfortable, warm, and inviting. There was talk about her taking on the bedrooms, but Chad resisted, comfortable with exactly the way it was.

Chad also took his mother's suggestion and asked Naomi out on a date. They went out a few times through the summer, but it never really developed into anything substantial. She was a smart, stunningly beautiful woman, and they had fun. But there was something missing between them that he couldn't put his finger on. Whatever it was, no one else around him could see it, nor did they care. They all thought he was nuts when he called it quits by the beginning of September.

He also decided to go away for a vacation for the first time in many years. To his mother's delight, he offered to take her and Samuel with him to Jamaica that fall for a week. While Denise was thrilled by the offer and excited about the trip, she couldn't hide her concern from her son. The discussion at the dinner table that Sunday afternoon about their plans developed into a conversation Chad had been actively avoiding for weeks.

"Do you think Jamaica is such a good idea, dear?" his mom asked as they flipped through travel magazines and brochures.

"Why not? We really can't go wrong with the choice of resorts. We just need to pick a spot. I hear the beaches in Negril are perfect," he replied.

"Chad, I'm not talking about the vacation. I just think you've chosen Jamaica for other reasons and I'm worried that it's going to make things worse."

"What reasons, Mom?" He didn't want to ask the question, but knew his mother well. If there was something she wanted to talk about, there was no way to avoid it.

"It was you who told me just a few months ago

that it's been too long since you've been back," he added.

"I know, and I'm really looking forward to going. But I'm not talking about me. It's you I'm concerned about."

"Mom," he said, grinning, "there's nothing to be concerned about, okay? I'm doing just fine."

She shook her head, looking sadder than he had seen her in a long time. "I know you're trying, baby, but you're not 'just fine.' I'm your mother, and it's time we talked about—"

"Mom," he interrupted, using the word as a warning.

"This is what I was afraid of, you know."

They looked at each other for several moments.

"I could tell right away how you felt about her, Chad. I had never seen you so happy, so fulfilled in a relationship. I knew you were in love with her. But I also feared she would break your heart."

He looked away from her eyes, staring out at his mom's backyard.

"That's why I told you not to get too involved. I didn't want to see you hurt. But you're a grown man, now. There's very little I can do to protect you from life."

"What does any of this have to do with our trip?" he protested, unable to listen to her words anymore. They were making him think . . . remember. . . .

"I know why you love her, baby. She's a beautiful girl, with energy and life inside her. That energy was in you too, whenever she was around. Then as soon as she left, it's like that energy, that light was gone in you too."

Chad couldn't meet her eyes.

"I was wrong to try and discourage your relationship. Maybe if I had been more supportive . . ."

He shook his head. "It had nothing to do with you. And you were right. This wasn't the life she wanted, that's all. I love her, more than I thought it was possible to love anyone. So I want her to be happy." He hung his head, hating the choking lump in his throat that was becoming a reoccurring obstruction, threatening to turn him into a weeping young boy.

"What are you going to do, Chad? You can't continue like this, mourning someone forever."

"I know," he replied, not bothering to deny it. "Eventually, I'll settle for a good Chicago wife and give you those grandkids you want. I'm just not ready yet."

"Is that what you still want—to settle?"

He finally looked at his mother, sensing her disapproval. "No, that's not what I want. I want Rebecca—in any situation she would have me. I would travel around the world with her if that's what she wanted. But she doesn't. So, when I'm ready to let go, and the memories aren't so fresh, I'll move on."

"Oh, Chad," Denise stated, cupping his cheek with her hand.

"I know, you think I'm being naive. That I'll just meet someone else, fall in love again, and forget all about her."

"No, I don't believe that at all. You're not a fickle man and I can see how much Rebecca meant to you."

He could only nod.

"So, you still want to go to Jamaica?" she finally asked.

"Yeah, I do."

"Good. So let's pick a spot. I'm thinking Negril also."

They eventually called Samuel back into the kitchen to get his input before finalizing their plans.

Chad left their house soon after, but his conversation with his mother stayed with him for some time. What he didn't tell his mom was how much he missed Rebecca, everything from the smell of her skin to the sound of her voice singing around the house. That he yearned for her during the day and dreamed about her at night. He was coping, going through everyday life, trying to create a sense of normalcy. His life appeared very much like it was before they met. But he was a different person now. Her absence from his life was like an open wound in his chest that would probably never heal. Yet, as much as it hurt, Chad would still never give up one moment of their time together.

The following week, the team at work was under a great deal of pressure to finish off a proposal for one of their largest clients. After four days of late nights and the hectic pace, their boss, Ivan, organized an evening out on Friday to unwind and celebrate the successful completion. Though Chad wasn't really up to hanging out in a bar, he went along for support.

The celebration started out like any other, at a local place in the suburbs near the office. There were trays of saucy wings and cheesy nachos, and drinks flowing freely from an open tab. Everyone in their party knew that Chad was not a big drinker, but there seemed to be a conspiracy to ply him with as much alcohol as possible, despite his strongest protests. By eight o'clock and after four glasses of scotch, he was more than a little tipsy and certainly too inebriated to drive. Satisfied with their accomplishment, no one objected when he announced he was leaving in a taxi.

"You sure you're okay?" William asked as they walked together through the pub and out the door.

"Why, are you feeling guilty?" Chad asked with a grin.

"Nah! You could do with a few drinks. It's good to see you more relaxed for once."

"What's that supposed to mean?"

"Come on, Chad." William smirked, tapping his friend on the chest. "You know what I'm talking about. You're always so . . . focused, intense."

"Not always," he mumbled, looking down the suburb street.

"No, not always."

They stood outside, breathing in the fresh air. There was a steady stream of cars going by, but no sign of a taxi.

"Come, I'll walk with you down the block. Maybe we'll catch one on the next street," William offered.

"Nah, I'll be fine. You go back inside, enjoy yourself. I'm good." Chad started walking before his friend could protest.

"I'll call you tomorrow," William shouted after him. Chad raised a hand in acknowledgment and continued walking. *It is a nice street*, he thought, with a mix of small, local stores and restaurants on one side, residential properties on the other. The character and age of the buildings reminded him a little of Hyde Park. Of those that he could see walking along the sidewalks that evening, the residents were a good mix of cultures and ages. *Rebecca would like it around here also,* he thought. She would have lots of great architecture and personalities to photograph.

As he walked down another block in search of a cab, Chad gradually felt less fuzzy headed. Perhaps he wasn't really that drunk, he thought. Maybe he was just light-headed from the lack of real food? He rubbed his stomach, hoping to find a bakery or café that was open. Maybe he could find one of those chocolate croissants that Rebecca had introduced him to? She claimed that the ones in Chicago were decent, but not half as good as in Paris. Chad remembered telling her that nothing could get any better, so he'd have to judge that for himself. The possibility that he would experience the historic French city with her as his tour guide was a real and exciting possibility at the time.

He was so wrapped up in his thoughts that he almost missed the sight of her. Then something caught his eye, maybe a cloud of springy curls, or the sound of her laughter that carried across the street, but the second he saw her tiny frame, Chad froze in his tracks.

It was a warm, sticky night, and she wore a simple cotton tank top with a pair of khaki shorts. Her small purse was slung across her body with a long strap.

And she was walking with a man, maybe average
height with a slender frame. While Chad watched,
they turned together to go up the walkway of an
apartment building.

Even as he stepped out into the road, dodging
cars as he crossed the four-lane street, Chad knew
he had to be imagining things. If he stopped for a
moment to think things through, he would have realized she was just a mirage created by his alcohol-
addled mind. But he was on autopilot driven by
instinct, and rushed forward at a hurried pace,
needing to catch up to her before she disappeared
into one of a hundred apartments. How he would
get inside past the security doors, or what he would
do if he reached her didn't occur to him.

As he approached the front entrance to the
building, another resident was exiting, leaving the
door opened behind him. Chad quickly squeezed
through the space, stepping into the brightly lit,
modern interior. The lobby was empty. He turned
around the open area, hoping to catch a glimpse of
where she may have gone. Deflated, and feeling a
little silly, he was about to head back outside when
the sound of voices echoed through the space. It
was coming from the rear of the building, but got
louder as the speakers made their way back to the
lobby area from an adjacent hall. They were muf-
fled and magnified, but one of them was still so familiar it froze him in his tracks.

There he stood like a statue, waiting for her to
emerge, all doubt gone from his mind.

Chad saw only Rebecca at first, looking sweet and

sexy in her casual summer clothes. She had a scarf tied as a headband, pulling back the untamable mass and accentuating her face. Her eyes were rimmed with darkened lashes, and her lips were shiny with rosy colored gloss. She laughed at something the other person said, throwing back her head and baring her pretty white teeth.

Then she looked forward and saw him standing there. Her steps slowed until she was also still. The man she was with put a protective hand on her shoulder as he looked back and forth between them. The movement caught Chad's eyes until he couldn't look away. The touch was like a familiar caress, brushing over her bare shoulder, pulling her closer to his body.

"Rebecca," Chad stated, surprised at how normal his voice sounded.

"Hi, Chad," she replied, as though they had been casual acquaintances who had lost touch.

"What are you doing here?" he asked, his brows deeply furrowed.

"I came back a couple of months ago," she replied.

"A couple of months," he repeated, more as a statement than a question. "I don't understand." His temples started to pound, and his stomach roiled.

"Rebecca," the man beside her interjected, looking back and forth between them. He was still touching her arm, and Chad fought the urge to snap his bony hand in two.

Rebecca politely introduced the two men, calling the man by her side Brian. She probably shouldn't have bothered since neither of them seemed to hear her, or even nod in acknowledgment.

"Brian, can you give us a moment, please?" she eventually asked as the tension in the air continued to build.

"Are you sure? I don't—" he objected, but was cut off sharply.

"Yeah, she's sure, *Brian,*" Chad added in a bear-like tone.

Rebecca added a nod to confirm she was okay. Accepting her decision, Brian bowed his head and walked away toward the elevators at the other side of the lobby. She looked back at Chad with a funny expression on her face. He suddenly felt flushed, and wiped the sweat from his brow.

"Are you okay?" she asked with concern.

"No, I'm not okay. I'm a little surprised to see you walking around Chicago, to be honest."

He meant to make light of the bizarre situation, but his comment came out sounding sarcastic. Chad wiped his face again and swallowed hard. His stomach roiled again.

"Are you feeling okay?"

Chad shook his head and closed his eyes. He tried to speak, tell her how he was feeling, but there wasn't time. Frantically, he looked around the lobby until he found what he needed. Chad quickly ran toward a spot in the corner, and promptly threw up into the garbage can.

Chapter 28

Rebecca's heart was beating like a drum in her ears. She knew this day was inevitable. Chicago was a big city, but it was still only a matter of time before she and Chad would run into each other. Yet, now that the moment was here, with him standing only a few steps in front of her, almost close enough to touch, all of that preparation went out the window. He looked bigger, harder, stronger than she remembered. *Sexier.* And of course, he appeared quite shocked by her presence. Rebecca had prepared for that as well.

She had spent over five weeks in California with Nadine and her family. The first week or so was not too difficult. She was quickly swept up in the opportunity to meet her adorable nephew and reconnect with her sister and brother-in-law. There was also lots of time spent resting to ensure her shoulder healed well and she would regain full mobility. Once she felt recuperated, there was plenty in San

Francisco and the surrounding areas to keep her occupied. Aaron became her little companion after school as she dragged him all over northern California.

Then somewhere around the third week, Rebecca woke up with a heavy feeling of regret.

She had observed her sister's day to day life as part of a loving family, their lives completely intertwined. Nadine was responsible for their well-being and them for hers. It was busy, stressful, and sometimes chaotic, but Nadine had purpose as a mother and wife, and also as a member of a larger community.

In comparison, Rebecca felt so separate and un-committed to any people or place. The irony was that that had been the goal when she left Jamaica and the world she knew. The loss of her mother had been so painful that she didn't ever want that kind of interdependence again. Traveling the world as a permanent observer almost guaranteed that she could stay unattached. She could see every-thing life had to offer through her lens and capture it in a photo, but not have to feel it.

That's why she had seized the opportunity to visit Nadine. She hadn't run to her family for refuge and recuperation after the ordeal with John, she had run away from Chad and the intensity of her love for him. Her happiness and contentment had become inseparable from his, along with the pain and suffering that were an inevitable part of life. She had been so worried about losing him and being hurt and she had left him instead to avoid the pain.

Unfortunately, it didn't work. She still loved him and it was still agonizing to be away from him. Her only option was to continue living the life she had planned for herself and hope that she would forget him with time.

By late June, Rebecca was actively seeking her next project or sale from her portfolio. Richard Kent was also talking about some work in Canada near the end of the summer, and she was happy to continue that client relationship. Then, out of the blue, she got a call from the New York news agency she had met with earlier in the year. Their Chicago office had just lost one of their staff photographers, and after seeing her portfolio from the recruiter, they wanted to meet her for an interview. Three weeks later, Rebecca was back there permanently to start her new job. With Julie's help, she had a short-term lease for a studio apartment until she was ready to buy a small home.

Of course, she had wanted to call Chad. It had taken all of her willpower not to. But despite what she had discovered about herself and why she had walked away, it didn't change the fact that he had easily let her go. Nor had she heard from him since.

Now that their inevitable encounter had happened and he was right in front of her, it was hard to remember all those logical and practical reasons why she was not the woman he needed in his life.

"God, I feel so much better," he stated as he emerged from her bathroom.

After he got sick in the lobby, Rebecca guided

him toward her apartment on the third floor of the building. He was in no shape to argue. They barely made it through the door before Chad covered his mouth again and she rushed him into the bathroom. He had been there with the door closed for another fifteen minutes.

"The kettle's hot," Rebecca told him. "Would you like some tea? I have peppermint. It will settle your stomach."

He shook his head and rubbed his tummy. "I'll take some coffee if you have it. I'm pretty sure there is nothing in here left to settle. That's part of the problem."

"What do you mean?" she asked, pulling out her French press and a tin of coffee grounds.

"Remind me never to drink on an empty stomach. Or on any stomach."

Rebecca grinned. It did explain what happened. She couldn't remember him drinking more than a half a beer when they were together.

"What was the poison?" she asked.

"Scotch, I think."

He was looking around the room, taking in all the details of the space. It was a tiny studio apartment, and his presence was making it feel even smaller. From the corner of her eye, she watched him walk around, touching pictures, running a hand over her sofa.

"Here you go," she stated when his hot drink was ready, sweetened with brown sugar and cream, just the way he liked it.

"Thanks."

He sat at the small bistro table near the kitchen,

but she stayed behind the counter to give him some space.

"Is this your apartment?"

Rebecca nodded. "For now. Until I find something to buy."

He nodded, putting down the coffee. "I'm probably still a little drunk. But what am I missing, Rebecca? How do you come back to Chicago and not tell me? For two months?"

She took a deep breath and gave him the speech she had rehearsed in her mind. "I got a job offer while I was in California, for a permanent staff position based here, so I came back."

"Is that a good thing? Doesn't that mean you won't be traveling anymore? I thought that's what you wanted to continue doing."

"I do want to continue traveling, and I'm sure I still will. But photojournalism gives me additional experience and some security. I kind of want that right now."

He nodded to himself, as though reaching a significant conclusion, then stood up. "I get it. See, I thought you left to do what you loved. To continue your career traveling around the world. But what you really left was me, and I was too blind or stupid to see it."

Rebecca was taken aback by the hurt in his voice. When she had played out this conversation in her head, she had imagined that he would be surprised by her decision, but not really upset. She had imagined he would have moved on, happily dating someone new. Rebecca felt unprepared and unarmed to respond to his questions and accusations.

"Chad, that's not what happened," she protested.

He raised his hands in surrender. "Actually, never mind. We're over. You don't owe me any explanations, Rebecca, and I have no right to ask."

"But you have it all wrong—"

He cut her off. "What else is there, Rebecca? Either you needed to be free to do your job or you wanted to be free of me. Which is it?"

"Neither! I'd been thinking about finding a staff role for a while, even before I met you. It always was an option, if the right opportunity came up."

"And you didn't think that was important to share with the man you were with? You didn't consider that I would want to know that?"

Rebecca was speechless for a few long seconds. "I didn't think it mattered," she finally stated in a small voice.

Chad just looked at her. "I think that says everything," he finally stated in a cold voice.

She watched with wide eyes as he turned away from her and started walking toward her front door. "Wait, Chad. You don't understand!"

"Rebecca, for the first time, I do understand," he stated in a much quieter voice, his back still turned. "Somehow, I had gotten so caught up in what we had that I forgot it was never meant to be long term. No expectations, right?"

"No, it's not like that," she begged, trying to find the words that would make him hear her. "Why won't you listen to me!"

He whipped around. "Because I'm dying inside, Rebecca! I've spent every hour, every minute of the last three months and eight days missing you—but imagining you happy, committed to your career, doing what you're good at. That made letting you go just a little more bearable. But none of that was real!

"You've been right here in Chicago, settling down with Brian, becoming a suburbanite. Do you know how that makes me feel? I would have done anything to be with you, including following you around the world living out of a suitcase if that's what you wanted."

He suddenly stopped, hanging his head as though in defeat. His pain was like a knife in her heart.

"Chad—"

"Please, Rebecca. I think it's better that I just go."

He was about to turn again, but she rushed forward, refusing to give up. "No! Just listen to me, Chad. None of that is true."

But he wouldn't stop. He was leaving and hating her and she had to make him listen. Rebecca started to cry out of sheer desperation.

"I left because I'm not what you need in your life, Chad," she whimpered, tears streaking down her face. "You told your mother that once I was gone, you'd find the perfect Chicago wife to settle down with. And I'm not that. I don't know if I'll ever be that woman. And one day, when the novelty wore off, you were going to realize that."

Chad looked down at her. "What are you talking about? I never said that," he denied.

"I overheard you, at her house when we were visiting your family that first time. Your mother warned you about getting involved with me, that I'm not the type of woman you could settle down with. And you said you weren't going to marry me. That I'd be gone soon, and then you would find the perfect wife. . . ." She couldn't continue as the sobs shook her body.

He gently took hold of her arms, clearly shocked by her words. "Rebecca, whatever you heard me say, I didn't mean it. I was just teasing my mom for being so nosy. How could you believe that those words were true?"

"Because it *is* true. Everything I owned fit into a suitcase, and I didn't know where I was going to be from one week to the next. All I've done is bring chaos and trouble into your life."

He pulled her closer. "That's ridiculous! I love you, Rebecca, and that's never going to change. Did you think that if you went away for a few weeks I'd just move on? Don't you understand? You're my whole world. I don't care where we live and what we're doing as long as I'm with you."

Rebecca looked into his deep, dark eyes and knew he was telling her the truth. She swallowed hard, starting to believe her worst fears were unfounded.

"I love you too, Chad," she replied, realizing it was the first time she had shared those words. "I've missed you so much."

He finally embraced her in his arms where they remained wrapped together for some time, experiencing the simple pleasure of holding each other again.

"So, you're really staying in Chicago," Chad stated as though the fact just became real to him.

"Yeah," she whispered back.

"And you'll come back to me?" he added, squeezing her a little tighter and pressing a gentle kiss on her temple.

Rebecca nodded. "It's the only place I want to be."

"Good, because I know I can't ever let you go again, Becca."

Neither of them seemed willing to end the tight embrace.

"I suppose we should talk about Brian," she eventually whispered.

Chad pulled back, his eyes stormy. "What about him?"

"I haven't shacked up with him. He lives on the second floor with his boyfriend, Taylor."

His body vibrated with laughter while she smiled into the curve of his neck.

"Good to know, so I don't have to kill him and bury his body somewhere remote."

Don't miss Zuri Day's

Love on the Run

Available now wherever books are sold!

Chapter 1

On a warm, overcast day in late September, the forever-grooving-always-moving female magnet Michael Morgan found himself spending a rare day both off from work and alone. After sexing her to within an inch of her life, he'd sent his latest conquest—all long hair (still tangled), long legs (still throbbing), and . . . well . . . perpetual longing—on her melancholy yet merry way. As usual when his mind had a spare moment, his thoughts went to his business—Morgan Sports Management Corporation—and the athletes he wanted to add to this successful company's stable. At the top of the list was former USC standout and recent Olympic gold medalist Shayna Washington, a woman he'd been aware of since her college days who he'd learned had just lost the mediocre sponsor who'd approached her two years prior. When it came to business, Michael was like a bloodhound, and he smelled the piquant possibility of this client oozing across the proverbial promotional floor.

Along with his other numerous talents, Michael had the ability to see in people what others couldn't, that indefinable something, that "it" factor, that star quality that took some from obscure mediocrity to worldwide fame. He sensed that in Shayna Washington, felt there was something there he could work with, and he was excited about the possibility of making things happen.

The ringing phone forced Michael to put these thoughts on pause. "Morgan."

"Hey, baby."

Michael stifled a groan, wishing he'd let the call that had come in as unknown go to voice mail. For the past two months, he'd told Cheryl that it was over. Her parting gifts had been accompanying him on a business trip to Mexico checking out a local baseball star, a luxurious four days that included a five-star hotel suite, candlelight dinners cooked by a personal chef, premium tequila, and a sparkly goodbye gift that, if needed, could be pawned to pay mortgage on LA's tony Westside. Why all of this extravagance? Partly because this was simply Michael's style and partly because he genuinely liked Cheryl and hadn't wanted to end their on-again off-again bedtime romps. But now, several years into their intimate acquaintance, she'd become clingy, and then suspicious, and then demanding . . . and then a pain in the butt.

Michael could never be accused of being a dog; he let women know up front—as in before they made love—what time it was. Michael Morgan played for fun, not for keeps. Fortunately for him, most women didn't mind. Most were thankful just to be near his . . . clock. He loved hard and fast, but rarely long, and while it hadn't been his desire to do so, he'd left a trail of broken hearts in his wake.

Broken, but not bitter. A little taste of Morgan pleasure was worth a bit of emotional pain.

But every once in a while he ran into a woman like Cheryl, a woman who didn't want to take no for an answer. So when entanglements reached this point, the solution he employed was simple and straightforward: goodbye. But sometimes the fall-out was a bitch.

"Cheryl, you've got to quit calling."

"Michael, how can you just dump me like this?"

Heavy sigh. "I didn't 'just dump you,' Cheryl. I've been telling you for months to back off, that what you're wanting isn't what I'm offering. This has gotten way too complicated. You've got to let it go."

"So what did that mean when we began dating 'officially,' when I escorted you to the NFL honors?"

This is what I get for being soft and giving in. If there was one thing that Michael should have known by now, it was that mixing business with pleasure was like mixing hot sauce with baby formula. Don't do it. *Any minute she's going to start crying, and really work my nerves.* As if on cue, he heard the sniffles, her argument now delivered in part whine, part wistfulness. Michael correctly deduced that she was sad, and very pissed off at his making her that way. "You've been my only one for years, Michael—"

"I told you from the beginning that that wasn't a good idea—"

"And I told you that I didn't want anyone else.

There is no one for me but you. I can't forget you"—
Michael heard a finger snap—"just like that." Her
voice dropped to a vulnerable-sounding whisper.
"Can I please come over just for a little while, bring
you some of your favorite Thai food, a few sex toys,
give you a nice massage . . . ?"

Michael loved to play with Cheryl and her toys.
And when it came to massages, he gave as good as
he got. And then there was the sincerity he heard
amid her tears. He almost relented. Almost. . .but
not quite.

"Cheryl, every time you've asked, I've been
honest. Our relationship was never exclusive. I
never thought of us as anything more than what it
was—two people enjoying the moment and each
other. I'll always think well of you, Cheryl. But
please don't put us through this. You're a good
woman, and there's a good man out there for you
who wants what you want, the picket fence and all
that. That man is not me. I'm sorry. I want the best
for you. And I want you to move on with your
life." He heard his other cell phone ringing and
walked over to where it sat charging on the bar
counter. *Valerie.* "Look, Cheryl, I have to go."

"But, Michael, I'm only five minutes from your
house. I can—"

*You can keep it moving, baby. I told you from the
beginning this was for fun, not forever.* Michael
tapped the screen of his iPhone as he reached for
his BlackBerry. "Hey, gorgeous," he said into the
other phone.

"Hey yourself," a sultry voice replied.

"Michael!" *Oh, damn!* Michael looked down at the iPhone screen to see that the call from Cheryl was still connected. "Michael, who is that bit—" Michael pressed and held the End button, silently cursing himself for not being careful.

"Michael, are you there?"

"Yes, Valerie."

"Whose was that voice I heard?"

"A friend of mine. Do you have a problem with that?" Michael had never hidden the fact that when it came to women, he was a multitasker, especially among the women he juggled. But the situation with Cheryl had him very aware of the need to make that point perfectly clear, up front and often. If a woman couldn't understand that when it came to his love she was part of a team, then she'd have to get traded.

"Not at all," the sultry voice pouted. "Whatever she can do, I can do better."

That's how you play it, player! "No doubt," Michael replied as his iPhone rang again. *Unknown caller.* He ignored it. *Sheesh! Maybe I'm getting too old for this.* Just then, his house phone rang. "Hello?"

"Hey, sexy!"

Paia? Back from Europe already? "Hey, beautiful. Hold on a minute." And then into the BlackBerry, "Look, Valerie, I'll call you back."

"Okay, lover, but don't make me wait too long."

"Who's Valerie?"

The iPhone again. *Unknown caller.* Michael turned off the iPhone. *Cheryl, give it a rest!* "Look, Cheryl—"

"Ha! This is Paia, you adorable asshole. Get it straight!"

Michael inwardly groaned. How could he have forgotten his rule about keeping his women separate and him least confused? Rarely call them by their given name when talking on the phone. *Baby* was fine. *Darling* would do on any given day. *Honey* or *dear* based on the background. Even *pumpkin* or the generic yet acceptable *hey you* were all perfectly good substitutes. But using names, especially upon first taking a phone call, was a serious playboy no-no. *Yeah, man. You're slipping. You need to tighten up your game.* He'd just promoted this beauty to the Top Three Tier—those ladies who were in enviable possession of his home number. He and Paia were technically still in the courting stage—much too early for ruffled feathers or hurt feelings. At six feet tall in her stocking feet, Paia was a runway and high fashion model, an irresistibly sexy mix of African and Asian features. They'd only been dating two months and he wasn't ready to let her go. He even liked the way her name rolled off his tongue. *Pie-a.* No, he didn't want to release her quite yet. "Paia, baby, you know Mr. Big gets lonely when you're gone."

"Uh-huh. Because of that snafu you're going to owe me an uninterrupted weekend with you and that baseball bat you call a penis. You'd better be ready to give me overtime, too!"

"That can be arranged," Michael drawled. "Where are you?"

"I just landed in LA. But we have to move fast. I'm only here for a week and then it's back to Milan. So whatever plans you have tonight, cancel them."

"Ah, man! I can't do that—new client. But I'll call you later." Michael looked at the Caller ID as an incoming call indicator beeped in his ear. "Sweet thing," he said, proud that he was back to the terms of endearment delivered unconsciously. *That's right, Michael. Keep handling yours.* "This is my brother. I've got to go."

"Call me later, Michael."

"Hold on." Michael toggled between the two calls, firing back up his iPhone in the process. "Hey, bro. What's up?" Just four words in and said phone rang. *Jessica!* Unbidden, an image of the busty first-class flight attendant he'd met several months ago popped into his head. *Was it this weekend I was supposed to go with her to Vegas?* "Darling," he said, switching back to Paia, "we'll talk soon." He clicked over. "Gregory, two secs." He could hear his brother laughing as he fielded the other call. "Hey, baby. I'm on the other line. Let me call you back." He tossed down the cell phone. "All right, baby, I'm back."

"Baby?" Gregory queried, his voice full of humor. "I know you love me, fool, but I prefer *bro* or *Doctor* or *Your Highness*!" Michael snorted. "You need to hone your juggling skills, son. Or slow your player roll. Or both."

The Hottest African American Fiction
from
Dafina Books